Wings

By *NEW YORK TIMES* BESTSELLING AUTHOR

NEAL TRAVIS

author of

MANSIONS

"FIRST RATE"
New York Daily News

CASTLES

"JET-POWERED"
West Coast Review of Books

PALACES

"A WHIRLWIND OF PASSION
AND ADVENTURE."
Publishers Weekly

Other Avon Books by
Neal Travis

CASTLES
MANSIONS
PALACES

Wings

NEAL TRAVIS

◆ **AVON**
PUBLISHERS OF BARD, CAMELOT, DISCUS AND FLARE BOOKS

AVON BOOKS
A division of
The Hearst Corporation
1790 Broadway
New York, New York 10019

Copyright © 1985 by Neal Travis
Published by arrangement with the author
Library of Congress Catalog Card Number: 84-091762
ISBN: 0-380-89802-0

First Avon Printing, July 1985

AVON TRADEMARK REG. U.S. PAT. OFF. AND IN
OTHER COUNTRIES, MARCA REGISTRADA, HECHO EN
U.S.A.

Printed in the U. S. A.

WFH 10 9 8 7 6 5 4 3 2 1

Chapter One _____

THE BIG JET ENGINES STRAINED AND screamed, striving desperately for that extra thousand feet where there was safety. Like a champion racehorse whose heart has burst yet still lunges for the winning post, Flight 73, Island Airways, bound from Honolulu to Hilo, was technically dead and stopped in midair. Burdened by its own weight and the 132 passengers and crew, it quickly began to drop, straight through the deadly clouds that had brought it to grief, down toward the ocean thirty-two thousand feet below.

The passengers in nonsmoking had sensed trouble first, as the stream of acrid metallic dust seeping through the jet's ventilators assaulted their lungs as no cigar smoke ever could. From the cramped galley, Jill Hewitt saw the call lights flashing on and she swore under her breath. Flight 73's passengers had already proved a particularly cantankerous lot. But she stopped stocking the drinks cart and stepped out of the galley to see what their latest demand was. By then the stream of dust was already a dense cloud swirling through the plane.

She heard the despairing scream of the engines and felt the plane scrabbling at the sky, clawing at the clouds, desperately defying gravity. Then Flight 73 began dropping like a stone. Jill was thrown against the roof of the cabin, along with plastic glasses and magazines, flight bags and sports equipment. For once, she thought, the passengers had taken the pilot's advice to keep their seat belts fastened. Odd, too, that time stopped just as Jill was suspended by the downward thrust of the plane. Then, amazingly, the jet was pulled out of its fall and began a forward motion. Jill crashed back to the cabin floor, feeling the violent slam as her shoulder struck a seat. But then she was on her feet, moving down the aisle to smile and nod and reassure the passengers. Just a downdraft, a bad one, yes, but they were all right now. Something to do with the cloud from the volcano. Keep those seat belts fastened, hear? We'll be starting our descent into Hilo very soon.

A small old man, white hair contrasting with his wildly floral shirt, was staring out the window.

"We're on fire!" he cried, voice pitched high. "The engine's on fire!"

She leaned across him, following his gaze, frowning. The last thing they needed was panic. People *always* thought the engines were on fire. But flames were pouring from the big engine, vicious red tongues licking back along the fuselage. She straightened slowly, trying to control her own panic. The passengers were murmuring, a growing chant beneath which she could hear the most ominous sound of all: silence. They were all listening to that sound, the silence of no engine noise at all.

A voice came over the intercom, a relaxed, reassuring drawl.

"This is Captain Nagle on the flight deck. Sorry about that downdraft we hit. Hope you didn't all spill your drinks in your laps."

They hung on his voice, eyes on the ceiling speakers. Even the most novice traveler knew something was terribly wrong.

"We've still got a bit of a problem," the voice said, calm and unhurried. "When we flew into that last cloud mass we struck a patch of heavy debris from the volcano and it got sucked up into the engines. That caused the engines to shut down for a few seconds. Those of you in the window seats probably saw a little bit of flame coming from the engines. What we'll have to do to put the fires out before we start the engines again is go into a long glide pattern. While we're in that pattern, there'll be a loss of pressurization, so we're going to drop the oxygen masks down and ask you to wear them until we're back to normal. Of course," he added, chuckling, "that means no smoking. Okay?"

The yellow oxygen masks came hurling down out of their holders, and a few of the sophisticates who made a point of never listening to the preflight safety spiel now wished they hadn't been so blasé.

"I'll keep you posted on our progress," Captain Nagle said. "Meantime, would whoever's handiest in the flight crew come forward and see me for a moment, please?"

Jill looked around. She was the one, so she walked calmly up the aisle, no hurry, smiling at the stony faces around her. It took her ten seconds to reach the cockpit, where she found none of the calm of the captain's speech. Nagle and his copilot were hunched over the massive console, jiggling switches, punching buttons, as if searching for some magical combination. Nagle didn't look up at Jill.

"Who is it?" he snapped.

"Hewitt, Captain," she said.

"Hewitt, we've got ourselves a situation here. It's not pretty. I've put the kite in a forty-five-degree glide, which means we've got about ten minutes to get the engines restarted. We don't know how badly damaged they are, and we won't know until—and unless—we can start 'em again. If they aren't running in five minutes, we'll have to get the passengers ready for ditching. Check with me in five minutes, and try to keep them calm in the meantime."

"You didn't see a singing nun on board, did you?" joked Eddy Cairns, the copilot. His face was white and his forehead wet with sweat.

She went back into the silent main cabin

and did what the rest of the crew were doing, moving around the plane offering confidence and comfort. Passengers gripped the arm rests and either stared straight ahead or shut their eyes. Jill sensed that behind the oxygen masks many were praying. She glanced at her watch and quietly passed on Nagle's instructions to the other members of the crew: in four and a half minutes they should begin ditching procedures.

The minutes passed with agonizing slowness while she prayed for the sound of engines starting, the power that would stop their long descent into death. But there was nothing, and soon it was time to tell the passengers their fate. The senior attendant, Glen Harvey, picked up the microphone, and Jill found herself noticing the way his eyebrows almost joined, the slight bend in his nose, the bright green eyes.

"As a precaution"—Harvey was speaking gently but without any pretense—"Captain Nagle has asked us all to put on life jackets. You'll find them under your seats. The crew will come by and help you with them. But you can take off your oxygen masks. There's enough air to breathe normally now."

Which meant, Jill thought, they were that much closer to sea level. She looked around and tried to smile at the terror-stricken eyes beseeching her. She went through the routine of donning a life jacket, demonstrating the ties and the whistles that would supposedly bring

5

help, the tube to reinflate the jacket when your chin slipped below the sea's surface. But the whole thing was a farce. The impact would break their bodies and the airplane into pieces. It would be like hitting a concrete blockhouse at two hundred miles an hour. She hauled a life raft from its storage compartment behind the bulkhead and set it by the emergency exit: it would be a miracle if anyone survived to climb aboard it.

Five more minutes and then the sea. People were praying openly now. Couples had linked hands; strangers touched each other. Near her a young couple gazed at their baby, trying to see a whole life in these last few minutes.

The volcanic cloud had been hanging over all of them, tourists and Hawaiians alike, for nine days, jangling nerves and straining emotions unbearably. Under the cloud it was hot, over one hundred degrees every day, and without the sun Hawaii was a bleak, inhospitable place, a glimpse into hell.

Tired, Jill had been unable to sleep and was up in time to hear the thwack of the paper landing on the sidewalk at six o'clock. The weather still dominated the front page. It was now, officially, the worst period in Hawaii's recorded meteorological history. Even the mayor of Honolulu admitted that pollution levels were dangerously high. He suggested staying indoors. But several accompanying stories told of the pressures of close confinement: It had been a week of drinking and quarreling, and Honolulu's jails were filled with brawlers and wife beaters. A social worker tried to suggest ways of coping with the pressures, but he had nothing more than patience to counsel. The cartoon showed a couple climbing on a plane bound for Los Angeles, where they were looking forward to some clean air.

"What are you reading that crap for?" Cindy Mason demanded, coming out of the house to join Jill on the lanai. "We have to live with this damn weather, but we don't have to read about it too."

Jill smiled at her friend. They'd lived together for a year, and their natures complemented each other nicely. Cindy was direct, explosive, outspoken, whereas Jill tended to take things as they came and wasn't crushed when things didn't turn out.

"What're we doing," Cindy said, "two great-looking broads living in a hick place like this? Paradise? Hell!"

"Come on, you love it here as much as I do. You've stayed twice as long."

"Only because the mainland airlines aren't hiring," Cindy said. "And because I can't stand cold weather, crowds, traffic, and gouging landlords." She poured coffee from the pot on the table and made a face. "God, between us we can't make a decent cup of coffee." She stood up and stretched; the short, sheer nightie barely covered her. She was short and blond and round, almost precisely the opposite of the tall brunette facing her. "What flight have you pulled today?"

It was Jill's turn to make a face.

"Hilo. Flying right into the heart of Volcanoville. I don't want to fly at all today. I don't want to fly again until this damned weather breaks. The passengers are getting worse every day—like it was *our* fault their vacations have been ruined. Demanding, rude—I should have stayed a schoolteacher. At least I was bigger than they were and could pull rank. On the run to Maui yesterday, this big fat oaf ran his hand up my skirt. Not just a pat on the fanny, either, but a real grope. I poured hot coffee in his lap."

Cindy laughed. "So? You felt better, didn't you?"

"So he reported me to the captain. And you know how it is just now, with the layoffs and all. They're looking for any excuse to fire us."

"You've got nothing to worry about. You were assaulted. Hell, *you* should have reported *him* to the captain. You did tell him your side of the story, didn't you?"

"I tried," she said, miserably, "but there wasn't much point. The captain on that flight was David Nagle. You know how Nagle feels about stews."

"Mmm, you have got a problem. Nagle doesn't like anyone, I don't think. He used to fly with us. Three or four years ago, well before you came out here. He was a great-looking guy and one of the top pilots. But he had a big chip on his shoulder, and when he quit to join Island Airways a lot of us were happy. I don't think I ever saw David Nagle crack a grin, except maybe when he was with that bunch of bums and old fliers who hang out at Andy Koa's bar.''

''Well, flying for Island hasn't improved him any,'' Jill said, frowning. ''And now he's deciding whether or not to put me on report. It's so damned unfair. I could get canned over this.''

''The worst they'll do is suspend you for a couple of weeks. So you'll have some time to spend on the beach with The Hulk.''

''You're forgetting it isn't exactly perfect weather for the beach,'' Jill said, gesturing at the dank grayness outside. ''And as for Jed Ramsay, I kicked him out last night—for keeps.''

''Hey! Good for you, kid! He was never your speed. Big, handsome, and dumb. She grinned wickedly. ''But if you're really through with him, would you mind if I, uh, tried to get a little closer to him next time he's crewing one of my flights? I know he's got mush for brains, but I've been lusting after his body for ages.''

''You're welcome.'' Jill shrugged. ''He's good in bed, but he's also a selfish, egotistical mamma's boy.''

''Sounds like a drag. But then, I only want

his body. I'm not looking to fall in love, like you."

Jill flushed.

"I'm not looking to fall in love with anyone," she protested. "I'm twenty-seven years old and I'd just like to be able to have a decent relationship with someone, a relationship that maybe went beyond the bedroom now and then." She glanced at her watch. "I better go shower and dress. I don't dare be late. Apart from everything else, the pilot on the run to Hilo today just happens to be David Nagle. It's my lucky week, I guess."

By the time she had dressed in the happy yellow uniform of Island Airways, called good-bye to Cindy, and gone through to the garage and her little red Mustang convertible, Jill was feeling positively cheerful. The car always put her in a good mood: just three months old, unmarked, frivolous, and fun. She hummed to herself as she negotiated Diamond Head Drive and turned onto the highway.

David Nagle hardly noticed the weather that morning as he drove his battered old VW along Nimitz Highway; everyone else might be moaning about it, but it suited his mood. Sure, it was making flying difficult—even dangerous—and he would give it all due respect when he was behind the controls of the big jet. But just then he had other things on his mind. Like the call last night from his ex-wife.

The call had started out friendly for a change, but ended in bitter abuse. Marion had just wanted to wish him a happy thirty-ninth birthday and remind him that it was David Junior's eighteenth the following week. Not that he'd ever forgotten the boy's birthday. He'd only been permitted to see David a dozen times in all those years, but he had tried to be a dutiful father from a distance. The situation was all his own father's fault: The old man dominated the whole family, always had. He'd sided with Marion when she divorced him and was now raising David Junior as his own son.

Marion seemed to like the arrangement. She lived in a Fifth Avenue penthouse provided from the Nagle fortune and—as she had often told him, voice dripping malice—she entertained a stream of increasingly younger lovers there.

"David's going to be a big success," she'd said last night on the phone. "Harvard this year, then your family's bank. Not like you, running off to fight in that ridiculous war, rejecting all the things your father wanted to give you. Look at you, a glorified bus driver. You're thirty-nine, David, but you're still the same stupid, romantic little boy you were when we met. That's why I'm so proud of young David. He's not at all like you."

She was crocked. She usually was when she called him. Sometimes he tried to remember what it had been like eighteen years ago, him twenty-one and already enlisted in the air force, Marion nineteen and drifting through Columbia with no real intention of graduating. They should never have married. She was so beautiful, though. And he was the son of Boston's finest family. The air force thing didn't worry her because she was sure his father would fix him up with a nice safe job in the Pentagon.

Except that David had applied for duty in Vietnam—to the bewilderment and, later, the utter contempt of both Marion and his father. Last night he had shut his mind off while she went through the litany of his stupidity and selfishness. Her bitterness over his leaving her, a new bride, to go fight an Asian war—he could understand that well enough. Her divorcing him when he signed on for a second tour of duty was not even a dull ache. But the boy, that still hurt.

At least David Nagle had some company in his bitter loneliness. In Hawaii there were a lot of vets like him, men whose wives had sent them Dear John letters, or who could not cope with the awkwardness, the guilt, the animosity provoked by the Vietnam War. Last night he would have tied one on with the boys at Andy Koa's after Marion's call, but David was a pilot who abided by the rules. He'd just had a few beers in his own apartment, the last at 10:00 P.M., the regulation twelve hours before he had to fly. He was brooding about the phone call and about being thirty-nine when he swung the VW into Island Airways' parking lot. He didn't even notice the bright red Mustang pulling into a spot ahead of him until his VW slammed into the side of it. The cars locked together and stopped.

She was out of the Mustang, around the side, and examining the damage before he had even gotten his long legs out of his car. She turned on him, her face white with rage.

"You goddamned idiot!" she yelled. "My car, my beautiful car! You've ruined it." She started to cry. The Mustang was indeed a sorry sight, all stove in down the side, the metal like an old crumpled piece of tinfoil. The VW didn't even look dented.

She hadn't really looked at him, hadn't focused on the very tall man with short sandy hair and hooded, cold blue eyes. She'd never seen him out of uniform before, so it took a few seconds to register.

"Oh, shit!" Jill Hewitt said, stamping her foot. "Captain Nagle! This really *is* my day." She savagely kicked the rear tire of the Mustang. "Okay. Seniority rules and I'll have to take the blame for this, too. But I really loved this car and now it's ruined."

"Hey, hold on, Hewitt," he said. "It was my fault. I was miles away. I wasn't looking. I'm sorry and I'll make it right. You're flying with me today, right? Well, by the time we get back from Hilo tonight I'll have that Mustang good as new. I've got a pal who can get *anything* done in a hurry. I'll just call Andy Koa

13

and he'll have a tow truck down here, get your car into a bodyshop, and it'll be waiting for you tonight.'' He reached into the VW and took his uniform from its hanger in the rear. ''Hold this a second, will you, while I park properly.''

As they walked toward the crew quarters, he glanced down at her and smiled, a first for Jill. ''I really am sorry. I had a car I loved once, a long time ago. Andy'll fix your car for you, and maybe you'll let me take you to dinner tonight, as part apology.''

She looked at him sideways. This wasn't the Nagle she knew. Maybe he was just trying to calm her in case she was planning to get her insurance company to come down on him hard. And there was still the matter of yesterday's complaint against her. She was still too angry to return his smile, but she did manage to be civil.

''That's very kind of you, Captain,'' she said. ''But if you can just get my car fixed, I can take care of myself for dinner.''

No one in the crew room noted how upset she was. Since the volcano cloud had been hanging over them all, the usual camaraderie had vanished. Each flight was more of an ordeal than the last now, and they had to save the pleasantries for the passengers.

Flight 73's cargo was no different from any other: disgruntled tourists who were watching their hard-saved dollars dissipate in the volcanic cloud. Everyone realized he would soon have to return to Grand Rapids without even a midwinter suntan to show for his trip to Hawaii. The passengers were complaining even before Flight 73 had left the apron. Some were demanding drinks, no matter what the regulations said, and the cabin crew served them; it wasn't worth the hassle of refusing. Cranky children sprinted up and down the aisles, refusing to be seated for takeoff. Hand luggage was strewn about carelessly, and Jill wasn't the only stew who snagged a stocking as she battled to get them all settled for take-off. It took so long that Captain Nagle himself came back from the cockpit to investigate the delay. At least it momentarily cheered the passengers to hear the crew being bawled out.

All the life rafts had been broken out and lay in the aisles, obscenely orange, like huge deflated sausages. The passengers tried not to look at the rafts but were mesmerized by them, and by the oxygen masks hanging from the ceiling, abandoned now; the flashing emergency exit lights, blinking on and off in ominous sequence.

The big jet continued its slow, graceful glide toward the sea. In the hushed cabin Jill could hear the first muffled sobs. She moved around, no longer giving her mechanical stewardess smile but trying to offer real comfort.

In the cockpit, David Nagle looked up at his copilot. He held up his hand, thumb and fingers spread, indicating five seconds to the moment when they would make their final effort to restart the shattered engines. What they were going to do was akin to starting a car in gear—except that this jet was coasting at 230 miles per hour.

Jill checked her watch. Eight minutes since Nagle had given her the orders. If it weren't for the cloud around them, they would be able to see the ocean, nine or ten thousand feet below. It was usually such a beautiful sea, as beautiful as the tourist photographs promised. She wondered who would tell her parents, who would trudge up the stairs to the faded South Side Chicago apartment and inform the elderly couple that their sole child was missing, presumed dead, in the tropical waters of Hawaii. Maybe someone from the airline would just phone. Her parents would already be prepared: they would have seen on the news that one of the jets their daughter flew was down. She tried to calculate the time in Chicago. Night; probably snowing. Her mother had written about the particularly cruel winter they were having in the Midwest.

They could hear it clearly in the main cabin, a kind of popping sound from the engines followed by a gruesome, grinding scream, the scream of machinery hopelessly chewing on its own metal components. Several children, shocked, began to cry loudly and were cradled by their parents. All the couples, family groups, friends, had formed tight-knit units, going to their fate together.

And then there was a bang, a big bang, followed by the familiar shriek of a working jet engine. Laboring desperately, sick for sure, but working. And then from the starboard side came the same sequence of sounds and suddenly they all felt a surge of power taking over from the aimless downward glide. Real power, slowing their descent. It leveled them and then slowly lifted them away from the sea.

At first they were afraid to react. It could be just a vicious trick fate was playing. The engines, strained far beyond capacity, might die again. The reprieve, if it was a reprieve, could be snatched away at any moment. But Captain Nagle was on the intercom in a moment.

"We've got the situation under control now," he said. Even his professional pilot's voice could not conceal his relief. "As I told you a while back, we lost our engines when they sucked in a cloud of debris from the volcano. It was one of those one-in-a-million things, not supposed to happen but it did. Anyway, we were about thirty-two thousand feet then and we had to drift down to about ten thousand before we could restart them." He actually chuckled. "They're running rough, as you can hear, and the engineers will be busy for weeks smoothing them out. But they *are* running, and I'm just going to head us straight on down to Hilo, where I figure we'll be landing in about ten minutes." He clicked off, then on again. "There's just one other thing I'd like to say. You all kept calm and conducted yourselves real well. Thanks, and thanks to the crew. Oh, and thanks for flying with Island Airways.'' They heard him chuckling again as he clicked off.

There was no jubilation. The shock was beginning to set in, the realization of how near they had come to the ultimate disaster. If they spoke at all, they spoke in whispers. As Jill moved around the cabin, restowing the life rafts, retracting the oxygen masks, her knees were weak and her hands shook. In a few minutes they were beneath the cloud at last, land visible below them. The jet banked gently to port and headed straight in to the strip. It was a smooth landing. It seemed to go on forever, though, because Nagle dared not use reverse thrust to slow the plane for fear of the engines' blowing up. The jet just kept rolling along the strip, emergency vehicles keeping pace with it on either side, until its own weight stopped it. Only then, when they felt the familiar bumping and lurching of the plane on the ground, moving slowly, only then did they know they were safe.

It started at the rear of the jet, a gentle clapping that grew and grew as the plane bumped its way up to the terminal. It came to a complete stop and then they were all on their feet, in defiance of the seat-belt signs, clapping, cheering, and crying. The cheers went on for minutes after the doors were opened;

no one would leave until they had all seen the man who had saved their lives. But David Nagle stayed locked in his cockpit, willing to wait them out.

"Nice work, Skipper," Eddy Cairns said casually as he gathered up the flight data and shoved it into his battered briefcase. "They ought to give you an award."

After Cairns had gone from the cockpit, David finally succumbed. His shirt was cold, soaked with sweat, and he began to shiver uncontrollably. There was a terrible pounding in his temples, as if blood were trying to force itself out of him; his hands jerked violently. He feared he was having a seizure, some kind of fit, but his mind told him it was only extreme shock. It would pass. He was almost back to normal when he heard the soft tapping on the cockpit door.

"Yes?" he growled, hoping to scare them off.

"I brought you some fresh coffee, Captain," Jill said as she entered. She passed him the cup. "They've mostly given up waiting for you." She grinned. "It should be safe to come out after you've had your coffee."

"Thanks," he said, using all his willpower to keep the hand that held the cup from shaking. He glanced up at her; a very nice-looking girl, he thought, not conventionally pretty like most of the stews working in the islands, and not tired and hard-looking as so many were.

She had a quiet, mature kind of beauty. He smiled.

"I bet you think I'm a jinx, Hewitt. I smashed your car this morning and I damn near had you on an unscheduled swim before lunch. You must have a great deal of confidence in me."

"We all do," she said quietly, ignoring the sudden scowl. "That was a miraculous piece of flying. Eddy Cairns said he doesn't know of any other pilot who could have pulled it off." She glanced out the window. "I'm afraid you're not going to be able to avoid the passengers. They're all standing at the terminal entrance waiting for you."

"I'll outwait them. I don't want their congratulations—just like I don't need their gripes." He glanced at her over the rim of his cup. "Like the guy yesterday, with you. That I don't need."

"But he . . . he assaulted me," she sputtered. "I should have had him charged, and instead it's *me* who's in trouble." Suddenly she laughed, a full laugh, her head shaking. "This is crazy! Twenty minutes ago I thought we were all going to die. Now I'm worrying about some sorehead. Frankly, Captain, I don't give a damn. I made a vow to myself while we were falling through the sky that I was going to stop wasting my life, and I'm starting right now. I don't care what you decide to do about his complaint."

"Ease off," he said, grinning. "I already

came down on your side. What you should have done, though, was report him to me and I would have had him charged. Next time you get one of those bastards, come to me, okay?''

She followed him across the tarmac. Their passengers were still grouped at the terminal entrance waiting to greet their savior. Nagle flinched, ducking his head and jostling his way through the outstretched hands. She wondered if part of his problem might just be excruciating shyness.

It was the same on the trip back to Honolulu late in the afternoon. While the rest of the crew sat together, celebrating quietly, Nagle sat alone talking to no one. There was an invisible wall around him, and none of them would risk trying to penetrate it.

The media were waiting when they came off the plane and Nagle tried to avoid them by mingling with the passengers, but Paul Prescott, Island's public relations chief, waylaid him.

''You've got to play along with them, David,'' he insisted. ''We've got to put this thing in the best possible light. The media could murder us if they played it like the incident was somehow our fault. I want you to stand up in front of the cameras and give 'em a spiel about how there was no real danger, everyone stayed calm, it was all standard operating procedure. Right?''

Nagle glowered at him.

"There was nothing standard about it," he snapped. "We almost ditched. None of the airlines should be flying while the volcanic cloud is there. You want me to tell the media that?"

"Christ, no! We can't afford to ground the fleet. You know how much trouble Island is in right now." He was wheedling. "Please, David, do the right thing. We'll be very grateful. A bonus, a couple of weeks' vacation . . . ?"

"For the crew as well," David insisted.

"No, just you," Prescott said. "We can't afford—"

"Let's get this over with," Nagle said, and Prescott led him to the interview room. The rest of the crew were waiting there with the reporters and cameramen.

Paul Prescott began to relax as Nagle fielded reporters' questions. It was obvious none of them knew anything about aviation; they only wanted a straightforward story about a hero pilot. No one wanted to know why the engines had failed or whether conditions were safe for flying. They mistook Nagle's abruptness for modesty. The whole thing would look real good on the six o'clock news, Prescott thought, when it might have been a disaster for Island Airways. Maybe Nagle wasn't such an SOB after all.

"Tell us, Captain, what are you going to do now?" a woman from the *Star* shouted at David. "Do you want to get right back behind the controls? Like jumping right back on a horse?''

He looked at her for a moment, and then, for the first time, David smiled.

''Well, ma'am,'' he said, ''all the crew and I would be real happy to fly again tomorrow. But Mr. Prescott here just told me Island Airways is so grateful to us for the way things turned out, they're giving us all a bonus and an extra two weeks' vacation. So I'll be lying on a beach for the next two weeks—if the sun comes out, that is.''

The crew whooped with joy at the news. Prescott had to admit it made a fine closing shot. He'd worry about explaining it to the bosses later.

David Nagle waited until the last reporters had departed before he wiped his brow. It had taken a massive effort to keep his voice steady and his hands from trembling. He was annoyed with himself. He should have been well over the tension by now, but he was still wound up tight. He headed for the crew lounge, where he showered and slipped into jeans and a shirt, then went out to the parking lot.

''Uh, hi,'' he said vaguely when he found Jill leaning against the door of his VW. Then he remembered. ''Isn't your car back yet? I'm sorry. Andy's let me down, I guess.'' He opened the car door for her. ''We'll drive over to Andy's and see what's happening with your car.''

"Would you mind stopping by my house first?" she asked. "I'd like to get out of this uniform."

At the house he accepted a beer from her and settled in the living room while she went to change. She showered quickly but took her time dressing. She wanted to look her best for him. She settled on a white halter top and blue wraparound skirt, brushed her hair out long and free, and put on bright pink lipstick.

He got quickly to his feet when she came into the room. He nodded approvingly, and she believed he was seeing her for the first time. She was right. Such a fresh look about her, he was thinking, different from the women he occasionally bedded, the too-willing, vaguely desperate girls who tumbled into his bed.

"If you've finished your drink we can go, Captain," Jill said briskly.

"Would you mind calling me David? I like to forget about all the airline bullshit when I'm not working. And the crowd in Andy's bar don't stand on ceremony."

She studied his profile as they drove down into Waikiki. Away from the airline he looked like a different man, more casual, even a little friendly.

Andy Koa's place was a few blocks back from the beachfront and did nothing to draw tourists. No garish signs outside; inside it was dark and cool, just one long businesslike bar and a few tables.

"Hi, David," Koa called as they sat down at the bar. "I heard on the radio about the fun you had going down to Hilo." Koa was a huge man, beefy rather than fat, with a dazzling white smile and a mass of tight-curled hair. He looked only about David's age but she guessed he would be closer to fifty; she'd been in the islands long enough to know how youthful the native Hawaiians appeared.

"It wasn't much," David said. "Give me the usual. And Andy, this is Jill. What'll you have?"

She asked for a vodka and tonic.

"Did you manage to get that Mustang fixed for me?" David asked when Andy put their drinks in front of them.

"You can have it back tomorrow night. Sorry, but they had to send out for a side panel. And it's going to cost you six hundred bucks. Those pretty little machines can't take any kind of knock. You've got to be nuts to own one."

"It's my Mustang," Jill said easily. "And it only crumbles like that if someone isn't looking where he's going and runs into it."

"Guilty." David shook his head. "I can attest there wasn't a mark on it before I came along in my VW. But I'm real sorry it's not ready for you tonight. With our unexpected vacation, I'd guess you'll want to drive off somewhere. Our grateful employers," he explained to Andy, "have rewarded us with two weeks off for saving their damn plane."

"Hey, great," Andy said. "I've been looking for an excuse to get out from behind here for a few days and do some sailing. You want to come out on the boat tomorrow?"

"In this weather? What's the point?" David said.

"The cloud will be all gone by morning," Andy said with certainty. "We're heading for a perfect day."

"That's not what the meteorological forecast says."

"Don't listen to them, listen to your brown brother. With my inbuilt knowledge, handed down from my forefathers, and by listening to the birds and watching the fish and smelling the sea—"

"Crap," David said.

"No, David," Jill protested. "Native people have a sense of the elements that's been bred out of the rest of us. If Andy says it's going to be fine tomorrow, then I bet he's right."

"Why, thank you, ma'am," Andy said, bowing. "Actually I just got off the phone to my brother in Hilo. He said the volcano shut itself down late this afternoon and there's a good northeaster pushing in and breaking up the cloud."

Jill joined in their laughter. She didn't mind falling for Andy's patter.

A couple of men drifted into the bar and waved to David; one of them, a man as big and burly as Koa himself, strolled over and clapped David on the shoulder.

"Good stuff, kid," he said simply.

"Jill," David said, "I want you to meet Burt Brydon. He's an Australian, so don't believe anything he tells you. But he's not too damn bad a pilot, even if the planes he flies are held together with wire and rusty nails."

Brydon kissed her hand gravely; his unkempt beard tickled.

"One day, my dear, Brydon Airlines will be a major operator and this bum will be working for *me.* In the meantime, I fly cargoes of chickens and copra and whatever else anyone wants to send anywhere in the Pacific. We're not fancy, but we're cheap."

Slowly the place filled up, mostly men and a few women, several of whom Jill knew as flight attendants. Most of the men were colleagues of David and Burt, fliers and ex-fliers, and the talk was of flying. The near-disaster of the Hilo flight got a brief airing but only to introduce other stories of greater risks; tales of seat-of-the-pants flying all over the Pacific, of planes patched up with wire and flattened cookie tins. They all drank a lot but no one got drunk and there was none of the macho competitiveness she would have expected from a group of younger men.

"I'm really upset at leaving you stranded without a car tomorrow," David said. "Whatever you want to do, I'll drive you. Or you can just borrow my car."

"It's no problem," she said. "I've got no plans. I'll just lie around the house."

He drained his drink and signaled to Andy for a final one.

"You ever do any sailing?" he asked suddenly. "Because maybe you'd like to come along with Andy and me. The boat's pretty rough, but it gets us where we want to go and it makes a nice change from work."

"I love sailing. I learned a little on Lake Michigan. Just summer-camp stuff in dinghies, but I guess I know my way around a boat. If you're sure I wouldn't be in the way, I'd love to come along."

"Andy," he called across the bar, "okay with you if Jill joins us on the trip?"

"Great," Andy called back. "She's a whole lot prettier than you, and I'm sure she's got a better nature. Anybody does. But warn her about my cooking."

David grinned. "Andy's idea of a gourmet breakfast is a cup of hot fat with a hair in it. We really do sail rough, though. It's not sitting around on deck in Bloomingdale's gear, sipping gin and tonic. It's dirty old shorts and cans of beer."

"I can cope," she assured him. "How long are we going to be away?"

"One night, maybe two. That all right with you?"

"That's just fine. I'm not responsible to anyone. Even my cat ran away from home a couple of months ago."

David did not sleep well that night. The day's drama played itself out again and again

28

in his head. He was intelligent enough to recognize the strain he was under and glad not to be flying for a while. But he could not understand why the tension would not leave him, why his hands still shook. The sailing trip was a good idea and he was glad he'd invited the girl. Three days in close quarters and he would learn if his hunch about her was correct.

The motorsailer *Wings* looked out of place among the huge, expensive boats on the Alamoana dock. She was big enough—close to sixty feet, Jill guessed—but her white paintwork was chipped and faded, the brasswork was dull, and the timber deck gray with age.

"Andy doesn't care what things look like," David apologized as they stood on the dock. "He bought this boat with some idea of doing charters for the tourists, but he doesn't really like to work too hard. If he spruced *Wings* up he could make a good living off of her, but—"

"But then she wouldn't be available when you and I want to take off," Andy interrupted as he came striding down the dock. "Hi, Jill. Wasn't I right about the weather?"

It was a beautiful day, just a few white clouds, and the sun was already hot. The whole island basked in it, the strain of the past days soothed away. All around them people were getting their boats ready to sail.

There was little for Jill to do. Andy and David handled the boat with an easy familiarity, motoring her out past the breakwater before putting up the sails. She was a big, beamy boat but moved decently under canvas, and within an hour they were out of sight of land. As the heat rose, Jill went down to her cabin and changed into a bikini. Belowdecks, *Wings* was cluttered and shabby, but she could see the boat's potential: sleeping accommodations for twelve in four cabins, a large galley, two showers and heads.

"It's a magnificent boat, Andy," she told him later. "A little bit of paint and a scrubbing brush . . ."

Andy laughed and winked at David. The men were wearing ragged old shorts, drinking beer from cans, and pretty much letting the boat sail herself.

"We like it the way it is. I guess we're slobs, Jill."

"No," she protested, "I see it suits you fine. It's just . . . a boat like this has so much potential. I'm always having tourists ask me if I know a boat they can go cruising on—not those little half-day tours but long overnight trips. This would be perfect."

"That's what he bought it for," David said, tossing her an icy can of beer. "Or at least, that was the justification he used at the time. But as you get to know Andy, you'll learn one thing: he's the laziest man in the islands."

"Yes," Andy said, "but I'm also the happiest." He shrugged. "Maybe I should do

30

something with *Wings*, but I like the life I've got now. I own a nice piece of the bar and I work there just as long as I please. I sail whenever I like. Carting tourists around would be such a hassle.''

They lunched on chicken and salad and later Jill stretched out on the deck, listening to laughter and talk from the men and thinking how happy and relaxed David Nagle was out there on the water. She was thoroughly at ease, too, Andy and David treating her like an old buddy.

''Nice girl, that,'' Andy said as he corrected the wheel a fraction. ''Doesn't seem desperate, like so many of the stews. And a real looker.''

''Yes,'' David said cautiously. ''I only just met her, but I think she's okay. She liked the company in your bar, though, so I'm not sure about her judgment.''

''Don't talk to me about judgment, Nagle. Those dogs you've been dating the last few years, ha! That's why I'm so surprised to find you with one who's not a bowwow.''

''Yeah,'' David said ruefully. ''But you know how it is. I just don't want to get involved. So I don't go around with anyone who really attracts me.''

''What about now?''

''It's too early to tell. Anyway, look after your own love life, Koa. What's happened to the little blond?''

Andy snorted with disgust. ''Her husband

left her, so all the excitement went out of it for me. And she started talking about making our arrangement permanent. She was moving her stuff into my apartment, piece by piece. I've had four wives and I sure as *hell* don't want another, de facto or otherwise.''

''You could have waited until she tidied your place up a bit,'' David said. ''It's a mess.''

David caught a tuna for their supper and they barbecued it on a hibachi on deck. *Wings* was swaying gently at anchor in a palm-lined bay, the tropic moon was rising, and Jill was about as content as she had ever been. She passed around the jug of mai tais she'd made but there was nothing else for her to do. The two men prepared and served the meal with practiced ease. They were used to each other around the boat, and Jill envied them their sense of belonging.

''This is what I dreamed about before I came to Hawaii,'' she said softly as they let the dark envelop them. ''Instead, it's usually like living in any American city with sand.''

''Yes,'' David said, ''you've got to get out of Honolulu to enjoy Hawaii. But once you do, it's heaven.''

Andy inhaled on the huge joint he was smoking and laughed at some private joke. Then he bowed to both of them.

''I shall leave you alone,'' he said, ''to let the tropics work its magic on you. Make as much noise as you like, but please try not to rock the boat." He leaned down and kissed Jill on the cheek. "Welcome aboard. I hope you'll make the Boston Brahmin very happy."

He chuckled to himself all the way down the companionway.

She didn't know what to do. Did David Nagle want to go to bed with her? She could feel him hanging back.

"What did Andy mean, 'the Boston Brahmin'?" she asked.

"It's his little joke," David sighed. "Andy's convinced my family are rich old New England Wasps and I'm some kind of remittance man banished to the islands. Trouble is, it's near enough the truth and I don't like being reminded about it." He drained his drink and looked out into the night. "But I guess it's not much of a price to pay for his company. Andy's one of the only two people I feel relaxed with these days."

"Why wouldn't your family be proud of you?" she asked, puzzled. "My folks think it's wonderful and romantic, my being out here, and I'm only a stewardess. You're a pilot, a respected one. And after yesterday's story gets back to the mainland, your family's going to think you're wonderful."

"Not my family," he said flatly. He stood up. "I'm going to turn in now. I'll see you in the morning. You know where everything is."

She stayed out on deck awhile longer, alone.

Rain woke her late that night, pounding on the deck above her head and slashing against the tiny porthole beside her bed. The boat was pitching in the storm, rolling and pulling against its anchor. She heard the thumping of footsteps on the deck and stumbled from her berth to help.

It was dark on deck except for jagged lightning flashes. There were whitecaps on the waves surging around them, and rain was sheeting down. In the bow of the boat, David struggled with the second anchor. She hurried forward and helped him get the anchor out over the bow. They played out the rope until the spikes bit into the sea floor. Then he grabbed her by the shoulder and steered her to his dimly lit cabin.

''Thanks,'' he said as they stood in the cabin, water pouring from them. ''When the squall hit she started dragging her anchor. I tried to wake Andy but he's dead to the world. Here,'' he said, throwing her a towel, ''you're drenched.''

She glanced down at herself. The thin nightgown was plastered to her and she felt more exposed than she'd have felt naked.

''I'll make us some coffee,'' he said. ''Would you like a brandy, too?''

''I'd love one,'' she said. ''But I'm going to find something to wear first.''

They sat for half an hour in a cabin near the galley, listening to the squall pass away, drinking coffee and brandy and talking quietly. Not about much. And when she stood up and gathered their cups and glasses, they both knew it was time.

He followed close behind her down the companionway, past the cabin where Andy snored contentedly, to the space in the bow where her berth was. She fumbled for matches and lit the hurricane lamp, then turned to face him.

David put his arms around her and drew her close to him. She raised her lips to his: the kiss began slowly. They explored each other, their kissing becoming more passionate. His hands moved down her back and cupped her buttocks, lifting her hard against him. She felt the length of his lean body pressing into her, the surprising strength of him.

He undid the robe she was wearing, letting it fall between them. She was naked underneath, and in the soft glow of the lamp her beauty was ethereal. Her breasts rose up to greet him, her thighs parted for his hand. He was in control of her, could play her body, but he didn't want it to be like that. He needed for all the sensations, pleasures, mysteries to be theirs together.

He eased her down onto the V-berth and stretched himself out beside her. Jill let her hands move over his chest, gently brushing his nipples and feeling them rise; she put her lips there and teased them with her tongue, tasting him. Her hand moved slowly down over his ribs to the flat, taut belly. He shivered when she circled his navel with a fingertip, and strained against her as she moved her hand lower. He sprang up to meet her hand, and she felt him long and hard but sheathed in satin; she stroked him gently, feeling the current of life throbbing, racing through her fingers into her own body.

His hands drifted up the inside of her smooth thighs, higher and higher, stopping just short of her core and retreating to trace new patterns. He kissed her nipples, then gently nibbled them, loving the sensation as they grew harder. His own body begged for relief, but he wanted to give her every pleasure. David was enjoying this new sensation of giving rather than plundering. He let his finger stray further, gently brushing her outer lips, and she shuddered, drawing closer.

He moved down her body and knelt between her legs. She watched, her eyes clouded with passion, as he bowed his head. His tongue entered the fiery center of her. It flicked and darted inside her, bringing her almost instantly to a crest. Her hands acted on their own, gripping his head and forcing him farther into her. She cried out when she came the second time, and she was almost afraid of the intensity of her passion. She forced herself to pull back, and she edged him up into the bunk beside her. She kissed him and tasted herself.

David returned her kiss, their tongues entwining, and swung his body over hers. He tried to enter her gently but her hips were already moving in a rhythm that pounded against him, sending him plunging deep inside her. There was a great empty space inside her that only he could fill. He felt bigger than ever before, better than ever before. Finally, as she arched her hips under him and dug her fingers into his back, he released his flood. All of him was inside her. Their pubic bones thumped together in a final ecstasy; he heard her cry out again.

They lay close together, sweat drying on their skin, and she studied his face hungrily. The hooded blue eyes were no longer cold, the features no longer stern. She kissed him on both eyelids and whispered, "It's never been like that."

"No," he whispered back, "not for me either."

They slept, snuggled in the small space, rocked by the sea.

"You going to sleep all day?" Andy called to them, leaning against the open cabin door, grinning. He held a cup of coffee in each hand. "Drink this and come up on deck. It's a beautiful day, and I already caught our breakfast."

David reached for the cups, telling Jill, "Keep yourself covered. The only reason this guy is hanging around is to get a look at your boobs."

"A fine sight she is, too," Andy said cheerfully, winking at Jill.

He left them alone and Jill sipped her coffee. She stole a glance at David squatting on the bunk beside her. She hated next mornings, usually so awkward.

"Hey," he said, "I think I love you."

They stayed close together all day, making opportunities to touch each other, looking into each other's eyes. Andy delighted in their obvious infatuation, kidding them as he steered *Wings* through the calm seas. They ate and drank and basked in the sun; Jill was in a happy daze most of the time, feasting her eyes on the man she had suddenly come to know so well.

David was just as dazed. He hadn't felt emotion like this in years. In fact, he had steeled himself against just this feeling. Last night, he'd decided he was safe. He felt a glorious happiness and was engulfed in gratitude to the woman who had caused it.

"As skipper of this tub," Andy rumbled, "I am empowered to marry the pair of you. Remember that."

"There's someone I want you to meet," David told her as they stood in the bow and watched the jagged Waikiki skyline approach. "Someone who's very special to me. I'm closer to him than I am to anybody. He's been

38

like a father to me for all the time I've been out here."

"I'll meet anyone you want me to," she said. "I want to show you off to all my friends, too."

He smiled down at her, thinking how pleasing a contradiction she was: so serious and mature at times, so ingenuous and young at others.

"He's Dr. Carl Cohen. If you know anything about orchids, you'll have heard of him. He's maybe the world's foremost expert on orchids. But before he came here and fell in love with the place, he was a doctor. And before that, a high-powered operative for the government. Very high-powered."

He didn't tell her of the circumstances of his first meeting with Cohen; that would have revealed just how important Cohen had been, and David knew the old man did not like anyone knowing that.

Soon after David had settled in Hawaii, trying to establish a one-man, one-plane charter business, he'd been sitting in the little tin shed that served as his office when the telex clattered into life. That was unusual enough: the machine often stayed silent for days on end. The message was even more unusual. Obviously misdirected, it was addressed to Dr. Carl Cohen and it was in code.

David found Cohen in the telephone directory and called.

"This is David Nagle, out at the airport," he

said. "I just got a message for you on my telex. I guess someone's got their wires crossed."

"It's most kind of you to call," said the gentle voice at the other end of the wire. "If you'll just give me your location I'll have someone stop by and pick up the message. I'm sorry to have inconvenienced you."

The real inconvenience came thirty minutes later when four menacing military policemen pulled up in a truck outside David's office.

"Where's the telex?" the leader demanded. No introductions. No pretense.

David bridled at the man's rudeness, but he had seen enough of the military to know there was no point in arguing.

"Here," he said, passing across the white message slip.

The man pocketed it, then said to the others, "Get the fucking machine on the truck."

"Hey, hold it right there!" David snapped, coming out of his chair. "That's *my* machine. You can't—"

The leader shoved him in the chest, forcing him back into his chair. "This is a security matter. Shut up and keep out of our way."

Speechless with rage, David watched as they hefted his telex out of the office and onto their truck. They drove off without another word. He was shaking with fury when he dialed Cohen's number again.

"Dr. Cohen? David Nagle again. I realize you're probably some kind of a big shot and

I'm only a struggling pilot. But I don't deserve to have four goons march in, rough me up, and take away my telex machine. I need that damned machine for my business. What in *hell* is going on?''

Then he really exploded; the voice at the other end was roaring with laughter.

''I'm sorry,'' Cohen finally gasped. ''I'm awfully sorry. You have just witnessed the military mind at work. I called someone and told them to pick up a telex, and instead they came and took away the machine itself!'' He erupted in laughter again.

''I fail to see anything humorous,'' David snapped.

''Of course,'' Cohen said, his voice gentle. ''I have seriously upset your business and I'll make amends. Since they've got your machine anyway, I'll order them to give it a full service and have it back in operation by this afternoon. In the meantime, let me send my driver for you. Come have lunch with me. I'm way up in the hills, but I hope you'll find the trip worthwhile. Please, will you accept?''

There was no work for David then anyway, and he was curious to meet the man who pulled so much weight. ''Okay,'' he said rudely. ''What the hell.''

''Thank you. My man will pick you up in thirty minutes.''

Cohen's driver was a Japanese—big, silent, tough-looking. The car was a white Cadillac convertible. They sped up out of Honolulu and into the hills, turned in a small gate, and entered a wonderland, driving through acre after acre of magnificent rain forest. Orchids bloomed everywhere, orchids of every color and size. At the end of the drive was Cohen's house—rambling, comfortable, perfectly suited to its lush setting. A short wiry man in his sixties was waiting for them on the wide balcony, and he hurried down the steps and opened the car door.

"Mr. Nagle." He was smiling. "Thank you for coming. I'm Carl Cohen."

It was a glorious lunch: fresh lobster, cold beef, fresh fruits, and several bottles of the finest French wine David had ever tasted. Through lunch Cohen continued to apologize. He explained he still did consulting work for the government and there were security elements involved.

Gently, Cohen drew from David much more than David ever told about himself. By the end of lunch Cohen knew exactly how perilous was the state of David's business, the mess his personal life was in, and the bitterness he felt about the Vietnam debacle and the way vets were currently treated by their countrymen.

It was to be the first of many lunches and dinners in the exquisite home in the wonderful rain forest. Cohen and David became the closest of friends, two loners who were at ease in each other's company and delighted in that.

David's offering to bring Jill to the older man's estate meant more than she could have guessed.

Chapter Two _____

TWO MONTHS LATER, IN A SIMPLE CERE-
mony in Dr. Cohen's lush garden, Jill and David were married. Her parents were there,
pale and small and blinking in the bright tropical light. They were overwhelmed by the
trip—New York was as far from home as they
had ever been. Jill had wanted his parents,
too, but he adamantly refused to invite them.
Jill wrote secretly to his mother in Boston. The
reply was stiff, just short of rude. She said the
Nagles did not recognize divorce. As far as
they were concerned, he was still married to
Marion. They would have nothing to do with
David until he stopped being a dropout in the
tropics and took up his family responsibilities
in Boston. Jill couldn't understand; surely
they still loved their son, didn't they?

   "Don't let David know you wrote his
mother," Andy advised her. "He means it
when he says he wants nothing to do with
them. They sided with Marion when she filed
for divorce and even when she denied him access to the kid. They thought he was a fool to

go to Vietnam, like the war was something only working-class kids went to. They had his future all mapped out, into Daddy's firm right after Harvard. But you know what David's like: he doesn't do what's expected of him.''

''But surely, after all these years, they can make up,'' she said.

''No,'' Andy said. ''He despises them, and part of that is because all the while his family was reviling him for being in Vietnam, the old man's company was making millions and millions of dollars underwriting loans for the big producers of war materials. David believes in everyone playing straight. He's been let down so many times now, he doesn't trust many people.''

''What about his son?''

''David's parents see young David as the continuation of the Nagle dynasty and they call the shots about the boy. I don't think the kid's mother gives a damn one way or the other. She's a New York rich bitch who lives for parties.'' Andy shook his head. ''David's closed those chapters of his life for good. Until you came along he pretty well lived just for flying and his small circle of friends.''

''God, I'm glad he had you and Dr. Cohen,'' she said, chilled. ''I remember how afraid of him we all were. He was so . . . prickly. Nobody could get near him. Who wanted to?''

Andy was standing alongside David as the marriage celebrant read the vows, and Cindy

Mason stood on Jill's left. Jill glanced out from under the short white veil. Just behind her, standing on the grass, were her parents, her mother dabbing her eyes with a lace handkerchief, her father blinking behind his horn-rimmed glasses. Dr. Cohen, small and old and gnarled, was looking full of life, beaming. She felt a rush of affection for all of them, for their being there on this beautiful day as she married the only man she had ever loved. David took her hand and she looked up into his eyes. There was peace there, peace and pride and happiness. She vowed to herself she would never do anything to cause him anguish.

The brief service was over and he bent to kiss her; her lips were warm and full of promise, her eyes moist and deep and loving. And then their friends were crowding around them, kissing and hugging, even—this from the dozen veteran pilots David had invited—throwing rice. And all about them danced the glorious blooms of Dr. Cohen's triumphant orchids.

Andy, bigger than ever in a billowing white suit, embraced them both and pulled them along toward a long table covered with fresh green banana leaves. The Hawaiian-style wedding feast was laid out. A few yards away, a trio of guitarists played the "Wedding Song."

"I don't want this day to end," she whispered to her husband before she was dragged away by the happy throng of friends. Just for an instant, she thought she saw a flash of fear in his eyes, or perhaps it was pain. But she knew she was mistaken: they were happy now and would be happy ever after.

"The best wedding I've ever been to," Cindy said, hugging Jill. "You really did it— you tamed the ferocious Captain Nagle. The airline should give you a medal."

"The airline," Jill laughed, "has given me three months' notice under the husband-and-wife clause. But I don't care. I would have quit anyway. I want to stay home and have David's babies."

"Have fun first," Cindy said, squeezing her arm. "There's plenty of time for babies." She put down her glass. "Now, you're sure you're all set for the flight tonight? It's going to be awfully cold in Aspen."

"Everything's packed," Jill said. "And thanks again for letting my parents stay with you."

"They're great," Cindy said. "Don't worry about them. They can have a few quiet days while you're gone. We'll do a little sight-seeing."

Dr. Cohen joined them, moving silently on his birdlike feet. He took Jill's hand and put it gently to his lips. She looked down on his bowed head and felt a fresh surge of affection. He meant so much to David. And already he meant so much to her. His wisdom, his calmness, his gentleness—he had all the qualities she and her generation had almost forgotten.

She felt a peace and serenity just being with him.

"Thank you, Carl," she said. "Thank you for this wonderful day and thank you for taking care of David so well."

"I'll always be here if either of you needs me," he said softly. "Come visit an old man now and then." He smiled at her, a sad, wise smile, and drifted away.

They glided off the chair lift and linked arms until they were far enough ahead of the following skiers to stop. The sky was sparkling blue at the top of the mountain; the sun shone on the fresh white snow. Jill looped her stocks over her wrists and breathed in as deeply as she could.

"We should have been up here hours ago," she mock-scolded David. "It's sinful to let half the morning go by."

"I didn't hear you complaining while we were in bed letting it go by." He grinned. They were conspirators, the tang of their lovemaking still enveloping them, the memory of their recent passion stronger even than the mountain beauty surrounding them.

"And I won't complain ever," she said, leaning out over her skis and kissing him. "But now we're going skiing. By the way, are you any good? I don't even know what kind of skier you are. God, David, there's so much we don't know about each other."

"We've got a lifetime to find out. Starting now." He bent to adjust his bindings. "See you at the bottom." He glided straight down the huge mountain, easily threading his way around the brightly colored knots of skiers dawdling in his path.

Jill watched him for a moment. He was very, very good, moving with grace and ease, perfectly balanced. She pushed herself off the lip of the slope but began with a gentle traverse. She was skiing hatless and enjoyed the breeze pulling at her long hair, the warmth of the sun on her shoulders. She swung back and forth across the side of the mountain, letting herself go deeper down the fall line on each pass, feeling her body loosening until she was ready to turn straight down the hill. She dropped into a racing crouch and headed toward the yellow flash of David's parka far below her. As she zoomed down the mountain, nothing in her ears but the swish of her skis racing over the powder, she wanted to shout for joy.

He was waiting for her near the chair lift, and she did a show-off stop, sending a wave of snow over him and halting inches from him.

"Pretty good," he nodded, brushing snow off his face. "A bit too hotdog for my liking, but good. I guess it's safe to take you right to the top next run."

"Worry about yourself, Captain, not about me. You older folks, your bones break easily.

If you bust something, don't expect me to hang around your bedside. I'll find myself a handsome young—''

''I love you, Jill,'' he said. ''This is the happiest I've ever been.'' He kissed her full on the lips, ignoring the skiers around them. He felt a tenderness in himself, something that had never been there before. His eyes moistened, shocking him. So many changes.

Later, after two exhilarating runs on the advanced slopes, they found a quiet trail and traveled for half an hour through a fringe of trees, gliding from sunshine to shadow in the stillness, side by side in a perfect white world of their own.

''We'll teach our children to ski just as soon as they can walk,'' Jill said. ''And we'll take vacations together in a place like this, you and me leading a procession of little Nagles down the slopes.'' She took the lighted cigarette he passed her. ''We're going to be so happy, David.''

''We already are,'' he said. ''At this moment there's nothing I want that I haven't got right here.'' He gestured to the trees and the snow and the sun. ''Someday I want us to run a little resort in the mountains, the kind of place nice people come to.''

''What would we do in the summer?'' she asked. ''You'd get bored sitting around on a bare mountain with no snow.''

''That's when we'll make all those babies you're talking about,'' he said.

They made four more long downhill runs, pushing their bodies to a stage of pleasant fatigue. As the sun was beginning to set, they made their final descent and went back to the lodge.

The lodge was a simple, comfortable place, all open fireplaces and exposed beams. It was owned by two of David's pilot friends and could sleep three or four couples, but they had it all to themselves. The caretakers had stocked the place with food and liquor and the lovers had no need to venture out into the hectic Aspen *après-ski* world. Leaning against each other in mutual weariness, they moved through the warm living room and up the stairs to their bedroom. One glass wall faced the mountain, and they stood a moment, watching the last of the skiers tracing patterns on the snow.

There was little room in the shower, but they squeezed in together and let the water flow over them. She took a bar of pine-scented soap and began to lather his body, feeling all the clefts and ridges, the muscles and bones, exploring him with possessive pride. His body was still a wonderful mystery, and she delighted in him.

David looked down through the streaming water as she knelt before him, her strong hands working on his thighs, kneading his buttocks, her sweet mouth taking him in and bringing him to the brink of ecstasy. He shuddered and felt his knees go weak. He gently drew her up to him, giddy with passion, and then he lifted her onto him, melding their bodies into one.

She gasped as his great shaft probed deep inside her, and she clung to him with her legs and arms. The water was still beating down on her, plastering her hair over her eyes, very hot, but not as hot as the heat inside her. Her frenzy grew into a string of orgasms like linked firecrackers, and then his own explosion shot inside her and she buried her face in his shoulder, trembling.

Groggy, they stumbled back to the bedroom, crawled under a goose-down quilt, and fell asleep in each other's arms as the last light touched their window.

Five days later, it was hot and steamy in downtown Honolulu and Dr. Cohen's guests appreciated the cool green quiet of his rain forest. They strolled among the magnificent blooms, talking softly out of deference to their surroundings.

"You're so lucky to know Dr. Cohen," Jill's mother said. "This place is truly a paradise. It'll seem like a dream when we're back in Chicago." She put her hand on Jill's arm. "Your father is so happy. He thinks David's a marvelous man. So do I."

"He *is* marvelous," Jill said happily. "No one has ever been as much in love I am. My only regret is that we didn't meet years ago, so I'm going to make every day with David count."

"When are you going to start a family?" her mother asked.

"We want to have lots of children. Soon, too. Which means we'll have to find a proper house."

"Just don't wait too long," her mother cautioned. "It's the one regret your father and I have, that we put off starting a family until a time when we thought we'd be better off. Well, as you know, your father never did get any promotions. We went ahead and had you and then it was too late for me to have any more. You have made us so happy, Jill. You've repaid us a thousand times over for all the struggle we had getting you to college."

"You're the best parents anyone could have," Jill told her. "It's awful we're so far apart now. Please come back soon, Mom. David's very fond of you both already."

"Ah, my two favorite ladies," her father called out, bearing down on them with a tall drink in his hand. Jill smiled at the change in him since he had arrived in Hawaii. His normal bookkeeper's pallor was gone. He had a light tan, and the solemn horn-rims now featured jaunty sun lenses.

"This has been the greatest time of my life," he said. "I wonder whether we might think about retiring here. Dr. Cohen was saying you can live cheaply here if you keep away from the tourist areas." He took Jill's hand. "Dr. Cohen thinks a lot of you," he said. "You can rely on him for help if you need it."

"I know, Daddy. He's already done so much for David just by being his friend. And he treats me like a daughter." She steered them back toward the house. "We can't stay out here now, though. This is your farewell party and you have to mix with the others."

Jill found Cindy swinging in a hammock on the porch.

"What are you doing out here on your own?" Jill asked. "You're always the life of the party. And no date?"

"Oh, lordy, you old married women," Cindy sighed. "You can't bear to see anyone single, can you? If you must know, I came alone because I didn't think it appropriate to bring my boyfriend. How do you think David would have reacted if I'd turned up with The Hulk?"

"Jed Ramsay! You're kidding!" Jill cried, then lowered her voice. "You're not going with him?"

"Take it easy," Cindy laughed. "We can't all be as lucky as you are. He hasn't got a brain in his head, just as you warned me. But he's good in bed and I don't have to make conversation with him. He'll do, for now. But out of respect for the newlyweds, I didn't invite him."

"David wouldn't have cared." Jill shrugged. "He's not jealous over my past. That's one of the things I love about him: he's so much more mature than most men."

"A twelve-year-old is more mature than Jed

54

Ramsay,'' Cindy said sweetly. ''Not as well hung, though.'' She swung out of the hammock and stood. ''I'm glad you're so happy, honey. It's all working out wonderfully for both of you. I was watching David watching you—the man's entranced. Who could have dreamed old sourpuss Nagle would turn into a love-struck boy? God works in mysterious—''

''He was just shy and lonely,'' Jill said defensively. ''Now that I truly know him, he's the kindest, easiest man to live with.'' She laughed. ''I hear from some of the crew that he's fun to fly with now.''

''I'm sure the airline will be very grateful to you for the transformation,'' Cindy said. ''Their gratitude and forty cents will get you a cup of coffee.''

''They're bastards,'' Jill said. ''I know. But being a stewardess beats working in an office or something. I wonder what I should do while I'm waiting for our first baby?''

Jill found her new involvement almost by accident. She and David were sailing regularly with Andy, and she wanted to do something to return Andy's hospitality. She took to dropping by the boat on days when David was flying and she wasn't. She enjoyed the sheer physical work of stripping and sanding the deck, of rubbing the brass fittings to glowing splendor. After a month of quiet activity, she had *Wings* almost as good as new. During that time, too, an idea grew.

"I know you guys aren't going to like this," she said, settling on a stool at Andy's bar. "But I want you to let me say it anyway." David and Andy glanced at each other.

"*Wings* now looks as good as she should. It's time we did something with her. Andy, when you bought *Wings* you thought you might use her for charters, right? Has she got a license?"

"Yeah, but I guess it's expired," he said vaguely. "I lost interest in the chartering idea, I told you."

"We have her surveyed," she said, "and renew the license."

"Hey, hold on," David said. "I see enough tourist traffic from the flight deck. I don't want to spend my spare time ferrying tourists around."

"Me neither," said Andy. "It's too much hassle."

"Is five hundred dollars a day—net—a hassle?" she demanded. "Because that's the minimum we'll make under the scheme I've worked out. Five hundred bucks a day, every day of the week if we want to work that hard. But," she smiled, "knowing you two, I suggest we start by going out just twice a week . . . until I've proved my point."

"What is your point?" David asked.

"I've checked out the other charter operations and I've talked to a lot of tourists about what they want," she said. "There's a gap in the market here between the two-hour cruises on an outrigger and the full-scale charters operating to the other islands. What I want to offer is classy day packages, say, nine A.M. to six P.M., restricted to ten or twelve people at seventy-five dollars a head. Everything's included—great food, wine, an open bar. I've costed it all out, and twenty-five dollars a head is more than it'll cost for fuel, food, and booze. I'll need one of you guys to sail the boat while I'm handling the food and fixing drinks. I'll need some help, but I figure I'll always be able to recruit a couple of off-duty stews who'll come along and lend a hand in return for the nice day out and a little money."

"Your catering figures sound right," Andy said grudgingly. "And the way prices run here, I don't suppose seventy-five a head will bother the tourists. But how will we get this started?"

"That's where we use our airline connection. It'll have to be done very discreetly, but we arm all our friends in the cabin crews with cards. Then, when they're chatting with the passengers about Honolulu, they mention this great charter operation and hand them the card. We'll kick back five dollars a head for every customer they get us. It's the best kind of selling."

"I don't want to hear this," David groaned. "Hustling the passengers is against every airline regulation."

"No one's going to know about it," she said. "And I promise we won't do any hustling on *your* flights. But doesn't it appeal to your sense of fair play to score something off the airline after the way they've treated all of us?"

"She's right, Dave," Andy said. "And it's a nice gimmick, having the stews along on trips. Fit 'em out in short shorts and tiny tops, turn on the charm, it couldn't miss."

"I've already talked it over with Cindy and she wants to come along. The other girls will, too."

"What do you think, Dave?" Andy asked finally. "You want to give it a try?"

"It's your boat," David said, "and since I fly at least three days a week, it's you who'll be doing most of the work. If you want to try it out, fine with me."

She kissed them both and ordered a bottle of champagne.

Jill didn't organize the first cruise until a week after she had quit the airline, needing time to prepare her menus. *Wings* had a good galley already, including a three-burner stove, refrigerator, and deep freezer. She wanted the food to be simple, abundant, and first-rate. With Cindy's help she devised a series of minimal-preparation dishes: cold soups, chicken in aspic, cold fillets of beef, cold poached fish. And there were also dishes to be cooked at home, then heated again on board, like coconut curries, a firehouse chili, some Chinese dishes.

"You know what we're doing?" Cindy said as they discussed the menus. "We're serving the kind of food the airlines would serve if they had any sense."

From the very first day, it worked exactly as Jill had predicted. They soon had more bookings than they could handle, as their unique sales staff went to work. Jill resisted the temptation to take more than twelve along on each trip: she sensed the key to *Wings'* success would be to keep the trips exclusive and give top value. They aimed at a certain type of clientele—well-heeled young-to-middle-aged couples, people who appreciated fine food and drink and didn't quibble over cost.

Andy surprised himself by getting caught up in Jill's enthusiasm. He still grumbled about having to play nursemaid to tourists, and professed to have no interest in the money they were making, but he enjoyed the sailing and hammed it up for the passengers, enjoying playing the wise, jovial old Polynesian sea dog.

David wasn't sure what to make of it. He was pleased that Jill was so happy, and he was proud of her business acumen, but when he was at the wheel of *Wings* he was cool and distant with the passengers. He couldn't banter with them the way Andy did. Still, he was polite and efficient, and that was enough.

"I think we need a second boat," she told

David one night as they sat on the terrace of their newly rented home. "I hate turning so many people away. We could make this into a big business."

"Don't hurry things," he said. "You've got a nice operation now; if you run a second boat you're going to have headaches about staffing it, about the provisions. I'm real proud of you, but I don't want you taking on too much."

"Don't worry, darling," she reassured him. "I won't do anything you and Andy don't agree with one hundred percent. We're all partners."

Chapter Three _____

HE CHECKED THEIR LANDING CLEAR-
ance from Honolulu tower and put the plane
into a long, gentle descent. It was a bright,
clear day, the flights to Maui and back had
been uneventful, and David was looking forward to a quiet evening at home with Jill. By
the time he was through at the airport she
would just about be back from the day's charter. He smiled. The charter business was
booming, three boats working now. All their
considerable profits had been poured back
into expanding the fleet, but neither he nor
Andy complained: they both knew it was all
Jill's doing. She was an incredible girl and David was a happy, proud man.

He turned to speak to his engineer and in
that moment he froze with panic: he was sliding out of consciousness, dropping away
without warning. He tried with all his might
to force his muscles to respond. He could see,
through a dark fog, his hands on the controls,
but he couldn't make them move.

"Are you all right, Skipper?" the engineer asked. "You're looking kind of strange."

David tried to speak but his throat had clutched. Cold clammy sweat broke out on his forehead. There was no pain, just that desperate helplessness, that feeling of slipping away from himself. And then, within fifteen seconds, he was suddenly in command again.

"I'm okay," he told the younger man. "Couldn't breathe for a second or two. I'm okay now." He continued their descent, careful to seem relaxed and unconcerned, and put the jet down in a routine landing.

He sat for a while in the parking lot, in the hot little car, trying to face what had happened to him. He forced himself to remember a similar time in Aspen and another time one morning when he was driving to the airport. He thought he knew what was going on, how his brain was betraying him, and he wanted fervently to be wrong. Finally he started the VW, turning it away from the direction of home and Jill, heading up into the rain forest instead.

Dr. Cohen was tending his orchids, wearing ragged shorts and an old shirt too big for him now. He glanced up when the VW drove into the compound, and walked slowly over to greet David.

He looked down into David's face. "You're troubled," he said simply. "Come into the house and I'll make tea."

David followed the old man up the steps

and into the house. Normally, these occasions gave him intense pleasure: the orderly calm of Carl's life, the sense of peace. Tonight, though, he walked in terror, waiting for the verdict.

When the tea was before them, Cohen sat down on a rush mat and waited for David to speak.

"Carl," he said at last, "I've been having . . . blackouts, I suppose they are. The latest one today, when I was at the controls." The words started rushing out then, David desperately explaining his terror, and just as desperately avoiding the dreadful word. Cohen listened, nodding, as the darkness deepened in the room. He did not speak until David had exhausted himself, and then he spoke without hesitation.

"Don't be afraid," he said. "You have survived far worse than this." It was all David could do not to sob. "Even without an examination," Cohen continued, "I would say that you may be suffering petit mal. It is controllable and it need never occur again."

"But flying . . ." Tears of anger welled in David. "I'll never fly again."

"No," Cohen said calmly, "not if it *is* petit mal. I know you, David. You would never place the lives of others in danger. What you described happening today—you won't risk that happening again, will you?"

David shook his head and Carl said, "It may be something very minor, like a reaction to medication. Do you take thyroid pills or anything on a permanent basis?"

David shook his head again. Cohen mentioned all the possible reasons for convulsive seizures, then said, "If you recall everything that happened during the episode, it may be a Transient Ischemic Attack. Epileptics don't remember. But you will need to be examined properly in any case. I'm not going to do that because if it is serious and is going to happen again, I would be forced to inform the airline. I do not want to be in that position. You must decide your course of action for yourself."

"But why should this happen to me?" David demanded, outraged. "There's no history of . . . anything like this in my family. How can I live if I never know when I'm going to black out? This means I'm practically an invalid."

"No it doesn't," the doctor said firmly. "It only means a few sensible precautions—avoiding stress and excessive drinking, a course of pills—could mean you'll never have another attack. In a year, say, you could have a clean bill of health. But not to fly, though," he said. He couldn't give David false hope. "When you tell the official medical examiner your symptoms, he will ground you and the airline will retire you on a disability pension. You are only forty years old, David. This thing may be a blessing if it moves you in new directions."

"I'm not going to be rubbed out by their

doctors," David swore. "I couldn't stand the pity, the snide looks, the jokes behind my back about my being sick in the head. No," he said, standing, "I'm just going to quit the airline for no reason at all. That way, I should be able to keep my private license. I swear to you I'll never fly commercially again. But please leave me this: that in a year, or whenever I'm cured, I can still fly for my own pleasure—risking no one else."

"You're giving up a lot of money by choosing that course," Cohen said. "Especially if it's not epilepsy. But I understand you. Yes, you will be able to fly again." He lit his pipe and watched the smoke curling upward. "What are you going to tell Jill?"

She was in the kitchen, working on the next day's meals, when she heard his car. She brushed flour from her hands and went to greet him at the door, and then she saw the terrible change in him.

"David!" she gasped. "What's happened?" He was deathly pale under his tan, and his eyes were blank. She held him to her but there was no response. He was as distant as the look in his eyes. After a while he stepped away from her.

"I've just been to see Carl," he said, his voice hollow. "I needed his professional advice. I spaced out, somehow, when I was bringing the plane home today."

"Spaced out?" she stammered, bewildered. "But you're all right now?"

"I'm not all right," he said. "It wasn't the first time. And it won't be the last." He swallowed and focused his gaze somewhere over her head. "Jill," he said, "I've got something wrong. Maybe epilepsy." He watched her closely then, looking for her reaction, expecting revulsion. He was so steeped in self-disgust over the collapse of his system that he assumed she would be repelled.

It did hit her hard, the word conjuring up childhood fears of a strange malady. Then, at once, the balancing element in her nature took over, reminding her of things she'd read about the disease.

David explained wearily that it might not even be petit mal. Carl had thought it might be a virus, the aftermath of last year's flu. David had had a bad case of it and, well, who knew?

She held him tightly, and felt a response after a moment or two. "It's no big deal," she said, her voice muffled by his sleeve. "They've got drugs now, and you can lead a normal life."

He stroked her head and held her closer to him.

"No big deal for most people," he agreed, and then his voice broke. "But I'm a commercial airline pilot. That's all I am, all I've been for years. And now I'm washed up, unemployable. My whole life's just been thrown into a tailspin because of some tiny nerve malfunctioning.'' He stepped away and flopped into a chair, letting his head rest in his hands. He felt he'd been in an unfair fight, caught by a sucker punch.

She sat down across from him. What could she say now? She could hardly say it didn't matter about flying. But she thought it didn't matter: all that mattered was that he would be all right.

''Can I fix you a drink, darling?''

A wry smile flickered over his face.

''Doc Cohen says drinking's bad,'' he explained. ''Oh, what the hell. One martini's not going to kill me, and I'm not responsible for anyone else now.''

She thought he was going to break down and cry, and she wanted to hold him, but she knew enough to resist the desire. She wanted to call Carl, but she resisted that, too.

She returned with the pitcher and iced glasses in a few minutes and set the tray in front of him.

''David,'' she said gently, ''we'll come through this. I think I know what a terrible thing it is for you to give up flying. I'm not going to tell you to look on the bright side, but I know how brave you are. You'll come through this. Just tell me *how I can help.*''

She burst into tears, cursing herself.

''You're helping just by being here,'' he said, his voice sad. ''If I didn't have you, Jill, there wouldn't be anything worth going on for. As it is, I'm so filled with self-pity right now I can't face the truth about what's happened to me. Please be patient with me for a while, just until I can face this.''

He sighed. ''I'm going to be even harder to live with than usual. Most of all, my pride's shattered. And my pride is going to cost us a lot of money.'' He explained his decision to quit the airline but forgo the medical pension. He'd been sure she wouldn't object, and she didn't.

''You're crazy!'' Andy sputtered. ''You don't quit a job like that. It's worth gold to have seniority in an airline, even an outfit as cheap as Island. Have you lost your nerve, man?''

David winced. But this was what he had insisted on: no one, not even his best friend, was to know the real reason for his resignation. Jill stole her hand under the table, found his hand, and clenched it.

He had refused a physical exam, having decided he knew his fate. He couldn't fly commercial airlines any longer: that was fate, and he would accept it.

''I just figure it's time I got more involved with the fleet you two are building,'' David said evenly. ''And besides, you seem to be having a hell of a lot more fun ferrying tourists around the water than I do ferrying them through the sky. And it was a good time to quit: Island was so glad to be rid of a high-salaried employee, they came up with a golden handshake, very generous.''

"And God knows we need David working full time with the boats," Jill said. "We averaged close to two hundred passengers a week for the past two months."

"Yeah, I know," Andy grumbled. "When you set this thing up, you told me it was going to be just a little hobby. Hell, I've never worked so hard in my life! And you know how I feel about work. Maybe with our third partner here working full time, I'll get to take it easier."

"Nope," David said with wicked glee. "Jill's got some big plans."

"No more boats!" Andy yelled. "Already I feel like a Greek tycoon." They were sitting in a dockside cafe, and he waved toward the wharf where *Wings, Orchid*, and *Frangipani* sat at their moorings. "Those three—there's a small fortune tied up there, but when are we going to realize on it?"

"The way we're going," Jill said, "the two new boats will be paid for in a couple of months. Then we'll use them as security to raise the money for the next stage. It's okay, Andy," she said quickly, "it doesn't involve buying any more boats."

"Look, I was only kidding," Andy said. "What you've done is real great, Jill. I just like to hear myself bitch and moan. You do whatever you want and I'll go along with it. I figure Dave will, too, right?"

"She's the boss," David nodded, meaning it. He liked Jill taking charge of things; he knew he would not have gotten through his crisis without her. She gave him strength. She would always have his total support.

"We're partners," Jill said slowly. "And what I want to propose is risky as hell. So we all have to be in agreement or let's not do it. But if it works, we'll get very big, very fast." She was suddenly nervous. "Have you ever been on Orpheus Island, Andy?" she asked.

"Sure," he said, "we've anchored there a couple of times. Pretty little place, nice beaches, palm trees. There was a resort complex there five or so years ago. It failed and they lost a fortune." He drained his beer and choked on it. "Just a minute," he coughed. "Don't tell me you want us to do something on Orpheus."

"I do," she said. "The lease on Orpheus is going cheap and all the plant is still there. We could bring it back to a good standard without laying out too much capital. Orpheus failed last time because it was too hard to get to. No airstrip. But we've got the means to get our guests there." She gestured toward the dock. "We take them in on our fleet, two hours each way, at the end of the day after we've done the regular charters."

"That sounds like a hell of a lot of work," Andy said. "Charter all day, ferry all night?"

"We hire more skippers," Jill said. "We already have a stack of good people on our books. But we've got to keep the charter operation going so we'll have a cash flow while Orpheus is getting established.''

''Okay,'' Andy said slowly, considering, ''but what makes you think we can make Orpheus work? It wasn't just access that killed the last resort.''

''We'll be selling the same concept that makes the charters so successful,'' she said. ''Upmarket, adult, a little hedonistic if you like. You know how sometimes there's a little dope smoked, topless girls, that kind of thing on the boats? Well, that's what the mainlanders are looking for, and the regular resorts are too family-oriented, too straitlaced for some of our clients.''

''What are you going to call this place?'' Andy laughed. ''Swingers' Retreat?''

''No,'' she said, ''we're going to call it Wings, like the company the three of us are going to have to set up.''

''We don't need a company,'' Andy protested. ''We've done fine on handshakes so far.''

''We'll need a company if you go along with Jill's scheme,'' David said. ''The money involved is heavy.'' He toyed with his lime juice and sighed. This was one time he could really use a decent drink. ''I got some money in settlement when I left the airline. *Wings*, which you seem to forget is still your boat, is worth around a hundred grand. So we start off with *Wings* as your stake, a hundred thousand from both Jill and me, the two new boats' value split between the three of us. Then we'll have to borrow two or three hundred thousand to fix the resort. It's not something the banks will finance on a handshake, Andy. We'll have to make everything businesslike."

"Shit!" Andy said. "You're trying to make this simple island boy into a suit. There's only one way I'll go along with it. If we seal it with a drink." He looked at David. "I don't know why you've gone temperance on us, Dave, and I'm not going to pry. But this evening, before we plunge in over our heads, let's have a drink." He called for three beers. "Look at it this way: we may never be able to afford a beer again." He sighed. "I think I've just seen the end of a happy, aimless life."

The Nagles hadn't told David they were coming. They arrived at the Royal Hawaiian and announced their presence with a curt telephone call to the house, which Jill answered on the kitchen extension.

"This is Celia Nagle." The Boston accent was pronounced, the voice cold. "Is my son there?"

"Oh, hi, Mrs. Nagle," Jill said. She was flustered but excitement was mounting. For as long as she had loved David she had wanted to repair the rift between him and his family, she could not understand how they had managed to grow so far apart. "This is Jill," she said, feeling strange at having to identify herself.

"Is my son there?" the woman repeated.

"He's in the shower," Jill said. "Just a minute and I'll get him for you."

David was toweling his hair and he grimaced when she told him.

"Be nice to her," Jill pleaded as he moved to the bedroom phone.

"Mother?" he said, his voice as cold as hers had been.

It seemed they were on their way to the launching of his father's new merchant bank in Sydney, Australia. They were at the Royal Hawaiian for two nights and wanted to see David.

"I guess Jill and I can come down in an hour or so," he said. He listened for a second and then growled, "That's the only way, Mother."

They drove down in silence. David was angry that his parents could appear out of the blue and demand his attendance, as if none of the bitterness and betrayal of the past twenty years had happened. And that his mother could suggest he not bring his wife with him. Jill was in a turmoil of her own: On the one hand she was hopeful, excited by the prospect of seeing the breach between David and his parents healed. Sure, he'd told her how awful they had been, and sure, the mean letter she'd got from Mrs. Nagle before the wedding still hurt. But all that could be forgotten, she believed. Her real worry was the change that had come over David when he learned his mother was calling. He was wound up like a spring, gripping the wheel and staring straight ahead. Dr. Cohen had told her how essential it was he avoid tension.

"Try and smile, just for me," she whispered as they reached the elevator. "I don't want your folks thinking I make you miserable. I wish you'd put on a better jacket." She was babbling, nervous, and he looked at her with a sudden rush of love and sympathy. She was such a trusting lady, so sure things could be put right with just some love and understanding.

His mother was sitting on a chaise, Boston correct in a short evening gown. His father stood awkwardly before the large windows, a drink in his hand.

"Mother, Father," David nodded to them, "I'd like you to meet Jill, my wife."

Celia Nagle looked Jill over and inclined her head slightly. She then gestured for David to come to her and he did so, bending down to peck her cheek. John Nagle raised his glass to Jill, but he too was clearly interested only in his son. He shook David's hand and clapped him on the back. Jill watched the two men together, the father older and fleshier, but strongly resembling David in his height and bearing.

"What will you have to drink?" John Nagle asked. "Champagne?"

"That would be fine, thank you," Jill said. It was a way of escaping her position near the door, and she crossed the room as he took the bottle from the silver ice bucket. She felt his eyes on her as he handed her the glass, and she drew herself up proudly. Their eyes met: she saw arrogance there, arrogance and ruthlessness. Then David was beside her, his hand under her elbow, reassuring.

"Come sit by my mother while Father and I talk," he said, leading her to the couch.

His mother was used to being paid court, and she did not stir when Jill carefully settled beside her. She held up her glass for David to pour her another Scotch and then she turned her head a little so she could see Jill.

"I believe you're from Chicago," she said in that haughty Boston drawl. "A Hewitt? I think we knew some Hewitts from Oakbrook Terrace. She was at Bennington with me."

"I don't think so," Jill said. "Hewitt was the name they gave my grandfather after he arrived at Ellis Island. From Poland." She noted Mrs. Nagle's quick frown. And she noted how quickly the Scotch had been drunk. Maybe Mrs. Nagle wasn't entirely the proper Bostonian after all.

"Well, welcome to Honolulu," Jill said. "You'll notice the change, after Boston. I don't think David or I could ever get through one of those northern winters again. We're spoiled here."

"Nonsense," Mrs. Nagle said, not rudely, but simply as a woman used to having her opinions accepted. "Climate means nothing

75

when it's a part of a city's culture, tradition. People who drop out into places like this are leading fools' existences. And denying themselves so much.'' She lowered her voice. ''I understand David has left that silly pilot's job. I hope that means he's planning to come home where he belongs.''

''You'd have to talk to David about that,'' Jill replied. ''But I think you'll find he's very happy—and very busy—here.''

There was a knock on the door and a waiter entered with a tray of canapés.

''John and I are working on a different time,'' his mother explained to the air. ''We thought a snack would be sufficient but we only ordered for three. We weren't expecting anyone except family.''

Jill saw David flush and she shook her head at him. She'd had years of dealing with graceless passengers; this rude dowager wasn't going to upset her.

''Come on, Mother,'' David said. ''That nonsense about different time zones doesn't wash with me.'' Turning to Jill, he said, ''My mother, for all her millions, would do anything to get out of paying for a meal. I guess that's one of the ways Father keeps getting richer.''

''David,'' his mother said icily, ''I don't think family matters—even when you're trying to make a joke—should be discussed in front of others.''

''You'd better damn well understand one

thing, Mother,'' he replied, and Jill could see a vein moving in his neck. ''If I am family, then Jill is family. She's my *wife* and I love her. Your attitude toward Jill—and yours, Dad—will determine whether any of us needs to bother keeping up this 'family' charade.''

There was a silence in the room, and then John Nagle, bluff and urbane, began to jolly them out of it. He filled the glasses again and pressed canapés on them all, beaming at Jill. A few minutes later she was standing by the window with him while David and his mother sparred verbally behind them.

''It's very beautiful here, despite the tourists,'' John Nagle said as they looked down on the night-empty Waikiki beach. ''But Mrs. Nagle and I used to come here, to the Royal, in the thirties, before the masses discovered it. So elegant then. So different.''

''I can't knock the tourists, Mr. Nagle,'' she said. ''David and I make our living from them. And they're the most important part of the islands' economy. Actually, I rather like to see ordinary Americans getting their couple of weeks in paradise.''

''Just what is it you and David are doing?'' he asked smoothly. ''He could only tell me he was 'messing with boats.' My son's forty years old. It's well past time he settled into a real career.''

''We've got a thriving charter business,'' Jill explained. ''And we're planning to expand it.

There's great potential in the hospitality industry—"

"Please," he said, holding up his hand to silence her, "you've lost me already. I guess I'm old-fashioned, but I never expected my son to end up in anything called 'the hospitality industry.' I wanted him to come into the family firm, as his son will." He was smiling, affable, so his next words stung badly. "You better understand from the beginning," he said. "Until and unless David accepts his responsibilities to the family, there will be no financial assistance coming to him from me. As long as he persists in the course he's on, he is on his own. And so are you."

She paled with anger.

"Neither David nor I want any handouts, Mr. Nagle," she said. "We're very happy here. And we have plans. We're not in your league, but we're building something of our own."

"We'll see," he said, with all the assurance of a man of great influence. "When David takes his rightful place in the firm, all this will seem like a silly little adventure. And I promise you one thing: the quicker you can persuade David to come home, the quicker Mrs. Nagle will accept you as his wife. You realize, of course, she doesn't approve of divorce. David is still married to Marion as far as she's concerned. I take a more relaxed view of that. You get David to see sense, and I'll see you are invested with all the rights and privileges that go with being a Boston Nagle.''

She might have laughed: this pompous man, steeped in the bigotry of old money and old family, would never understand what she and David cared about.

David and his mother were talking in increasing volume.

''You don't want to understand, do you, Mother?'' he said. ''For the last time: I am married to Jill, she's my wife. I can't follow your morality—my ex-wife is a whore. She cheated on me while I was fighting a war! She's a goddamned—''

''Don't use bad language, David,'' his mother said. ''It's common. And I'm sure if you thought about it, remembered what you were taught, you would understand my position.''

He stood up, tired of fighting. He crossed the room and shook hands with his father. ''Have a successful time in Sydney,'' he said.

Mrs. Nagle didn't get up as they left. She fluttered a hand at her son and gave Jill a stiff nod. Mr. Nagle ushered them out of the suite, still affable and urbane, as if this were just a business conference that hadn't resulted in what he wanted, but eventually would.

As the elevator door closed behind them, David kissed Jill. ''For all their money and position, they haven't got one one-hundredth of what we've got. Thanks for going through the ordeal. They can now drop out of our life again, maybe for another five years.''

Chapter Four _____

IT WAS AFTER MIDNIGHT BEFORE JILL felt she could leave the bar in the care of Maggie Stewart. The guests were noisy and some of them a little drunk, but it was a crowd without troublemakers. Maggie could look after them.

Jill slipped out of the palm-fringed, open-sided bar and strolled down the jungle track to her bungalow. As she got closer she saw lights on and she could hear Jackson Browne on the stereo. David was still up. She was glad. Often in these past months their schedules were so awry, one was going to bed as the other was getting up. She pushed open the thatched door and stepped into the softly lit living room.

"You got away early," he said, standing up from the dining table and pushing aside the account books. "That's great. I was missing you, but I couldn't come visit. I've put off the books for too long."

She walked over and kissed him and some of the tiredness went from her. They were all working too hard, she and David on the resort island, Andy supervising the charter work and the ferrying of the guests. David felt good against her, big and strong and lovable.

"Thank God we get such nice people here," she said as they broke their embrace. "I wouldn't work like this for a bunch of typical hotel guests."

"It sure isn't a typical hotel," he said, grinning. "Our grosses are wonderful but, hell, the money going out on food and booze and staff terrifies me."

"It's all we've got going for us," she said, "the concept of everything free and everything the best. For their two hundred and fifty a day we give 'em all of it. That way they don't notice their bungalows aren't exactly Sheraton standard." She went into the kitchen and found a chilled bottle of white wine in the refrigerator. "You want some?" she asked casually. She was happy when he nodded. If David took an occasional drink it meant he was confident the epilepsy was still controlled. "How are we doing, anyway?" she asked, waving to the accounts.

"The overheads are starting to level out at last," he said. "There aren't as many hidden costs now, and our marketing is getting better. If it weren't for the mortgage, I figure we'd be clearing sixty or seventy a head a day."

"The advance bookings are looking good," she said. "I liked it better when it was word of mouth, but those ads in the glossy magazines do get results.''

''Yes,'' he said, taking a glass from her. ''Wings Resort is starting to take off. Another year of this and we'll be making big money.''

''You're still happy about it, aren't you?'' she asked, anxious. ''Running the charters was one thing, but now—we're so caught up in this. Not enough time for each other, having to do tasks we never even thought about.'' She laughed. ''Look at you, the old fly-boy, working as an accountant!''

He came and stood behind her chair and gently rubbed her neck, then bent down and kissed the top of her head.

''I love it,'' he said, ''because I love you. You had a vision and it's working for all of us. I'll work at anything we need to make this a success. Anyway, it's fun to find out what you can do. Hidden talents. I never thought I'd be an innkeeper but, if I do say so myself, I'm not bad at it.''

''You're holding the place together, darling,'' she said, meaning it. She put her hand on his and stroked it. He was wonderful, a man who could cheerfully apply himself to anything from fixing a stopped-up toilet to doing the books. He had even allowed himself to relax enough to be at ease with their visitors. The experience seemed to have made a whole person of David; he was leaner, fitter, looser. There was real companionship and trust in their love now.

"You want to come to bed?" he murmured. "It's very late."

"No," she said, teasing him. "I want to take a bath. Why don't you join me?"

Hand in hand they moved to the big sunken tub off their bedroom; they watched the steaming water rise to the tips of the ferns surrounding the bath, then undressed each other. They marveled in each other's bodies, so familiar but still a wonderful rediscovery. They anointed each other with fragrant oil before sliding into the water. Every part of her body yielded to him, opening for him. He felt a tender strength, a need to possess her while being owned by her. They coupled in the womblike sanctuary, their bodies locked but liquid, unhurried until the climax that sent shudders through them.

Jill lay against the side of the tub, her arms around David, feeling him still inside her. She brushed a green frond away from her eyes and nuzzled his neck.

"You know," she whispered, "this isn't a bad resort, not bad at all. I think I'll come here more often."

The television people had taken over the island, disrupting the routine, harassing the staff. The tranquillity had disappeared with their arrival. They had to be fed at odd hours and nothing was ever quite good enough for them. After five days of their presence, David was edgy and strained, so Jill persuaded him to switch roles with Andy and run the charter operation until filming was finished. Al Cola, the television producer, had paid a hefty premium to gain the exclusive use of Wings for fourteen days while he shot an episode of ''Brute Force.'' Jill hadn't wanted to turn the place over to him, but he had booked the island well in advance, so no ordinary guests needed to be canceled, and the money he offered was enormous. There was the clincher, too—a location credit on the show, which was regularly seen by forty-five million viewers.

''I still haven't gotten close to Don Messner,'' Cindy complained as she helped Jill clean up the remains of a 5:00 P.M. lunch for fifty cast and crew. ''That was the only reason I gave up my vacation to come help you with this mob. Messner does something to me.''

''You and just about every other woman in America,'' Jill laughed. ''The hottest thing since Burt Reynolds. It's odd, having them all here when I've never seen the show.''

''Cathy snuck around to the back beach yesterday when they were filming,'' Cindy said. ''He was doing a karate scene, stripped to the waist. She said he was the strongest-looking guy she'd ever seen.''

''Tell Cathy and the others to keep out of the crew's hair,'' Jill cautioned. ''That was the other reason Cola wanted to use Wings: all the staff are airline or ex-airline, so he figured they'd be used to dealing with stars. We can't have anyone getting in the way.''

''They're not being bothered,'' Cindy said. ''Only when they want to be. Sonny Ramos seems to have established some kind of . . . rapport with them.''

Jill glanced at her quickly.

''You mean he's dealing drugs to them?''

''Just coke and grass, I heard,'' Cindy said. ''And only small quantities.''

''I figured he's been dealing all along to the guests who want it,'' Jill said, frowning. ''And I'm damned if I know what to do about it. Grass is all but legal in the islands and coke's a way of life to some of the people we get here. I'd kick him off the island except for two things: he's the best guitar player around, and some of the guests *expect* to be able to buy drugs.''

''I think you've got to pretend it's not happening,'' Cindy advised. ''It's a pretty high-flying crowd you cater to, and if you try and stamp out drugs on the island you'll lose your clients.''

''It's just so stupid,'' Jill said. ''Who needs drugs in a place like this? I can understand them snorting coke in New York and L.A., but here?''

''The kind of crowd you pull, some will want stuff wherever they are. I think you've just got to keep it at arm's length. It's always going to be a problem in resort areas. I hear there's so much heroin around at Pipeline—''

"At least that's one horror we haven't got," Jill said. "The Wings crowd is too smart to get mixed up with heroin."

Cindy yawned. "The only drug I need right now is sleep," she said. "I've been up since dawn and so have you. Let's go grab a couple of hours' nap before the evening rush."

Maggie Stewart, Jill's assistant manager, woke Jill about 9:00 P.M.

"Mr. Cola's just been by," she said. "He said when they break tonight, he wants to party. Don Messner's not needed for the next couple of days, so he and Cola and a few of the others want a special dinner around midnight."

Jill wanted badly to go back to sleep. But she would have to see the evening went well.

"We can do it," she said to Maggie. "Have you set up the kitchen staff?"

"They're all prepared," Maggie said. "And Andy's gone out in the outrigger to catch some tuna. That and roast duck, beef, and the usual salads and fruits."

"Sounds fine," Jill said. "Just be sure there's a couple of cases of Bollinger on ice. Cola won't drink anything else. He says it's part of the diet he's on."

Jill showered quickly and slipped into a brightly printed sarong; the night was soft and warm, but there was no moon and she had to feel her way down the jungle track to the bungalow Cindy was using.

Her friend was up and ready, dressed in a

tie-dyed cheesecloth skirt and blouse. Against
the light Jill could see clearly that Cindy was
wearing nothing else but tiny bikini panties.

''You're determined to make an impression,'' Jill laughed.

''It may be my only chance to talk to Don
Messner.'' Cindy grinned. ''I want him to see
what he's been missing.''

There was an air of excitement in the restaurant; the tables and the bar were decked with
tropical flowers, and the hurricane lamps
overhead cast a warm glow on gleaming sil-
verware and sparkling white cloths. For the
occasion, Andy had put himself behind the
bar. A sarong covered his lower torso, a white
lei decorated his gleaming brown chest, and
an orchid protruded from his great mass of
curly hair. He grinned at Jill.

''Nothing's too much effort for our star,'' he
called to her. ''If Messner likes this place,
we're on the map for sure.''

Even Sonny Ramos, the entertainer, had
dressed for the occasion. Usually the painfully
thin Filipino appeared in scruffy jeans and
T-shirt. He figured, rightly, that his brilliant
guitar playing and reedy singing voice were
what intrigued the guests. But tonight he was
wearing black dress pants and a starched
white shirt. His long hair was slicked back and
he had a look of extreme nervousness.

''Mr. Cola told me,'' he confided to Jill,
''there might be a spot for me in the show,
playing in the background. Hell, if he likes

what I play tonight, I could be the next Don Ho.'' He sniffed and rubbed his nose.

She walked around the room, checking that everything was just right. A soft breeze came through the open walls, stirring the palm fronds and carrying gentle night sounds. It *was* beautiful; Wings was becoming what she had planned—laid-back luxury combined with genuine island charm.

Cola arrived first, a small, fat, fussy man, eternally frowning. He nodded vigorously as he surveyed the room, gulping a glass of champagne. And then they all sat back and waited for the star and his guests to arrive.

Even Jill caught her breath when Don Messner walked in; he was simply one of the most beautiful men she had ever seen. A glorious body, muscled but not beefy, a fine handsome head, a way of walking proudly but without arrogance. He wore jeans and a white T-shirt and made the outfit look like exclusive tailoring. Messner nodded to the other members of his party and crossed the room to where Jill was standing by the bar.

''Good evening,'' he said. ''I'm sorry I've been so antisocial these past days. But I try not to let anything interfere with my work.'' He smiled at her, all white teeth and liquid brown eyes. ''I just wanted to tell you, though, how great your place is. I want to come back and stay when this circus has moved on.''

''We'd love you to,'' Jill said. ''But it's usually a lot quieter than this.''

"I think it's beautiful," he said. H
across the bar and shook hands with
"Hi, Skipper," he said, "thanks for the ⸝ᵤₑ
trip across the other day. Any chance of you
and me going out fishing in the next couple of
days?"

"Sure," Andy said. "Just tell me when. If
you've got the time, we'll get you a marlin."

Then the food and drink started flowing;
everyone had relaxed because Messner was
obviously enjoying himself. Sonny played
better than ever before and Cola nodded approvingly. The champagne flowed and the
noise level grew; Jill tried not to notice that
Messner and most of the party were also
sniffing cocaine throughout the meal. Cindy
had given up all pretense of hostessing; she
had accepted Messner's invitation to sit by
him, and was wearing a look of stunned bliss.

At 3:00 A.M. there was still no sign of anyone leaving. The tables were pushed back and
dancing began, Cindy clinging tightly to
Messner as they moved around the tiny floor.

"I'm bushed, Andy," Jill said quietly. "No
one will miss me if I slip away. Do you mind
keeping an eye on things?"

"Be my guest," he grinned, downing a bottle of beer in one long gulp. "This is a great
party and I wouldn't miss a moment of it."

Jill hurried down the trail, glad to be away
from the noise and fuss but glad the party was
such a success. She went straight to her bed-

room, cast her clothes on the floor, and fell into bed. She was asleep within moments.

She was still asleep when he climbed in beside her. At first, dreaming, Jill thought the naked body beside her was David. She murmured something as his lips brushed hers, and allowed herself to be turned on her back. It was only when she felt the great weight move onto her that she began to pull herself from the depths of sleep. It couldn't be David; David wasn't there.

She struggled to get away from the body lying on top of her, frantically pushing him away. She screamed, and a hand came over her mouth, choking the sound off.

"Keep it quiet, baby," he whispered. "It's okay. It's me."

And then the bedroom light was switched on and Don Messner, entangled in the sheet, reared up in confusion. She saw the shocked look in his eyes. All he had time to see was skinny Sonny Ramos beside the bed, a chair raised high. The chair came crashing down on Messner's head and the star gave a grunt of pain, his eyes unfocused. Slowly he toppled off the bed and crashed to the floor.

She and Sonny stared at each other over Messner's body, and then she remembered she was naked and hastily covered herself with the sheet. Sonny just stood there, the chair in his hand, waiting to be told what to do.

"I followed him down the track, to see he

was all right," Sonny explained haltingly. "He was pretty far gone when he left the party. I saw him come into your bungalow, Jill. I didn't know . . . I thought maybe you'd invited him. But then you yelled, so I rushed in. I guess I'm in trouble."

"No, Sonny, you're not in trouble," she said, her voice shaking. "I'm very grateful to you. You saved me. It doesn't matter how big a star Mr. Messner is, he can't do what he tried to do to me."

She heard someone pounding across the living room floor and Andy was there, looking ridiculous in his wilted lei and drooping sarong.

"What in hell?" he demanded. "I heard a scream. You, you little bastard." He turned on Sonny and grabbed him by the throat.

The musician tried to speak but the grip on his throat was too hard.

"No! No, Andy!" Jill finally managed. "Sonny saved me. The guy who broke in is on the other side of the bed—on the floor."

Andy moved around to look.

"Oh, shit," he said simply. "Messner. We got trouble."

"Is this a private party, or can I join in?"

The three of them turned to Cindy standing in the bedroom door, draped in a flimsy white negligee.

"All the noise you guys are making woke me," Cindy said. "I thought everyone was all partied out."

"Don Messner had other ideas," Jill said.

"He came in here and tried to rape me. I was lucky Sonny heard me scream. Your dream-boat lost a fight with our Sonny."

Cindy seemed to be holding her breath. She crammed a fist into her mouth and her cheeks reddened. Then the laughter couldn't be stifled any longer.

They stared at her, angry and bewildered.

"I'm sorry," she gasped. "It's all my fault. I, uh, invited Don to my bungalow. We were both pretty loaded. He said he'd follow me down in just a moment and I told him where to find me. I fell asleep waiting for him. And he went into the wrong bedroom! Gee, I'm sorry, Jill, it was just a mix-up. Are you all right?"

"Yes, now," she said grimly. "But your pal isn't. And when he wakes up he's not going to be pleased about this."

Andy bent over Messner and checked his head.

"No bleeding, just a lump," he pronounced. "He should be okay in a little while." He picked up the star and flung him over his shoulder. "I'll put him to bed in his bungalow. Maybe when he wakes up in the morning, he'll think this was just a dream. We hope."

They were up early, blinking in the bright morning light, and silently they set about cleaning up. No one mentioned the incident, although they all glanced down the track toward Messner's bungalow from time to time.

The star appeared about nine, stumbling up the path in a bathrobe, blinking and pale. He was a mere shadow of the glamorous man who had strolled into the party the night before.

"I need," he said, "a cup of coffee and some details." He slumped in a chair and put his head in his hands until Andy brought the coffee. "What in the hell happened?" he asked. "I recall I had a . . . a date. With Cindy. Right?" He looked around to where Cindy was sitting in a corner. She nodded. "And I thought everything was going fine. And then she started yelling and some maniac whacked me with a chair." He touched the back of his head and winced. "It's the kind of thing that happens in my TV show. I don't need it happening in real life. What in hell happened?"

"Don . . . Mr. Messner," Cindy piped up, her voice faint. "You made a mistake. You went to the wrong bungalow."

He shook his head.

"But I remember being in bed with someone, just before the lights went out, so to speak." And then his eyes widened. "Don't tell me." He looked at Jill. "You live in . . . the next bungalow down from Cindy, right?"

She nodded.

"Oh, shit," he said. "Well, *gosh*, aren't I a moron?" He stood up. "Look, I'm sorry about all this. It's about the most embarrassing thing that's ever happened to me. You're okay, aren't you? I mean, nothing, uh, happened, did it?''

''No, Mr. Messner, nothing happened,'' she said coolly.

''Except I got my head stove in.'' He started laughing then, though it caused him pain, great whooping laughs that infected them all. The tension dissipated in the laughter and they stood in a loose circle, laughing, the laughter building on itself.

Down on the beach, filming, Al Cola heard it.

''I hope that noise doesn't mean Don's starting another party,'' he grumbled to his director. ''That boy's a very valuable property. I wouldn't want him hurting himself.''

Messner found Jill alone in the office late that afternoon. He tapped on the open door, and when she looked up, he smiled.

''May I come in and talk to you for a moment?'' he asked.

''Sure,'' she said. ''Pull up a chair. How are you feeling?''

''Fine,'' he said. ''I came to see how you were. I can't tell you how sorry I am about what happened. I don't usually go around forcing myself on women. It was just an awful mix-up and I hope you can forgive me.''

She smiled. ''It wasn't really your fault,'' she said. ''And I hope Sonny didn't hurt you too badly. We don't usually beat up our guests.''

''I didn't think so,'' he said. ''Like I told you last night, I love this place and I want to come back on my own.'' He looked down at his hands. ''Would I still be welcome, after what happened?''

''Well, since nothing really happened,'' Jill said, ''if you don't count the lump on your head, you'd be most welcome here. But, as I told you last night, it's usually a lot quieter.''

''Amen,'' he said, nodding.

David's first reaction was rage; he wanted to find Messner and beat holy shit out of him. Then there was intense jealousy, and, finally, concern for the shock she had suffered. David figured his response was probably typical of any husband in those circumstances: he knew none of the happenings had in any way been Jill's fault, yet he somehow blamed her. It wasn't until they had made long and passionate love that night that he managed to get it all in perspective.

''You're wonderful,'' he whispered as they held each other. ''I wouldn't be surprised if Don Messner knew exactly whose bed he was trying to get into.'' He chuckled. ''You realize millions of other women would think you were crazy? I guess it's some kind of back-handed compliment to me.''

She cuddled him close, so happy to be with him.

"Just don't leave me alone again," she whispered. "I can't bear to be apart from you." She stroked and teased him and aroused him again. "Next time you abandon me, I might not holler quite so loud when a tall, dark stranger invades my boudoir."

"I'd better stay close then," he murmured as he moved between her thighs. It was such good love they made together, he thought as she quickened with him. "Or maybe you'd like me to wear a black mask." He heard her throaty chuckle and it brought him to a sudden, thrusting climax seconds ahead of her own.

Jill lay back, feeling the warm strength of his body on hers. She stroked his head and shoulders, feeling his muscles. He seemed wholly well again; it was months since there had been any sign of his illness. Soon, she thought, they would talk about having a baby.

"I love you, David," she whispered. "I'm so lucky."

Their policy was to close Wings to guests for four days at the end of each month. It enabled them to do all the routine maintenance, to keep the island fresh and sparkling. And it gave them all a break from the strenuous routine of pampering strangers. Usually, David and Jill used the break to go across to Honolulu and see old friends, especially Carl Cohen. This time, though, Carl had agreed to come to them, to spend a couple of days at

Wings. Jill was nervous. It was a major tribute to their friendship, his agreeing to make the trip; she knew he seldom left his home and orchids. She so wanted him to approve of what they were doing.

She was at the dock when David berthed, and she felt a surge of affection when she saw Cohen standing at the bow, formal in a starched white linen suit, small and gnarled and indestructible, like a little old tree.

"Welcome to Wings," she said when he came ashore. He kissed her hand, a quick, birdlike motion that was more intimate than a thousand of the close embraces and cheek kissings all the smart, modern people affected.

"I'm honored to be here, in your home," he said. He glanced around. "But where are all the naked nymphets, the millionaire jet-setters, the hedonists? Did you send them away because a strange old man like me would cast a pall over their pleasure?"

"We wanted to have you all to ourselves." Jill laughed as she put her arm in his and started up the path to the village. "I never believed we'd get you here."

They were walking through a tunnel formed by the verdant tropical rain forest, tall flowering trees bowed by the profusion of vines entangled in them, garlands of wild orchids splashing their delicate colors on the lush green background. Huge butterflies drifted nearby.

His eyes darted everywhere, taking it all in.

"You have worked well with nature," he said approvingly. "Even hedonists must appreciate the beauty of this place."

"David and I love it so much we sometimes wish we didn't have to share it with the guests at all," Jill said.

"But the guests make it possible," David said, catching up to them. "And we're lucky with the kind of people we get here. They don't come expecting high-rises and golf courses and discos. They actually find, after a few hours here, they like being out of reach of telephones."

That evening, while David was preparing a barbecue on a point high over the ocean, she and Carl strolled around the island, moving silently on the sand, listening to the birdsongs and the surf.

"David is truly at peace here with you on the island," Dr. Cohen said. "I'm happy you found each other and this place. His illness has never come back and I don't see any reason why it should recur. I told him right from the first there was no reason to hold off having children, but you know the kind of man he is—proud and stubborn. He was afraid that somehow his illness would be passed on to his child. Now he sees there's no danger of that, or I think he does." He bent forward and righted a tiny crab lying on its back in the sand. "I think you should start the child very soon, before it is too late."

"Too late?" she said. "I'm still under thirty, Doctor."

He shrugged.

"My dear Jill, never put things off, particularly something you both desire so much." He sighed. "I waited far too long to find what it was I wanted; now, every day I spend in my paradise I thank God for it. I curse myself for every day I wasted before finding it."

They sat by the embers of the fire as the night came down and the birds and insects fell silent. David lay back against a tree trunk, content here with the two people he loved best in the world. He had listened to Dr. Cohen on the boatride over, and he accepted what Carl had said. They would have their baby: life would be complete. It was funny, the way things worked out. If the volcano hadn't vented itself, imperiling his plane and passengers, he and Jill might not have come together. And if the trauma of that flight had not led to his grounding, he'd still be flying and would never have known the joy of their life on this island.

"The volcano is acting up again," he heard Carl say. "I have a friend, a vulcanologist, who tells me it could be very bad this time. All the signs of a major eruption are there: the sea has risen a few inches in some places, and the land has risen by a similar amount in others. But no one pays heed, except people like my friend. He argues there should be plans—rescue, evacuation. But the authorities fear any hint of a possible major eruption would wreck the tourist industry. So nothing is done. At least, if it comes, you will be safe here.''

''I don't think anything will ever touch us here,'' Jill said. ''The real world seems so far away. And I'm selfish enough to want to keep it that way. Always.''

Chapter Five _____

MOUNT MATUTAVI WAS AGAIN REMIND-
ing the islands that it was asleep, not extinct.
For two weeks the gray, gritty cloud had
spread into the atmosphere until all of Hawaii
was enshrouded. It was, Jill thought, just like
the last disturbance, the one in which she and
David had been thrown together. This time,
though, the atmosphere did not depress her
for she was hugging a secret to herself. She
was—and her calculations were exact; there
could be no mistake even though she had
yet to confirm it with a doctor—two weeks
pregnant. She hadn't told David yet, but
she knew he would be overjoyed. Everything was perfect. David, his illness
apparently controlled, had sailed through
his pilot's medical and begun flying light
planes as an occasional hobby; there seemed
no reason why he shouldn't. Even Wings
was surviving the volcano's lousy weather;
the tiny resort was deemed by its guests the
best place to be if they had to face bad conditions at all. Everyone stayed cheerful; the

wine flowed and the food was still the best in the islands.

Jill knew from the aircrews who worked for Wings on their days off how bad it was. Worse than the last time, Cindy told her. The cloud was more dense, more coarse, and flying was extremely hazardous. Many of them wanted the airlines grounded until the eruption was over, but the airlines were holding off, knowing such a move would destroy Hawaii's tourist season.

"It'll get worse before it gets better," Andy said as they sat around the bar talking about the weather. "My grandfather was a kid when Matutavi last blew its top, and he says all the signs are here again."

"I'm staying right here for the duration," Burt Brydon said, reaching over the bar for another cold bottle of Foster's beer. "I did a cargo run to Maui Thursday and I had to turn back. So I said, 'Burt, it's time to take a vacation.' I'm glad you had a vacancy, David."

"There'll be lots of vacancies if this keeps up," David said grimly. "The Waikiki hotels are down to fifty percent. Our chartering has stopped altogether. No matter how charming we think Wings is, it'll affect us soon."

"If it does, we'll all just sit here and party until things are back to normal," Brydon said. "If you'll run a group discount, the rest of my boys will come over and wait it out here with us."

Jill listened carefully to what Burt Brydon was saying. Of all David's old flying cronies, Brydon was the one who'd fly anywhere, anytime. He had to: he owned three ancient DC-3s and he made a precarious living ferrying freight and foodstuffs from island to island. He usually worked around the clock, aided by a bunch of unemployed pilots and a team of aged mechanics who kept the Dakotas flying with inspired feats of cannibalization. Burt himself was fearless, a big, bluff Australian David's age. In Vietnam he'd been a spotter pilot for the Australian artillery. If Burt refused to fly, things were bad.

"I heard they finally agreed to issue a stage-one alert for Hilo," David said. "I guess there's little enough tourist traffic left there. It won't be a loss."

"What's a stage one?" Andy asked.

"Carl explained it all to me," David said. "There's supposed to be four stages in a volcano alert. One is simply a declaration that there's a future danger. Stage two means it's likely to come in a matter of a few months. Stage three means a matter of days, and mass evacuation begins. Stage four—red alert— means the volcano will blow in a matter of hours."

"My granddaddy doesn't know about all those stages," Andy said quietly. "But he remembers the last big bang, and from what he tells me, we're much worse off than stage one or two, Dave."

"Dr. Cohen and the vulcanologists agree with him," David said. "They figure it's close to a stage three already. But the local people are fighting any kind of declaration. They've lived with the volcano so long they're fatalistic about it. And they'll be ruined if the tourists are scared away."

"Someone must know what they're doing," Burt Brydon said. "I'm not going to worry about it." He reached over the bar again and came up with another cold textured large bottle. "You sure you got plenty of this Foster's in the cellar, Dave? I can't ride out a disaster without a real Aussie beer in my paw."

The earthquake was tiny for the region, scarcely rippling the lake in the blackened crater of Mount Matutavi; the only visible sign of it was a fresh burst of sulphurous steam rising from the near-boiling water. The quake was recorded on the graphs in the seismic laboratory and it confirmed the pattern of the past three months. Seismic "events," as they were called, had increased to thirty times above average.

In the magma chamber deep below Matutavi, the latest quake stirred the lake of molten lava; the lava surged and bubbled, expanding all the time, seeking the easiest release spot. The magma chamber extended for a hundred acres under the mountain and out to sea; if a quake was of sufficient force to open the ocean floor, the release of energy would occur there and create a *tsunami*, a tremendous wave a hundred and twenty feet high, racing away in all directions and destroying anything in its path.

"They've gone to a stage-two alert," David said. In the past few days he had become fascinated by the volcano and its activity, and he now monitored the civil defense radio network. The others in the bar professed boredom with it all; their only concern was for the cloud to disperse and the sun to return.

"My granddaddy says they can declare anything they like," Andy shrugged, "but that old mountain will do as she pleases. He says it's just like the last time—rumble, rumble for months on end, till everyone's used to it, then she blows and everyone nearby dies."

"What was it like, the big one?" David demanded. "What does he remember?"

"He says it was just like this time. The volcano had been acting up for months and then a string of earthquakes started, spread over five or six days. He says it was like the surf was running under the land. All the old-timers went around shaking their heads and pointing at the mountain and saying it was going to punish them."

"Didn't they run away?" Burt asked. "If they were so sure the explosion was coming . . ."

"It was the same as now," Andy said. "You

live under a volcano, that's your choice. If you ran every time she acted up, you'd always be running.'' He frowned at the murky dusk outside the bar; it was early afternoon. ''Anyway, the day she blew must have been like today. Dark at noon, another earthquake—maybe a bit stronger than the rest—and then a couple of hours later a series of very big blasts, like bombs exploding.

''There wasn't just the one volcano, either. Matutavi was the spectacular one but there were two others, just out to sea. One of them was a little rocky island that was a five-hundred-foot cone within hours. The other came up from the ocean floor, where there had been nothing before. Then all three of the cones were pouring out this mass of smoke and ash, thick as molasses, going maybe five miles up into the sky.

''He says there was lava pouring over the lip of Matutavi and big rocks shooting out of the craters. That lava and stuff wasn't what killed most of the people, though. It was when the ash started coming down again; it mixed with the rain that was pouring down and it all turned to liquid mud. It flopped on everything, crushing houses, knocking down trees, blocking all the roads. You couldn't escape. And the ash and the sulphur fumes and the heat all combined so you couldn't breathe. Most people suffocated.''

''But a tidal wave did the real damage, didn't it?'' Burt asked. ''I've seen pictures of it, with cargo ships carried half a mile inland, everything devastated.''

''There was a wave, all right,'' Andy said. ''Not a tidal wave, but something called *tsunami*, which is peculiar to earthquakes and volcanoes under the sea. But by the time it came along, most of the damage had been done. The people had escaped or else they were dead. The wave just buried a lot of bodies. After the wave, ships tried to come into shore to carry away the survivors, but the volcano had seen to that, too. The sea was blocked with pumice stone to a depth of six or eight feet. The ships couldn't get through it.''

Jill shuddered. She knew there was no danger to them, far from the angry mountain, but she despaired at Andy's description.

''And then, after it was all over,'' Andy continued, ''people returned and started again. They rebuilt their villages and made new gardens. The soil was excellent and, as a bonus, they got miles of new black-sand beaches. That brought the first tourists—that and the novelty of walking inside a volcano. Nature takes away, nature gives.''

The earthquake registered 7.6 and triggered the first step in the chain; Matutavi split open and began to vent itself straight up into the already choked sky. It was as beautiful and as horrible as any atomic cloud, and the heat contained in the spire of ash was as intense as a nuclear blast. The red alert was proclaimed then, when it was already too late. The main airstrip was destroyed when the tarmac cracked from the heat and the pressure formed high waves and deep fissures. The roads were quickly impassable, blocked by mud slides and fallen palms; those who could walk abandoned their vehicles and struggled through the choking fumes in search of safe ground.

They sat in the bar and listened silently as the radio documented the disaster. The reports were of complete confusion, chaos; there were spasmodic broadcasts from a ham operator, his voice strangely calm, speaking from his garage less than a mile from the vortex. The ham operator told of wave after wave of torrential rain that carried mud down from the clouds and deposited it in waist-deep drifts; of lava flows moving down the mountain at a steady, majestic pace, engulfing everything in its path; of wayward boulders flung from the crater, smashing down like meteorites. He was in radio contact with the local flying club; their small airstrip had so far escaped damage. Now, lit up by the headlights of vehicles ringing the strip, the club's small planes were ferrying out handfuls of the desperate hundreds grouped there. More small planes were desperately needed, the operator said, and quickly, before this strip, too, was destroyed.

Brydon listened intently, nodding. Then he stood, stretched his huge frame, and scratched his beard. He went around behind the bar and came up with two six-packs of his beloved Foster's.

"I've got my rations," he said. "If someone will run me over to Honolulu in the speedboat, I reckon I'll try flying one of the Dakotas down there. Hell, those pissy little Pipers and Cessnas aren't going to move the number of people they've got waiting."

Jill watched, unable to move or speak, as David stood up and joined Brydon. She knew what he was going to do: she could not stop him. But if she told him about the baby now . . . No, she loved David because of the man he was. She knew what he had to do. He walked toward the door with Brydon, then turned and came back to her. As she looked up into his face, she knew she wouldn't tell him about the baby.

"Don't worry," he whispered, bending close to her. "Those DC-3s are indestructible. And I won't take any risks. I've got too much to lose. I love you." He kissed her while the others looked away.

He hurried down the path with Burt, neither speaking. The speedboat roared into life, and he headed it for the mainland while Burt got on the ship-to-shore radio and arranged for two of his planes to be fueled and made ready. As the boat bounced over the waves, David took one last look back at Wings, so safe and beautiful, where he had spent the happiest days of his life. He would do his duty; then he would hurry back to his sanctuary, back to Jill.

The airport was pandemonium. A score of light planes had already taken off for the disaster site and another score were lined up waiting to be allowed into the area. He and Burt were assigned air force volunteers to navigate for them and they were moved to the head of the takeoff parade. He followed Burt up into the sky and lost him immediately in the gray cloud.

"Two hours five to destination," the navigator shouted to him over the roar of the twin engines. "*If* we don't run into one of the weekend fliers on the way."

David nodded. The plane was dipping and bucking in the cloud and he was glad of his recent experience as a weekend flier of small planes; these were different skills than those needed in the cockpit of a commercial jetliner.

Jill stayed by the radio, beyond fear for David. She was suspended, all emotions held at bay because she couldn't do anything to change what was happening, anyhow. Several helicopters were at the disaster scene, but the turbulent conditions were playing havoc with helicopters. A radio reporter had arrived on one of them and was broadcasting from the chaos.

"At least two of the choppers have tipped over and are being pushed off the strip," he cried, voice cracking. "The wind is frightening, roaring in from all directions. The light planes seem to be able to cope with it better than the choppers, but those planes can only take a handful of people off. There are still more than a hundred people here at the airstrip, praying to get out of here. There is no other escape route. We are cut off all around us; it's like being under shellfire—boulders crashing down, debris flying around. And all the time there's this thundering sound of the volcano erupting.

"This airstrip is down near the beach, and the sea is an unbelievable sight. The sea itself seems to have retreated, as if it's being sucked down some huge hole. And right out there, when the wind clears the air for a few seconds, we can see a new island forming in the sea in front of our eyes, just pushing up out of the seabed. It's an ugly thing, a boil about to burst. We think it's a new volcano forming. We are all very afraid but there's no panic here. The small planes continue to land and take off with their human cargo, flying them to a strip on the other side of the island, then returning for another load. If there's time, they will lift us all out of here. But none of us knows how much time is left."

For a moment, there was only static crackling. Then, "Just a minute. I hear something above the noise. Motors, *big* motors! My God, it's a DC-3! That wonderful old workhorse of the airways, the Dakota, the greatest plane ever built. One of them has somehow gotten here and he's coming in to this tiny strip, flaps down, nose up into the gale, almost in a stalling position. He's coming down . . . he's down safely! Another's coming in right behind him! Incredible! Two big DC-3s! People around me are crying and laughing and cheering. These two planes mean life for us here. They'll take, oh, thirty or forty each, maybe more.''

David wrestled the controls as they bucked against the gale, his hands slippery on the joy stick, and wrenched the plane to a stop only yards from the end of the strip. He gunned the port motor and spun it around to taxi back to where the people were huddled under the concrete control tower. All the way over and during the landing he'd been waiting for that fuse in his brain to blow again, waiting for the trigger to go off. Nothing had happened. He had come through this harshest of tests and he had won; he had beaten the volcano.

The crowd was orderly: after those in charge loaded people on board, well past the safety limit, he looked down from the cockpit at the white and strained faces of the ones who had to be left behind. He nodded to them, trying to tell them he'd be back soon. Then he revved the engines and sent the plane careering down the runway, only seconds behind Burt's plane. The engines strained and altered pitch under their great load and the palms at the end of the strip came racing toward him, but he knew his craft, and when he pulled the stick back hard into his lap, the plane jumped into the air, kissing the tree-tops.

The navigator called the course for him and they swung away from where the volcano was sending fireworks into the black clouds, across the island to the receiving strip on the other end of the island. It was almost normal day-light there and he took the plane straight in, touching down moments before Burt did. They each disgorged their passengers right there, swung around, and took off again, heading back into the maelstrom.

At Wings, they listened without speaking, hanging back against the walls, respecting Jill's solitude by the radio; all the guests and staff were gathered in the room and they all felt for her in her anguish. The radio reporter continued his broadcast, the hysteria in his voice only just barely controlled now.

"The sea now seems our greatest danger, surrounded as we are by so many dangers," he said. "The sea looks like it's boiling, surg-ing, deciding what direction it will go in. There are still about fifty of us here waiting to be taken off, but the wind has gotten worse, as if that were possible. The small planes haven't been back for fifteen minutes and we're afraid they won't make it again. The helicopters have all been beaten back.

"But I can hear it again, that wonderful sound of the Dakotas coming in! These brave pilots have returned, one more run against all the odds, braving the hellish volcano to take the last of us off. What a majestic sight they are, dropping out of the storm onto this strip.''

Andy watched Jill carefully, noting the chalk-white face, the hands clenched together. He gauged the distance between them in case she fainted.

David was exultant, sweat streaming off him in the close cockpit, as he watched the last of the refugees scramble up the little steel ladder into his plane. He glanced across to Burt's plane, already loaded and starting its takeoff, and gave the answer to his friend's thumbs-up sign. He was grinning madly.

Then he looked past Burt's plane and everything in him stopped.

It was the worst of all nightmares, every fear bearing down on them. A wall of water, three or four times the height of the tallest tree, solid, like a huge gray concrete block, coming out of the sea and up the beach, aimed straight at them.

The reporter, last to board the plane, saw it when David did.

''Oh, God!'' he cried. ''Hell is coming to get us. A wave, a giant wave . . . The other plane is just going to make it,'' he sobbed, ''but we won't.''

A dreadful roaring noise engulfed him then,

a noise that went through his microphone just before drowning it and everything else.

David felt the wave pick up the plane and turn it over. The plane and all in it were crushed under tons of surging water.

"Jill," he whispered as he died. "Jill."

She screamed once. "David," and Andy caught her before she hit the floor. He carried her, so small and frail in his huge arms, to her bed in the bungalow. Cindy followed and he told her to stay with Jill while he radioed for a doctor.

"There's still a fifty-fifty chance," he whispered to Cindy. "We don't know which plane got away."

Jill stayed unconscious throughout the long afternoon; the others could hope and pray, but she knew David was gone. She willed herself to stay unconscious to avoid the shattering of her life. Waking might destroy her mind.

The doctor was at her bedside when she finally opened her eyes.

"Give me something to make me sleep a long, long time," she whispered.

He nodded and prepared a needle. She whispered again, "The fetus . . . ?"

"You don't have to worry about side effects," he said. "It won't affect the baby." David's child. She didn't want it now. There was nothing to live for anymore.

David came to her during her drug-induced trance and spoke to her, gently and lovingly.

He told her she must live for both of them. "I love you," she heard him say before he departed. "I will always love you."

"Don't leave me like this," she cried, desperate. "Take me with you, *please.*" But he was gone.

They buried David on the highest point on the island, between a stand of palms overlooking the pretty little resort. During the brief service, Jill stood between Dr. Cohen and Andy. She swayed and began to fall as the brown earth showered onto David's coffin.

Later Dr. Cohen sat alone with her, holding her hands in his.

"Go away for a little while," he said gently. "But you are coming back here; you must come back. This is your home. And David will always be here waiting for you. His spirit is here, as yours is." He squeezed her hands. "And I will always be here. I promised David long ago that I would watch over you. I shall keep that promise, Jill."

Her eyes misted over and she managed only a nod, no words.

Winter in America and winter in her heart. After three months in Chicago Jill was still a stranger, even with her parents. There was grayness everywhere, in the skyline and chilly lake Michigan, in the drab dress and unsmiling countenances of people. Her sense of aloneness was absolute. She fought against tears and despair but there was nothing to hold on to, nothing to hope for. She lived in the old apartment with her parents and would never have stirred from there if it hadn't been for their grave concern. She saw their looks of helplessness, their tears, and she made supreme efforts to appear to be recovering. She started going for long walks on the lakeshore, and her body, at least, was soon firm and strong again. But when she went out with old friends, to a restaurant or the movies, she felt even more hopeless and alone. It didn't seem right that the rest of the world should be going on as if nothing had happened to David.

"I'm very worried for you, Jill," her father said one afternoon. "Your mother and I love having you here with us, but I don't think it's the right place for you. You need your own apartment, and a job to keep you busy. You can't grieve forever."

Why not? she wanted to shout.

"It's time for you to have a life," he continued. "You were happy here in Chicago before. You can be happy here again."

She was moved; it was the most forthright he had ever been. What an effort it must have cost him.

But she knew where her future lay. It would never be the same without David, but at least she would be living in the tropics they had loved together, amid those vibrant colors. That night, while yet another vicious storm swept in from the Great Lakes, she dreamed of a warm blue ocean rolling up to golden sands.

She ignored the baby until her body wouldn't let her do that anymore, and then one afternoon she locked herself in her room and got undressed very slowly and stood in front of the mirror, looking at the curves and the round belly and thinking, ''This is real. I can't make it go away.'' And in a rush she understood that she wanted the baby, wanted it as badly as she'd wanted a baby when David was alive.

The revelation cheered her a little, and it softened her. She no longer had to worry about loving the child; she wanted it and she was sure of that. It. Him. It was a boy, she knew that, too.

Embarrassed by the feelings the mirror had set off in her, she turned away and got dressed. But she'd reached an awakening and she was glad. From then on, she didn't ignore the baby for being there when it wasn't wanted; it *was* wanted.

She had a task to perform before returning to Hawaii. First she flew to Boston and telephoned David's mother from the airport. Jill had written them on David's death and eventually received a very correct, almost terse note; there had been no communication since.

''Yes?'' his mother said as Jill announced herself on the phone. She sounded nervous. Jill explained that she was in Boston, and Mrs. Nagle told her to visit Mr. Nagle at his office.

Jill arrived there exactly on time and was shown in immediately. Mr. Nagle was sitting in one of two big leather chairs in a corner by a window, a silver coffee service on the table beside him. He rose when she came in.

"My dear," he said, advancing and taking her hand, "come sit down and have coffee." He fussed over pouring it. "What brings you to Boston? We thought you were firmly entrenched in the islands."

"I'm on my way back there now," she said. "I just wanted to see you, to—to tell you how it was when David died."

He scowled. "The tragedy was just the damn fool kind of thing the boy did all his life. He could have achieved so much." He gestured around his office. "He could have had all of this. Instead he ran away from his duties. He became a bum."

"David wasn't a bum," she said, voice rising with anger. "He was a fine pilot. He was a wonderful husband. And he died a hero. Please try and remember David as he *truly* was. David was happy. He loved his life."

"Self-gratification," he sighed. "Is that all you young people think about? What about responsibility, loyalty? Don't things like that count?"

"They do, Mr. Nagle, and David was loyal, loyal and responsible," she said. She found herself wanting desperately to form some link with him and Mrs. Nagle. "Maybe when you and I and Mrs. Nagle can talk together, you'll come to see that David was doing what he had to do. You should be proud of him.''

''I'm afraid talking with my wife is out of the question,'' he said. ''She does not wish to be reminded of David at all. It's all been too upsetting for her.'' He lit a cigar and drew on it. ''I suppose you feel entitled to some kind of settlement.'' She shook her head furiously but he appeared not to notice. ''You weren't married all that long, and there were no children,'' he said, ''but I am prepared to be quite generous. On one condition. You must revert to your maiden name.'' He blew a smoke ring and watched it floating in the afternoon light. ''You'll think me stuffy and old-fashioned, but we Nagles are intensely proud of our name. There has never been a Nagle with a lowly job, like David's. You'll understand how embarrassed we were when David was running a guesthouse on an island. Or being an airline employee.''

''Wings,'' she said, her voice icy, ''is a lovely business. And I can't understand your embarrassment over his being a pilot. He was a hero. I can't begin to understand you. No wonder David despised you.'' His face flushed but he said nothing. ''I feel sorry for you, Mr. Nagle. I have lost the man I loved, but you lost him a long, long time ago.'' She started for the door. ''You can keep your money. David gave me his name and I'll bear it proudly. Not because of what you or any of your goddamned ancestors ever did, but because of David, the man he was." She fumbled with the door and hurried out through the reception area and into the elevator, ducking her head to hide the tears.

She was on a flight to Chicago within an hour, and packed for Hawaii by midnight. Her parents were sorry she was leaving them but happy she had a sense of purpose again. They promised to come visit soon, and to stay for the baby's arrival.

They were all there to meet her at Honolulu Airport: Dr. Cohen in his white suit, Andy huge and bearlike in a flowered shirt, Cindy tan and beautiful in slacks and a pink cotton blouse. She knew as she saw them she had done the right thing: she had come home. They all hugged her and Cindy cried a little.

"Look at you, so pale," Andy said. "You better get your tan back. You look more like a guest than the co-owner of Wings."

"And so thin, too," Cindy said.

Dr. Cohen held her hands and looked into her eyes. He smiled. He could tell she was pregnant.

"Jill is going to be all right now," he said. "She's back where she belongs."

Andy and Cindy went off to find her bags and Carl stayed with her.

"You are young and brave and intelligent," he said to her. "You will prosper, and the love you and David knew will make you more capable of loving again, of giving love to all people and all things.''

He rode with her to the dock and waved them good-bye as the boat churned toward Wings. Jill watched the Waikiki skyline recede and thought about how many times she had made this journey. But this time there was no David waiting for her at the other end. Andy took one hand off the wheel and draped it around her shoulder. Cindy touched her cheek. Soon her island was before her, welcoming her like another old friend. She was home and she was glad.

Her parents arrived a week before the baby was due and Andy squired them around. Jill was too big to move much. She had dinner waiting when the three came home each evening, and twice Burt joined them. It was a nice evening, candlelight and a three-quarter moon and soft conversation. Nobody mentioned David because he was everywhere they looked and in everything Jill and Andy and Burt were doing with Wings.

Two days after the baby's due date, Jill was gazing out at the mist when a couple of things happened at once; it began raining in earnest, and the pains began. The doctor met her and her parents at the hospital, and with very little pain and almost no struggle at all, Jonathan David Nagle made his quiet appearance. He was healthy and everything went well and as Jill was holding him she suddenly burst into the kind of hysterical sobbing she had allowed herself only once since David's death. None of the nurses or the doctor seemed to find anything unusual in this, and Jill was left to sob herself out, which she did gladly and with a sense of great relief.

When she finished crying, she took a long, long look at the baby and saw little of David in his face, which was all to the good. He was not a shadow of his father, he was Jonathan. An hour later, she fell into a contented sleep.

In the morning, when her parents came to see her and the baby, she told them firmly that Jonathan looked a little—only a little—like Jill's mother and nobody else, and they understood what she wanted them to understand: there was to be no mention of David until she was ready.

Chapter Six _____

THE CHAIN OF ISLANDS RAN AWAY TO
the north, each one a bright green jewel in the
blue ocean. As the airplane passed over them
Jill saw that each was different. Some were
wild and rugged, covered by dense jungle;
others were trim and neat beneath regulated
rows of coconut palms. But all the islands
were ringed with golden beaches and, wherever there was a break in the reef, perfect
waves rolled up to the shore. The plane
banked steeply and began its descent to the
coral airstrip on the main island, Petit Bougainville.

"It's even more beautiful than you said,
Burt," she told him before leaving the cockpit
and returning to sit with Cindy. There were
only about forty other passengers on the plane
and she figured Burt would be battling to
make a profit on this charter. He had been flying down there to the South Pacific once a
month for the past six months; if there had not
been such an overabundance of aircraft available for lease he could not have afforded to

keep going. But Burt had faith in the little-known group of islands; he was convinced the newly independent island nation of Garokan was just the place for rich, jaded American tourists looking for something new.

She glanced around the plane: the passengers didn't look much like tourists. Investment bankers was more like it, coming to see whether Garokan might become an offshore, tax-free haven. She and Cindy waited for Burt to come out of the cockpit and left the plane with him. The heat greeting them was not unpleasant, in the mid-eighties but with little humidity. They walked across the white airstrip to the terminal, a long, low shed of wood walls with a thatched roof.

"Hi, Mr. Burt," a smiling brown customs officer greeted them. "Good to see you back. We'd be out of business without you." He waved Burt through the gate. "These ladies are with you? Lucky man." He waved Jill and Cindy through, too.

"They're all very relaxed, very friendly," Brydon said as he carried their bags through the tiny terminal. "It's no place to expect fast service, but what is there to hurry about on this place?"

He dumped their bags in the trunk of an ancient Chevy taxi.

"Woody Kelly's hotel," he told the driver, and they settled in the lumpy rear seat.

It was a slow progress along the narrow

dusty road; they had to stop several times to avoid big, slow-moving cattle.

"Charolais," Burt said. "Some of the best beef anywhere. Don't expect Mrs. Kelly to serve it, though. Like a lot of the other residents, she doesn't consider buying local meat and fish, so everything is shipped from New Zealand, frozen. We'll change all that, I hope."

Jill glanced at him and smiled. Burt was determined that she investigate Garokan as a prospective site for a new Wings resort. Andy was all for it.

"It's not as if you're needed here," Andy had told her bluntly. "We're booked up for the next year. Everything's under control; the place runs like clockwork. Go find us somewhere new to start a place: I'm getting bored here."

She knew Andy was mostly concerned with keeping her occupied, anxious for her. She had buried her grief deep inside her, but Andy and Cindy and the rest of her friends continued to treat her with an excessive care.

"They do it out of love for you, and for David," Dr. Cohen explained. "Be patient. Soon they'll see you've found your inner strength."

And there was Burt. She'd been back three months and was heavy with the baby when he appeared at Wings. He was as big and disheveled as ever, but somehow changed, as if he were carrying a great burden. It was in his eyes all the time and it came out when he got crying drunk one night.

"It should have been me, Jill," he mumbled as they sat alone in the bar. "I'm just a drifter, with no one who cares about me. If David had taken off first . . ."

She shuddered.

"Cut it out!" she snapped. "You knew David. There was no way he wasn't going to try and rescue those people." She patted him on the shoulder. "Please, Burt, it was fate. Now the rest of us have to carry on without him. David wouldn't want this."

After that he contrived to visit often and was always trying to help her, this way or that way.

They were passing through the coconut plantations now and she noted the variety of livestock grazing among the trees. Cattle, pigs, goats, sheep, and chickens all looked content and strong.

"It's an incredible place," Burt said, waving out the window at a group of natives. "Everything grows here. A good chef could have a ball without ever having to use anything brought in from outside."

They hit a stretch of sealed road and the cab speeded up, its battered top flapping, casting bits of material behind them. The sealed road ended right outside a ramshackle structure nearly buried under flowering creepers. In the midst of the wild vegetation was an ancient wooden sign: WOODY'S PUB—COLD BEER. They followed Burt up the creaking steps to the wide verandah that ran around the building. A couple of old, pink-faced men in soiled white suits were collapsed on cane chairs; they did not look up as the newcomers stepped into the cool gloom of the bar and reception area. Burt thumped a bell on the bar and they heard curses from somewhere in back. Woody Kelly appeared.

The only reason she wasn't as well known a character as Apia's Aggie Grey was that Garokan was harder to get to than Samoa: there weren't many visitors to spread the legend. There had been a Mr. Kelly once, forty years before, but he had been captured by the Japanese, or eaten by the natives, or packed off home to Ireland by Woody—depending on who was telling the story. For forty years, Woody had run the hotel on her own. She had been known to knock down men—and women—she didn't like, but, far more serious, she often blackballed those who displeased her. Being barred from Woody's Pub meant being locked out of the social center of Petit Bougainville.

"Brydon, you big Aussie bastard!" the woman boomed as she saw them. "Why didn't you say you were coming? The place is filled up. Did you bring this month's *Cosmopolitan*?" She turned to Jill. "It's hell in these islands, honey. The natives are about the most licentious people anywhere in the Pacific, but they elected a mission-educated guy as their first president and he's banned all my favorite magazines.''

''I brought it, Woody,'' Burt said. ''Lucky your customs guys are so lax. They didn't even want to look at the pictures.'' He swung himself onto a barstool. ''How about long cold gins for Jill Nagle and Cindy Mason, and a cold Foster's for me?'' He drank straight from the large, textured bottle, wiped his hand across the foam clinging to his moustache, and called for another.

''What's this bullshit about no room in the inn?'' he demanded. ''I cabled you two weeks ago saying I was bringing a party down.''

She shrugged. A huge woman, she was more than six feet tall and massive across the shoulders. She had a rawboned face, thin gray hair, skin burned amber. She must have been close to seventy, Jill thought, but she had so much vitality it was hard to tell. She suddenly winked at Jill.

''You know what the cable service is like here, Brydon,'' she said. ''Still, I'll see you right. It's about time I sent those two old codgers out front home to their wives and children. So, I can get you two rooms. But what's this about a party?''

''I brought forty people down for the week,'' Burt said. ''Most of them in suits. They should be arriving on your doorstep any time now.''

''Humph!'' she said. ''They'll have to sleep in the longhouse. Bloody bank clerks. Most of them don't spend a cent at the bar. We need some real tourists, people who come here to have fun.''

''Isn't there anywhere else to stay on the island?'' Cindy asked. ''Your place doesn't look that big.''

''I'm not equipped for a lot of guests,'' Woody said. ''And I wouldn't be bothered with them if I were. I make my living off the bar and the dining room. The bar stays open as long as I'm on my feet; the dining room opens when I get back up again.'' She drained her drink and gestured to Jill and Cindy to follow suit. ''Apart from my place, there's two hotels in town, the Snake Pit and the Cafard. Most people take one look at them and settle for bunking in my longhouse.''

She was interrupted by a flurry outside: through the open louvers Jill could see ducks and chickens scattering as two rickety old buses staggered down the road and drew up at the front of the hotel. Their companions from the flight, plus Burt's flight crew, all emerged. The two stews and the engineer knew the ropes, so they vanished around the back of the hotel to stake out the best beds in the male and female dormitories. The visitors didn't know what to do, so they crowded into the bar, looking around.

''Where's reception?'' asked one of them, an owlish young man, sweating in his gray suit.

''Right where you're standing,'' Woody

told him. "You can go dump your bags out back. Men to the left, women to the right. Then report back here for drinks and you can sign the register."

They sensed there was no point in grumbling: the young bankers were inured to the deprivations of hunting out new tax havens, and the few tourists in the party decided to treat it as an adventure. They trooped off meekly to their spartan accommodations.

Jill watched them go and laughed.

"You sure know how to handle them, Mrs. Kelly," she said. "I guess there's a lot to be said for having the only game in town."

"Call me Woody," she said. "Everyone does, even people I'm not speaking to."

"Jill's in the hotel game herself," Burt volunteered. "She owns Wings Resort in Hawaii."

"I read about that," Woody said. "Don Messner—now *there's* a hulk—mentioned it when *Cosmo* interviewed him. You ever meet him, dear?"

"Actually, yes," Jill said, grinning. "I got to know him quite well when they were filming on the island."

"You going to start a place around here?" Woody demanded. "God knows, we could use it."

"I don't know," Jill said. "Burt thinks there's a big tourist potential in Garokan, but I'd have to talk to people who know, like you, before we decide. Anyway, it's good you wouldn't think of us as competition."

"Hell, no," she said. "Like I say, I'm happy with the bar trade. If you opened up a nice little resort, I'd get a lot of custom from you. People coming over to see the crazy old lady who runs the pub."

"What else is there to do here, for tourists, I mean?"

"Plenty, if you're willing to travel around all the islands," Woody said. "Over on Sabot, for example, they've got the best and most beautiful dancers in the whole Pacific. The few visitors we get, they really get turned on by a visit to Sabot." She leered at Burt. "You better take the girls over there," she said. "Biggles can fly you tomorrow."

A man had drifted into the bar. He was tall and spare and sported a flowing moustache; despite the heat he wore a battered leather jacket and grubby white silk scarf. It wasn't hard to see why he had been nicknamed for the dashing pilot hero of an English children's story.

"Hello, Burt, old chap," the newcomer said. His accent was very English. He turned to Jill and Cindy and bowed from the waist. "Harry Ashworth, remittance man and first-rate pilot," he said. "But everyone calls me Biggles—though I'm damned if I know why."

"Cindy Mason and Jill Nagle," Burt said. "I've been trying to get them down here for months. Jill runs a resort in Hawaii and I figure there's an opportunity for her to do something similar here.''

''Well, we could certainly use some tourists,'' Biggles said. ''What about the party you brought in, Burt? Any of them want a flight to the outer islands?''

''Most of them are bankers,'' Burt said, ''but there's a few who'll want to do some sight-seeing. We were thinking about going over to Sabot for a night.''

''Ah!'' said Woody. ''Here comes our resident spy.''

The latest arrival in the bar scowled; he was a slim, dark, small man, neat in shirt and shorts and long white socks. He nodded to Burt and Biggles and swung himself onto a stool.

''A martini, Mrs. Kelly,'' he said. ''And, please, do stop trying to turn me into local color. I am *not* your resident CIA man; I am a humble lawyer trying to establish a practice on this godforsaken atoll.'' He turned in his seat and looked at Jill. His smile was wry. ''There's no excitement here,'' he said, ''so the locals have to manufacture it. My name is Clint Donnelly.''

She nodded to him. ''Jill Nagle. I'm sorry you're not a spy. I could use a good intelligence briefing about Garokan.''

''Oh, I can give you that,'' he said. ''As a lawyer, I guess I know most of the little secrets of our proud new nation.''

''Jill's thinking about starting a tourist resort

here," Woody volunteered. "So I guess she'll need a local lawyer. And you're the only one around, Donnelly."

Donnelly took out his wallet and passed his card to Jill.

"Anything I can do to help," he said. "You'll find land acquisition is a nightmare here. The various tribes each own their own land and you have to deal with village councils to get a lease."

The bar had filled up, Burt's passengers realizing there wasn't much else to do but drink. Some of them were griping about the accommodations, but only out of earshot of the forbidding Woody.

"Cindy and I want to take a walk downtown, Burt," Jill said. "See what Petit Bougainville has to offer."

"Very little," he said, "but I'll come with you."

It was a quarter-mile stroll along the beach behind the hotel to the town. There wasn't much there. A pair of crumbling wharves, hardly used since the copra trade had gone into decline, some tumbledown sheds, three general stores selling out-of-date goods, a post office, a police station, a native market, and two decrepit hotels. But for all its seediness, the town had charm. In the evening light the buildings had a soft pink glow, and the people walking in the dusty main street were bright and smiling.

"I guess it all looks a little tired," Burt said

defensively. "But the kind of people you'll be bringing to Wings won't care about the town. Wait till you see the beaches. And the coral reefs. And some of the best marlin fishing in the world. I tell you, Jill, this is about the last unspoiled paradise in the Pacific."

"I'm looking forward to seeing it all, starting tomorrow," she said. "But I'm already convinced about the climate. It's marvelous."

"Yeah, and it stays like this for ten months of the year," he said. "The only bad time is the rainy season, December through January. Everyone who can do so leaves the islands then. But that wouldn't be a bad thing in your business—shut down for two months of maintenance and R and R for the staff."

"What about local staff? Will I be able to find trained people here?"

"Some," he said. "Before the French pulled out they instilled fairly high standards in the natives who worked in their houses. You could probably rustle up fifty or so good domestics and kitchen hands. And there are several good native chefs kicking around. What you see now," he added, gesturing to the town, "and what you get at Woody's, doesn't indicate the potential of the place. Like all the islands, there's a certain torpor that's set in. It needs someone like you to come along and shake it into life."

"Is the place politically stable?" Cindy asked. "It's only been independent for a year, right?"

"I think it's pretty safe," Burt said. "They're very hospitable to tourists. They know that's their only growth industry. The government itself is very straight up and down." He grinned. "That's what Woody meant, calling Donnelly the resident spy. Most people think he's the CIA's man here."

"Why would the CIA have a guy in a little place like this?" Jill asked.

"Well, like I said, the government is very careful to try and do the right thing. They don't want to become the pawn of any of the big powers. So they've refused both the U.S. and Russia diplomatic representation here. Except that they did accredit the Cubans, so a couple of times a year the Cuban ambassador to Japan flies down here to show the flag. And that makes the Americans crazy, so the theory is they've put a CIA guy here to keep tabs on the situation."

"And poor Mr. Donnelly is the suspect," Cindy said.

"Yeah," Burt said. "He's got a nice little business as the registered office for a lot of tax-dodging companies. I hear he's got something like seven hundred company titles on the wall of his office, and each one of them paying him a hundred bucks a year for the privilege. And he does a little conveyancing work, leases, that kind of thing. So it's a decent business. But in a place like this, everyone gossips and the gossip about Donnelly is that he was in some odd spots—like Cambodia and Thailand—before he turned up here. So they figure he's CIA.''

After breakfast the next morning, Burt took them around the island. It was a bone-shattering four-hour drive on the coral roads, but the reward was the beauty of the coastline and the mysterious, awesome rain forests on the mountain range that split the island. There were at least two locations, palm-fringed coves, suitable for Wings, so Jill returned to the hotel very pleased. Biggles was waiting for them in the bar, drinking what she hoped was a soda or mineral water.

"You ready?" he said, wiping his moustache. "I radioed the chief chappie this morning and told him I was bringing a big spender in to see him, so they'll lay on the works for you."

He had rounded up two tourist couples to fill out the Beechcraft, and Jill listened in on their conversation as the plane droned across the water to Sabot.

"The Island of Love!" one of the wives gushed. "I've read about it for years. The handsomest people in the Pacific, untouched by missionary influence."

"They're handsome, all right," Biggles said, turning in his seat. "Over the past hundred years they've intermarried with the French planters, so you've got this tribe of light-skinned Polynesians. There's no one like them. You gentlemen better watch out for your ladies—and vice versa," he added roguishly.

They came in low over the lagoon in the center of the island and touched down on the narrow airstrip. There were no buildings, only a stack of forty-four-gallon gas drums indicating any commercial activity. Beside the drums was a flower-decked wagon with bench seating; four handsome gray horses were harnessed to it.

Cindy clapped her hands with delight. The others worked their cameras. It was all so beautiful, light-years away from the world they lived in.

At the wagon, a smiling youth awaited them, a boy, tall and slim, fine featured, with light cocoa skin. His eyes were blue.

"Welcome to Sabot," he said, presenting each of them with a garland of tropical flowers. "Our island is your island for as long as you wish." His speech was lilting, English with a French accent.

They climbed into the wagon and began a slow and gentle progress past the huge palms of a long-established copra plantation, past a green hillside dotted with big cream Charolais cattle, down to a village by the sea. There were about fifty houses in the village compound, attractive places built of palm trunks and thatched with palm leaves.

"Construction wouldn't be any problem here," Jill told Burt as they trundled through the village square. "Their houses have the perfect look for a Wings resort as it is."

"They put them up in a matter of days and they'll withstand hurricanes and earthquakes—both of which you're liable to get here," Burt said.

The wagon deposited them in front of a large, open-walled assembly hall; waiting on the wooden steps was a crowd of children and teenagers, smiling and waving to them. The children were entrancing, the youths handsome, the girls beautiful—and naked to the waist.

"The bra never took on here," Biggles told his party as they were escorted into the hall.

It was dark inside after the bright sunlight, and Jill waited for her eyes to adjust. Then she saw the figure of the chief rising from his carved wooden throne to greet them. He was tall, very tall, and his bare bronzed chest rippled under the open cloak of bird-of-paradise feathers.

"My God, he's gorgeous!" Cindy whispered. "And so young. He can't be more than twenty-five."

The chief fixed them with his bright blue eyes and threw his arms wide, revealing more of the sculptured body.

"Welcome," he said. "Please come sit at my table and take refreshment with me after your journey." He stepped down from the throne and walked to the head of a long, low table covered with fresh banana leaves.

Wooden bowls of fruit—guavas, mangoes, tiny oranges, soursops—had been distributed across the table and at each place setting was a hollowed-out coconut filled with yellow liquid. They all sat down and then the chief lifted his coconut and drank deeply, indicating they should follow suit.

Jill sipped; it was tangy, refreshing, potent.

"This sure isn't kava," Cindy said. "Thank God for that."

The chief smiled.

"No," he said. "The French convinced us kava was like drinking paint stripper. Over the years we developed this, *motu*, made from fermented sugarcane, soursop juice, and lime juice."

He chatted with them, relaxed, urbane, educated.

"Perhaps you would like to stroll around our island," the chief said, rising. "There are many willing guides and they will have you back here in two hours for the feast and dancing." He turned to Jill. "Perhaps, madame, you will stay with me. I understand you wish to investigate business possibilities on Sabot."

The others trailed out of the hall, the women glancing enviously at Jill.

The chief watched them go, then sat down again.

"Would you like another drink?" he asked. "It's really quite safe. No more potent than a rum and Coke." He turned and called into the back of the hall. "Moya! Two more drinks."

He settled back into his chair and undid the pearl-shell clasp on his robe. "You don't mind if I get rid of this damned thing? It impresses the few visitors we get to the island, but it's hot and it tickles." He was now wearing only a white lap-lap, as near naked as the beautiful girl who brought their drinks and disappeared back into the gloom. "Now," he said, "what kind of business are you in and how might it fit on Sabot?"

She gave him a quick rundown on Wings.

"But," she concluded, "I don't know that it would work here. There'd be some difficulty in getting the people here. The airstrip would have to be enlarged."

"No need," he said. "We are a seafaring people—legend says we sailed here from South America—and we maintain a dozen large outriggers. It would be no trouble to bring fifty or sixty visitors up from Bougainville each week. At most a four-hour trip and surely a spectacular introduction to the resort. And if any of them were fainthearted sailors, there would always be Captain Biggles to fall back on." He stood up. "Do you ride?" She nodded. "Good," he said. "Come and I will show you some possible sites for your village. May I call you Jill?" She nodded again. "I am Jean-Paul," he said. "But I would appreciate it if you would call me Chief when in the presence of members of my tribe." He laughed. "I have so little to preside over, it's important to preserve the dignity of the office."

They cantered easily down the white beach on two black horses, riding around a headland and along the side of a placid lagoon cut off from the ocean by a coral reef. In the middle of the lagoon sat a long, low island, palm trees along its center, giant banyans lining its shores. He reined in where an old man was sitting by a dugout canoe mending a net. The man struggled up and bowed when he saw it was the chief.

"Good afternoon, Tavu," the chief said. "I would like you to take the *senubada* and me across to Karakato."

"I am honored, my chief," the old man said. They stepped into the little boat and he sent it skimming across the shallow water.

"See," Jean-Paul said, indicating the lagoon. "It is safe for swimming and sailing and fine for exploring sea life. You would not lose any of your tourists to danger. There is none here."

The old man ran the boat up on the white sand and they stepped ashore.

"This was a plantation until the French left," Jean-Paul said. "The whole island is only about twenty acres square, but it has many coves and the heavy vegetation would allow you to build bungalows that had a strong sense of privacy." They were walking up a narrow path. "And here," he said, "is the old plantation house. It is in disrepair but it could easily be restored." They explored the wide verandah. "Perhaps it would serve as your central building, your restaurant and bar.''

"It's all wonderful!'' Jill said. And it was. Once she got them onto this little island, her people would be totally isolated from the outside world. Here they would live in beauty and peace. "You've won me already," she said. "I'd love to put a resort here. But," she asked, "aren't you worried that such a development will affect your people?"

"Not too much." He grinned. "For one, you would be comparatively isolated here on this island within an island. Only those of my people you chose to employ would come here. It is something of a holy place to my people— one of our gods resides here—and they visit only on that god's days. But of course," he grinned again, "the god would not mind his people earning a wage on his island. We are a practical people."

Jill was trying to think of disadvantages; she didn't trust her initial enthusiasm. It seemed too easy.

"Utilities would be a problem," she said. "It will be damned expensive to put in a generator."

"True," he said, "but offsetting that, my people will build your accommodations from free materials, and they'll work for, say, five dollars a day. Better, I think, than the going rate in Hawaii?" It certainly was.

They completed a tour of the hidden little island, Jill noting where she could put tennis courts and where she could scatter thirty bungalows.

''If you decide to accept my offer,'' he said, ''I promise you absolute cooperation. No trouble with the lease of the island. No labor problems. Because the truth is, Sabot is desperate. Since independence, those fools on the main island of Garokan have been squeezing us. They don't like us because we were close to the French. Most of us are at least a quarter French; many, like me, had some part of our education in France. When the vote was taken on independence, only Sabot voted against it. Now they try and punish us by denying us a share of the central revenue. So we must have an industry of our own. Frankly, yours is the only offer we've had.'' He smiled. ''We would make you very welcome and I would smooth your path.''

When the remains of the feast had been cleared away, the dancing began. Ten young men and women came out of the surrounding jungle to take up positions on the ground in front of the guests. The tropical night came down fast, and the dance was lit only by guttering flares ringed around the dancers. In the flickering light, illusions wove through the dance. It was a dreaming time. The dancers were young, beautiful, incredibly lithe, and, other than their woven flax skirts, naked. The flames flashed on gleaming bodies as they moved through intricate steps. It was clearly a dance to celebrate the rites of courtship; the dancers coupled and uncoupled, changing partners, each seeking the perfect mate. Jill was glad of the darkness: she could feel her face flush from the sheer eroticism of it, from the increasing tempo of the drums. The dancers, the whole scene, were arousing passions in her, passions she was determined to keep in check. Cindy was sitting beside her and she felt a shiver run through her friend's body. Burt, on the other side of her, looked dazed.

The dancers paired and the pace increased; they writhed together, wet gleaming bodies locked limb to limb, oblivious to the onlookers. The rest of the tribe approached the dancers, edging forward and encouraging them with a soft, hissing sound. The dancers were not just simulating the act of love, they were on the verge of doing it. From the corner of her eye Jill saw the chief rise from his place and make his way over to her. He held out his hand, inviting her to join the dance. But Burt placed a heavy hand on her arm. The chief shrugged, gave her a little smile, and turned to Cindy, who scrambled to her feet and moved into the dance with him. It was the signal for all the others to join in too, and within seconds there were thirty bodies moving to the hypnotic drumbeat.

Soon only Burt and Jill were left outside the dance.

She caught glimpses of Cindy dancing: a white dress swirling wide, slender thighs flashing, blond hair flung this way and that. The mighty body of the chief enveloped her. After a while, the drums slowed and the native couples began to melt away into the jungle, embracing, stroking. Only the tourists were left in the square, embarrassed by the recent passion. Jill saw Cindy's white dress far off in the trees.

"Burt," she whispered, her throat dry. "Shouldn't we see if Cindy's safe?"

He ran a hand across his forehead, wiping away the sweat.

"Cindy's a big girl, Jill," he muttered. "She knows what she wants." As he got up, he said, "Jesus, what a turn-on! With a floor show like that, Wings would be booked forever."

Chapter Seven _____

"I'M WORRIED ABOUT YOU," DR. COHEN said. He poured another cup of the astringent green tea for her and slumped back in his deck chair. Below them a puffy rain cloud was depositing a late-afternoon shower on the hot sands of Waikiki. "You're not having any fun, not meeting new people. You live for the baby and your business."

"I'm too busy," Jill protested. "We're opening new resorts all the time. Garokan is doing more business than the original Wings, the Malaysian place is already ahead of projections, and now I've got a proposal to open Wings in the Greek Islands. I'm meeting new people all the time—thousands of 'em every week."

"You know that's not what I mean, my dear," he said gently. "You're a young woman, successful businesswoman or not, and you need someone special. You surely don't intend to remain a widow forever? David would not have wanted that."

She did not resent his probing. He, of all people, had the right.

"Someday, Carl," she sighed, "someday someone may come along. But for now, I'm happy, in my way." Not quite true. There were nights of agonizing loneliness, when only the exhaustion of working could bring her to sleep.

"Don't wait too long," he said. "And do not confuse worldly success with happiness. You would do well to adopt a little of Andy's attitude toward life."

They laughed together.

Time. There just wasn't enough time for everything, she thought as she drove down to Honolulu. She was already running late for a meeting with Burt in her office. She resented the office, preferring to spend her time in the resorts, but an office had become a necessity. As head of the burgeoning Wings chain, she had to present a good, responsible front to the world.

The streets of downtown Honolulu had already emptied of office workers, so she parked right outside her building. The bottom three floors were in darkness, but all the windows of the Wings floor were ablaze.

"Hi, Burt," she called as she dashed in. "I'm sorry I kept you waiting." She took the sheet of messages her secretary handed her. "Come on through and we'll fix a drink," she said.

She found a cold Foster's for him and a soda for her; she had pretty much stopped drinking lately, finding she needed a clear head at all times. She sat down on a white couch and smiled at Burt as he lowered his big frame into a chair opposite. The Australian appeared to be making an effort to smarten himself up; the beard was neatly trimmed and his shirt and jeans were crisp and clean. Oh, there was no way anyone was going to make a pinstriped tycoon out of Burt Brydon, but he did look more . . . civilized. He had always been there, Burt and Andy both, looking after her. Two big, cuddly brothers.

"I've been missing you," Burt said. "You're always off someplace and I've got all the charters I can handle. I guess we're doing well." He toasted her with his beer bottle. "You look tired, Jill."

"I'll get by," she said. She was tired of being told she looked tired. "I've got to go to New York next week and I plan to turn it into a vacation. What about you? We're pushing plenty of business your way, aren't we?"

"Oh, yeah, thanks," he said. "I do real well out of Wings. And I moved seven planes between here and the mainland this week. Everyone's looking to save a buck and the charter business is booming. I'm moving onto the Japan–Hawaii route soon. There's plenty of planes available to me. It's better than trying to run a regular airline. But," he added quickly, "your operation will always be my main concern." He grinned at her suddenly. "I took a group down to Garokan a couple of weeks ago. Looks like Cindy's doing fine. Still

149

head over heels with the chief. She seems happy.'' He eyed Jill speculatively. What did she really think about that love affair?

''Well, if it makes her happy, fine,'' Jill said noncommittally. ''There hasn't been any trouble since we opened Wings on Sabot, and the place is always packed, so I guess you had a great idea, Burt.''

''You seem to be getting a different crowd down there,'' Burt said. ''I noticed on the flight, they were mostly young guys. Not many women. And they were all booked in for three-week visits.''

Jill nodded. ''Cindy says it's because the local girls are so beautiful. The word is out and it's becoming a Mecca for single guys. I guess there's nothing to worry about, though. The islanders were into swinging long before we came along.''

''How's Jeff working out in Penang?'' he asked casually. ''I haven't made that run yet.''

''We'll go there together sometime,'' she said, brushing her hair back. Why was he looking at her so strangely? ''That's the prettiest beach in Malaysia. Jeff's fine. I'm glad you sent him to me. I didn't think he'd become manager so quickly. He's got a great deal of skill. I like him.''

Burt glanced away.

''He was copilot for me a few times,'' he said. ''He's bright and funny, a good kid. A bit wild . . . but I guess he's over all that by now.''

She concealed her smile. Jeff Thompson was her age, yet to Burt he was "a kid." She had worked with Jeff for two months while establishing the Penang resort, and they had gotten to be good friends. In fact, if she hadn't placed such constraints on herself . . .

She and Burt ate at a little seafood place on Alamoana and she relaxed enough to share a bottle of wine with him. He was always good company; she was safe with him. It was such a cozy feeling. Good old Burt. They sat outdoors and watched the big yachts rocking in their berths.

"Are you sorry you let the Wings fleet go?" he asked her quietly.

"Yes, but it had to happen," she said. "It was getting too difficult to find reliable skippers, and the guests are just as happy to be whisked over in the launch." She looked out over the harbor and sighed. "But it was great when we started it, the charter business, then ferrying the first guests over in the evening. Still, progress means changes. Andy's kept the original *Wings*, but we sold the other two and paid off some of the bank loan." She made a face. "Those damn loans! The more we expand, the greater the gross but the more we have to go into debt. I tell you, Burt, if this business suddenly went bad, we'd be in big trouble."

"You've got nothing to worry about," he said. "Your product's right—small luxury resorts for bored people who've got money.

New destinations opening all the time. No, there shouldn't be any trouble, Jill.''

After that, he fell silent. When she began thinking about going home, he began to talk faster and faster, the words falling over each other.

''Jill,'' he said, ''these past few months I've been . . . tidying up my affairs. My business is going so well, and I thought I better get some things straightened out. Like, I finally got around to giving my wife a divorce. We've lived apart for years, but until now there didn't seem much point in doing anything about it.'' He leaned toward her, tense. ''What I mean is, it's all done and I'm free and I'm doing okay. Look,'' he stumbled, desperate, ''what I need to know is, could there be . . . is there any chance you and I . . . oh, damn, you know what I mean.''

For a moment she wanted to lean against him. He was so big and strong and she almost loved him. Another extension of David, one of the men who had been so close to David. She kissed him on the cheek and he put his arm around her, misunderstanding. Gently, she pulled away.

''I know what you mean, Burt,'' she said softly. ''And I'm very touched. Your friendship—you'll never know how much you mean to me. Please, let's not spoil it. I'm still confused about what I want. I can't make any decisions of the kind you're talking about. Do you see?''

"Yup," he said, trying to shrug it off. "I just thought I'd let you know I was available." His voice dropped. "I can wait, Jill. Just don't do anything without giving me a shot. Hear?"

Cindy groaned with pleasure, her hands caressing the long, hard back, as Jean-Paul fell away from her. She kissed him, clinging, wanting him not to leave. But it was almost dawn on the island and they had agreed he should never be seen leaving her bungalow.

"Darling," she whispered, "one more time. I don't care who knows about us." Her body could never get enough of him; they'd been making love since midnight, but she still cried out for more.

"No, *ma petite*," he said, placing a finger to her lips. "My people would no more approve of my being here with you than would your guests." He stood up, his handsome body gleaming, and wrapped the strip of white cloth around his waist. He bent and kissed her. "Next week," he said, "I will again have a dozen of my special guests coming to Wings. You will be able to accommodate them?"

"Of course, Jean-Paul," she said. She kissed him one last time and then he was gone, a silent shadow moving through the jungle, down to the beach, and to the canoe. She was so tired but she couldn't sleep. Jean-Paul's special guests concerned her and she knew she should tell Jill about them. But they paid the going rate, caused no trouble, and she saw nothing wrong. They were all men on their own who, instead of enjoying the usual pleasures of Wings, spent their time working out on the beach or exploring the island with Jean-Paul. In the evenings they spent some time at the bar, mingling with the other guests. There didn't seem to be anything wrong. And it was what Jean-Paul wanted; she would do anything for Jean-Paul.

Jill tried to get some work done on the flight to New York but the delegates from the Pacific Area Travel Association were determinedly whooping it up. She and Wings were to receive a PATA award at the New York exposition, and she was happy about the publicity—mentions in the travel magazines and a chance to show the travel agents what Wings had to offer in all its locations. So she gave up trying to work and joined in the general merriment. She gently turned down a couple of proposals, one from a man and one from a woman agent. And she turned down invitations for dinner. She would be quite busy in New York, apart from the travel show. Sebastian Judge was going to spell out the Greek Islands proposal for her.

Seb Judge had sought her out in Honolulu a couple of months earlier. He'd been staying on Garokan, he said, and loved Wings. She was a little surprised because of course she knew who Seb Judge was, one of America's eminent trial lawyers, an adviser to several governments, a wheeler-dealer. A very tough customer, Seb Judge was used to high-rise, five-star hotels, not the casual ambience of a place like Wings.

"But that's the whole point!" he'd said. "It was so different from the kind of place I usually go. I was entranced. I'm going to tell all my friends about it. You don't think having a lot of geriatrics like me will spoil things for your other guests, do you?" Seb was in his early sixties.

What he wanted her to do, he said, was investigate setting up a Wings in the Greek Islands. He had good contacts within the Greek government; he could smooth the way for her. He could arrange finance, for instance. He didn't want anything from Jill, just the assurance that he could always get a reservation in a Wings resort in his favorite places.

His Rolls-Royce and driver were waiting at JFK, and the PATA delegates looked at her with new respect. She smiled as the plush car swept her through the rainy streets into Manhattan; limo was the only way to arrive in the big city. She was staying at the Stanhope, and the usually imperturbable staff of that hotel noted Judge's Rolls and treated her with extra deference. There were flowers from the great man in her room and a message to call him as soon as she could.

"Delighted, my dear," he crowed when she reached him. "Hearing your voice takes me right back to the tropics. Why did I choose a profession that requires me to slave in dank canyons of cities? Will you lunch with me tomorrow? 21?''

She unpacked, then sat for a while at the window, watching the evening strollers on Fifth Avenue. It was a fine spring night and the city was clean and glistening after a shower, bathed in a soft twilight glow. The steps of the museum were dotted with couples holding hands, glorying in the end of another long, hard winter. Everyone in New York seemed so young, she mused.

It was still early and she wasn't tired. She tried to think of anyone she wanted to call in New York. And then the idea hit her. The telephone directory was by the bed and she picked it up and flipped through the pages until she found the number.

''Hello,'' she said when a young man answered, ''is this David Nagle?''

''Yes,'' he said. ''This is David.'' He waited through a silence. ''Yes?'' he said finally.

She could detect the impatience of *her* David, the refusal to observe social niceties. She plunged in.

''I'm Jill . . . Jill Nagle,'' she said. ''I was married to your father. I arrived in New York today and I thought—''

''You want money?'' he demanded. ''Grandfather said you'd make an approach sometime.'' His voice was flat, bitter. ''You've called the wrong person. I just live here, with my mommy. You like that? A twenty-three-

year-old who still lives at home because he
hasn't gotten his act together yet. You're sure
wasting your time talking to me if you want
something.''

''I don't want anything from you!'' she
snapped. She took a deep breath. ''I loved
your father and I thought you and I might
have things to say to each other. I already had
dealings with your grandparents, and no
thank you. I only wanted to make contact with
David's son. But if you're just an asshole like
your grandparents are, young Mr. David Nagle, you can go to hell!''

She was hanging up when she heard his
laughter. She brought the receiver back to her
ear.

''I'm sorry,'' he gasped. ''Really. I'm sorry.
It's just the family always portrays you as the
wicked witch of the west, using our noble
name and eager to pluck our family fortune.
I'm sorry,'' he said again. ''I didn't mean to
come on like that but, see, I've been indoctri-
nated by the rest of them. Dad wrote me how
great you were, how happy you were together.'' He chuckled. ''They—we—*are* a
bunch of assholes. I'm sorry Dad and I never
got together before it happened.''

He barely paused to breathe. ''Look, can we
meet? For a drink or something? I'd like to
meet you. What are you doing right now?''

''Just sitting in the Stanhope,'' she said,
''wondering why I'm risking yet another re-
buff from the Nagle family.''

"Meet you in the sidewalk bar in twenty minutes," he said.

She recognized him as he came striding up Fifth Avenue. She shivered, the resemblance was so acute. He was tall and spare, like his father, the hair cropped, the eyes blue and questioning. It seemed he *was* David, and for one strange moment she expected him to know her and to come right to her table. When he stood at the entrance, looking around, she rose to catch his attention.

He crossed the space in a loping stride.

"Hi," he said, "you're very pretty and very young. The family didn't tell me either of those things." He sat down across from her and signaled for a waiter. "What are you drinking? Gin and tonic. Bring two more," he told the man.

"I hope I didn't mess up your evening," she said. "It was just—I don't know, I wanted to talk to you. David cared so much . . ." She couldn't help it, she was crying in front of all those happy, sophisticated New Yorkers and David was looking pained. She ducked her head until she felt his hand on her cheek, urging her to look up.

"Hey," he said, "cry if you need to. Don't be ashamed. I know you and Dad loved each other a lot. *I* should have gotten in touch with *you* before this. I wanted to, but the family . . . oh, hell."

The drinks came and she stopped crying, but she couldn't stop the fierce rush of memories flooding through her: she was with David again, a younger, flippant David, but David.

"What are you doing in New York?" he was asking. "I thought you were running a little guesthouse or something, in the islands. By the way, whatever it is, it makes Grandfather mad as hell. He's always bitching about how the great Nagle name is being used to attract *paying guests*." He chuckled.

She picked up her glass, sipped, and looked at him steadily. "Last year we made three million dollars."

He coughed and she went on, "I don't run 'a little guesthouse.' I run one of the most successful resort chains in the world. Your father and I started it on nothing. I've kept it going, expanded it. We didn't do it on inherited money, either, or on Boston connections, or on the old-school-tie network. Your father and I worked hard—and I still work damn hard—to create this. I do not need the Nagles or their money or their breeding. And I don't need their name, but I keep it because David gave it to me and it's mine."

He held up his hands. "Please. I'm sorry I came on so strong." He leaned on the table, chin resting in his hands. "Tell me how it was with you two, what Dad was like in those years after the war. Mom won't talk about him at all except to bad-mouth him, and the grandparents have kind of written him out of the family history." He sighed. "It's my fault, too. If I'd been a little braver I could have . . .

But I never knew my old man. So please, tell me.''

For the next hour, while young David sat quiet and attentive, she talked about his father, their life together, their love, the business they built. She talked about his tempers and his kindnesses, his bravery and the way it brought him to death. Obliquely, she told him about her grief and loneliness.

''I'm sorry,'' he said softly when she fell silent. He touched her hand. ''In this family, we don't love like that. I've been insensitive to it all my life for that reason. I wish I'd known him when he was with you. Because I do know he was happy then. That's one thing I do know.''

They had more drinks, sitting in an easy silence by then. She might have stayed there forever, suspended in time with a make-believe David. She knew it was an illusion but she couldn't stop wanting him to be David.

''Is there something else you want to do?'' he asked quietly. ''It's only a little after eleven. You want to eat? Walk? Or just stay here? We can go in and listen to the jazz, if you want to.''

She nodded. ''As long as I'm not keeping you from anything.''

There was a good trio playing, but the room was almost empty and they had their pick of the tables. He took a corner one and ordered cognac for them.

There were more cognacs while they sat

there, mostly silent, and once his hand
touched hers and remained there. It was late
when the last blues was played and they
stepped out into the lobby. She turned to say
good night to him but he was right beside her.

"Do you have your key?" he asked her.

She nodded, and when the elevator arrived
he stepped in with her, took her key, and
pressed the button for the sixth floor. She
didn't want to know what would happen
next. This was a time warp, a few hours given
back to her from a past she thought she had
lost forever. She pretended it was her David
there beside her, walking down the corridor to
her room.

She heard the door shut quietly behind her
and she turned around, not knowing whether
he was gone or not. He was leaning against
the door, studying her, watching her.

Her eyes met his and she knew what she
must do. Going to the desk, she moved some
papers, glossy brochures for Wings, and
watched her hand trembling.

"It's very late, David," she said softly. She
turned back to him and smiled. "It's been a
wonderful evening, a great comfort to me."

He nodded. He understood and accepted
her decision.

"It's been a comfort to me, too. Please, Jill,
can we see some more of each other while
you're here?"

"I'd like that," she said, knowing it was all
right. "My days here are pretty well filled up,

but if you've an evening to spare . . . I'd love to see you."

She lay awake long after he'd gone, sounds of the never-sleeping city floating up to her. She knew how close she had been to breaking a taboo, how much she had wanted to stay in the fantasy world, the world that brought David back for a time.

Burt banked the Boeing 707 to starboard and passed low along the palm-fringed shore.

"Those of you on the right," he announced over the intercom, "can look out and see the main beaches of Penang and all the big hotels where ordinary people stay." He moved the jet onto a port swing. "And now those of you on the left can see Wings, the island resort you've been smart enough to choose. We'll be landing in five minutes."

As he put the plane down at George Town, Burt saw another jet in the green and white livery of Brydon Airlines on the runway. That would be Chuck Henry taking the Australian visitors back home. Burt grinned: he'd come a long way since the days of ferrying cargo from island to island around the Pacific. A dozen planes under long-term charter now carried the Brydon logo.

There were three Wings coaches waiting to take them all to the resort and Burt climbed into the last of them. He accepted a mai tai from the smiling hostess but shrugged off the garland of flowers she offered. He didn't want to be mistaken for a tourist. He lit a cigar and relaxed in his seat as the coach turned off the highway and began moving through a rubber plantation. He could see the resort island now, a hundred yards offshore, sunlight falling on its golden beaches and jungle greenery. Jill sure could pick the spots, he thought admiringly. All of them just isolated enough to be exclusive, all set on tiny, beautiful islands. She'd stuck to the original formula of providing the best food, free and abundant liquor, attentive staff. It was all understated luxury. She wasn't as big as Club Med but she charged five times as much and the guests loved it.

They crossed to the island in Malay fishing boats, skimming over the warm, clear water, ducking through gaps in the reef and running gently up onto the sand. Jeff Thompson, dapper in white shorts and shirt, his lean brown face shielded from the sun by an enormous planter's hat, was welcoming the arrivals. He broke away when he saw Burt.

"Hey," he said, grinning and flashing white teeth, "you finally made it. I've laid on everything for you. I want this to be a real experience for you." He pumped Burt's hand. "I'll never be able to thank you enough for getting me involved with Jill Nagle. This is the best job I ever had."

It was impossible not to like Jeff. He was the epitome of boyish charm, but it was genuine charm. He was good-looking, funny, considerate. Except for that one time when he'd almost ruined Burt . . . still, everyone deserved a second chance. And from all reports, Jeff was a fine young man.

"I thought I better check you out," Burt said. "I've been hearing only good things about you and that makes me suspicious. You were never happy unless you were raising hell."

"I've grown up, Burt," Jeff said solemnly. "All I needed was a little responsibility."

"Being my copilot wasn't responsibility?" Burt punched the younger man's arm. "Just as long as you're flying straight now. Jill's a very special lady. You must never do anything to mess her up."

"How's she getting along?" Jeff asked as they walked up the beach to his house. "You're close to her, Burt, aren't you?"

"As much as anyone is." Burt shrugged. "Andy and I do what we can. And I expect you to do the same. She's given you a big chance here."

They climbed up onto the verandah and Jeff called for a house servant to bring them drinks. The sun was just going down behind the palms and soft music drifted up from the open-air cocktail bar.

Burt drank his beer and remembered some of the flights he'd made with Jeff. The boy had been a fine pilot and would have been one of Burt's most trusted fliers if it hadn't been for that one time. They'd been taking cargo down from Jakarta to Darwin, a routine flight. Just before takeoff a friend from the Australian embassy drove a jeep up to the side of the plane and beckoned Burt out of the cockpit.

"You haven't got anything on board you shouldn't have, do you, Burt?" the friend asked. "Because when you land at Darwin the customs are going to turn you over."

He'd worried all the way across the Timor Sea and finally went into the body of the DC-3 to check his cargo again. He found what he was looking for a half hour out of Darwin: the burlap bail was stamped COTTON GOODS, but when he picked open a seam and pushed aside the batik fabrics he found the marijuana, fifty pounds of it, enough to get him five years in a Darwin jail.

"Put her in a slow turn," he told Jeff when he went back to the cockpit. "I've got to get the hatch open and dump some stuff." The boy was white and trembling but Burt said nothing. He manhandled the bail to the open door and watched as it went spinning out of the plane, down into the green sea below.

At Darwin, as he'd been warned, customs men went through the plane three times. They were obviously expecting to find something. Burt didn't like the way they looked at him when they finally gave up.

He had still said nothing to Jeff. But that night, safely away from the airport, relaxing in their motel, he walked the boy outside, spun him around, and knocked him to the ground.

"You don't fly for me anymore," he'd said, and left him there bleeding from the mouth. It was another year before he spoke to Jeff again. He still agonized over Jeff's meeting Jill through him, but she seemed well pleased with Jeff, so maybe . . .

"Snap out of it," Jeff laughed. "People are supposed to have fun at Wings. Let's go over to the bar and see if there are any nice-looking ladies in the group you brought in. We usually get lookers here. One of the benefits of this job."

The cab dropped her at Fifth and Fifty-second and Jill walked quickly through the lunchtime crowds to the entrance of 21. Sebastian Judge was waiting for her in the lobby. She couldn't have missed him, even in that crowded, bustling place: among the dark sober suits of Manhattan's movers and shakers he stood out in white jacket, pink shirt, blue tie, blue pants. He should have looked out of place, dressed for a Hamptons summer party, but the intense aura of power about him offset the garb. He came loping through the crowd to embrace her, his mane of white hair flowing over his collar.

"Yes, indeed," he said, taking her hands as he admired her. "You brighten up this gloomy old place. I'm so glad you could find the time to lunch with a dull lawyer." He turned and waved to one of the owners and called, "Where can we seat this lovely creature so your jaded patrons can best admire her? Not my regular table, thank you. Today I want us to be on show.''

They were ushered to a banquette in the main upstairs room of the handsome restaurant, a position where they would be the center of attention. Seb Judge always attracted a lot of attention anyway. His dress, his manner, the reputation as a killer in the courtroom. Some of the regulars shook their heads as they saw Seb's companion. She would probably be one of his divorce clients, in which case some poor husband was in for hell, or Seb's date, the latest in the succession of beauty queens Judge squired around town to combat the rumor that he was gay.

The captain hovered, waiting. ''A bottle of the Krug, Adam,'' Seb said, waving away the menu. ''My doctor's being strict with me again. I'm only allowed a simple salad. I do hope you have a good appetite, though,'' he said to Jill. ''It gives me pleasure to see others eat while I nibble on my three kinds of lettuce.''

He nodded approvingly when she ordered the New York cut, rare, with fries and a salad. She sipped the robust champagne and found her confidence was all there. New York and 21 might be foreign territory and Seb Judge one of the most powerful men in the country, but she had nothing to feel hesitant about. She was a success.

''You fit in well here,'' he said, reading her

mind. "You really should have a New York office, a presence here. You're getting quite famous, Wings, but you've got to make 'em sit up and take notice in New York." He swirled the champagne in his glass. "If you do the thing I'm going to propose in the Greek Islands, you'll be a lot bigger a lot faster. And as I told you in Hawaii, I can smooth your way there. I've a friend in the State Department we'll meet with. If you're willing to try this venture, he'll arrange all the right introductions."

"Why?" she asked bluntly. "Why are you putting yourself out for me?" She was watching carefully and, just for an instant, she saw something in his heavy-lidded blue eyes.

"I have everything I need," he said. "So sometimes I indulge myself doing things just because they interest me. I like you. At the same time I have friends who'd like to see this place in the Greek Islands developed along the right lines. All I'd want in return for setting things up is the guarantee of being a welcome guest and being able to send my friends to Wings, knowing they'd be welcome, too."

"Do you want to buy into Wings?"

"No, not me, but I do think you should have some new investors and I have them waiting in the wings. Bad pun. Just corporate money, of course, not anyone who'd want any say in the way you're running things."

"I don't know," Jill said. "So far we've made it on our own. The cash flow's great; the bookings are steady. But the overheads are crushing, and since I didn't start with much cash, servicing the debt is a real hassle. I still wake up nights shivering about what would happen if we hit one bad season, or there were some disaster in one of the resorts.''

''Don't worry,'' he said. ''Here in New York you're seen as a major success story. Any time you want to sell off a piece of the action, it can be arranged. I'll take care of it. You just go on expanding and I promise you we can finance this new venture—and any other—at most attractive terms.'' He toasted her with his champagne glass.

She was on the run all the next day, attending the PATA convention and meeting with Judge's State Department contact in the afternoon. The man seemed as eager to help her as Judge had been.

At dinnertime, David was waiting in the lobby of her hotel. A smile lit up his handsome young face when he saw her. They decided to walk over to the East Side, to one of his regular hangouts. The crowd was young—very young, it seemed to Jill.

''Noisy, isn't it?'' he said as they sat down in a booth. ''I guess I spend too much time in joints like this.'' He drank a beer and a look of puzzlement came into his eyes. ''Today I was talking with Mom. We don't talk much.'' He shook his head. ''She's got so many hang-ups. I think she's jealous because you and Dad were so happy, for one thing. Anyhow, my grandfather called her today and they had this bitching session about seeing you on a television show last night. What in hell happened? You'd think Wings was a tropical club for swingers.''

Jill winced. The TV guy *had* pushed the sex-in-the-sun angle pretty hard.

''I'm sorry your grandfather saw the show,'' she said. ''We both know how he feels about the sainted Nagle name. And,'' she added gently, ''I hope you don't think you have to defend me to your family.''

He started talking about himself, telling her his life was just drifting along. He was supposed to be doing his MBA at Harvard but he kept putting it off because completion of the degree meant joining the old man's firm. That was ordained. He was a Nagle, a David Nagle.

''Oh, I don't know about that,'' she said. ''Your father didn't take holy Nagle orders.''

He looked startled, then hopeful, as the impact hit him.

He walked her back to the hotel and kissed her lightly on the cheek outside the building. She watched the familiar stride as he loped away down Fifth Avenue, then turned and entered the lobby.

A woman was sitting in the lobby, older than Jill but handsome, wearing full-length ermine despite the mild evening. She rose when Jill walked in.

''I'm Marion Nagle,'' she said. Her voice was almost a hiss. ''Stop messing around with my son. You were welcome to David. He was useless. But I'll not see my son end up a useless bum too. Keep right away from him, hear, or I'll ruin you.''

Jill stared at the ranting face, and then suddenly her palm came up and whipped across the perfectly made-up cheek of Marion Nagle. The woman staggered back. Jill gave her a little push to clear a way to the waiting elevator. Just as the doors closed she locked eyes with Marion Nagle again. The woman's face was suffused with hatred.

''You're a very sick person,'' Jill said. ''David was right.'' And the elevator doors closed on Marion. Even when she was safely in her room, Jill shivered. She had had enough of the Nagles.

Chapter Eight _____

SEB JUDGE DIDN'T DO ANY OF HIS really important deals in his office, or in places like 21: he liked the anonymity and the safety from bugging he could get with a roll of quarters and a phone booth in Grand Central Station. Today he set the coins on the shelf and dialed the number his office had passed on to him.

"It's Seb," he said when the man answered. "You called."

"What in hell's going on, Seb?" The voice at the other end was agitated. "When are we going to get this damned woman out of the picture? She was on television the other night, carrying on like she still owned the place."

"She does. I told you all along this couldn't be done in a hurry. She has no intention of selling out, so we'll have to infiltrate slowly. I told you—"

"Yes, but now I'm getting pressure about the whole situation from another quarter, a family matter . . ."

"You must be patient. The others are.

They're willing to wait until we've got everything we possibly can out of the situation. There are other areas where it would suit us to have her system operating. In fact, she's going to Europe today."

"Europe! I thought, damn it, we were only really interested in the island, what's-its-name, Garokan. Now you've got her traipsing all over the world."

"You know what the others are like. Sure, we want Garokan for our own purposes, but the Texans feel, while we're at it, it would be a good idea if we could expand. Places where the scheme might serve the national good. A little bit of patriotism mingled with capitalism, eh? The new places we're interested in . . . well, put it this way: they're countries supposed to be our allies who don't always act like allies."

"You mean those goddamned Dutch? Or the Greeks? The French, the Italians, even the bloody West Germans and their ridiculous Green Party? I tell you, Seb, NATO isn't worth a cunt full of cold water."

Judge winced. It was always a shock to hear profanities delivered in that fine, cultivated accent.

"Right," Seb went on. "A lot of them need propping up, and we need to establish a good cover. Wings would be good cover. We could put some of our people in place and maybe do a little destabilization."

"Okay," the man sighed, "I guess I'll have

to bide my time. But this better pay off in the end.''

''It will,'' Judge promised. ''The other thing about it is, the more I can talk her into expanding, the more new capital she's got to take on. That'll make the take-over just a formality. First we'll soften her up. I've got something arranged for her Malaysian resort that'll leave her reeling. Then Garokan. Then we take the whole chain and use it to fit our needs.'' He chuckled. ''Actually, the whole damn business is so well run, I think we'll make a big profit, apart from the island. She's a smart cookie.''

The man grunted and hung up.

Judge dialed the Houston number.

''Seb,'' he announced when the phone was picked up. ''She likes the idea, the Greek thing, so I'm sending her there today. Make sure your people take care of her there, make everything go smoothly. She's got no idea what we're all about. I don't want her being scared off. I can't go appealing to her patriotism or anything like that because, like most people her age, she's not a hot patriot.''

He listened.

''Sure,'' he said at last. ''I never thought there'd be any problems with the training program. But we can't rush things, understand? Maximum benefits for all is what we're after. In the old days, something like this would naturally have been done as a matter of course. No need for people like us. But we know how things have changed—the Agency with its balls lopped off, all those good people sacrificed. No leadership anywhere anymore, so we'll provide it, but it'll take a little time.

"Also, we've got to convince our side the Cubans really are trying to exert their influence. So far their ambassador's only made the trip from Tokyo to the island twice. I'd like to see him down there in Garokan hobnobbing with that Uncle Tom president a few more times before we make our move. And we have to get the Greek thing in place, and maybe a couple of others." He nodded into the phone. "Right! That's what it's about. And may I just say I'm proud to be associated with you all. Hell, it's just like the old days!"

Within hours of Jill's arrival in Athens, the cultural attaché from the American embassy and an official of the Greek Tourist Board were standing beside her on the deck of the hydrofoil as the tiny island of Practos rose out of the blue Mediterranean. It was all so different from her beloved Pacific, the colors softer, the weather crisp, almost cool. She wondered if she might be moving into an area she wouldn't understand as well. The hydrofoil set them down on a long stone dock, reversed, and sped away to its next port of call. At the end of the dock was a guardhouse. A bored and rumpled Greek soldier emerged and frowned at them.

The tourist board representative showed a

pass and they were waved through. There was total silence as they started up a rocky path through stunted trees and spiky bushes. There was a scent of wild herbs, unfamiliar odors. The trio paused and looked back to the sea and the nearby string of islands.

"It's got such a wild beauty," said George Smith, the man from the embassy. "Like something from another world. But you grow to love it very quickly." They started up the track again. "In a moment, you'll see why we brought you here. This apparently untouched island has actually had one hell of a lot done to it."

They crossed a rise and there it was, laid out before them. It was a shallow valley, facing the sea, and in the center of the valley was a vast, low, white stone house, almost as big as a palace. It was surrounded by smaller cottages tucked away in groves of olive trees. The valley was carpeted in wild flowers and lush green grass. The place was an emerald in a setting of dusty rocks.

"It has the best water of any of the islands," the Greek explained. "Huge concrete tanks have been built inside the hills and there's storage for hundreds of thousands of gallons. There's even a desalinization plant in case there's ever an exceptionally dry season. No expense was spared."

They walked up the white marble steps of the main house; no expense had been spared there, either. The massive doors and window shutters were all of burnished mahogany; the fittings were bronze. The terrace was made of an intricate mosaic depicting the legends of Greece; at regular intervals terra-cotta pots were set in the mosaic with lush green vines hanging down from them.

The Greek selected a huge key from the chain at his waist and swung the door open. They stepped into a handsome entry hall of gleaming floors and stark white walls leading to a center courtyard where a fountain played. They wandered through the house, via bedroom suites, a banqueting hall and ballroom, ten reception rooms, and an enormous kitchen. When they emerged from the house by the side entrance, they faced the tennis courts and swimming pool; beyond were some of the cottages, each a tiny replica of the main building.

"It's breathtaking," Jill said at last, breaking the silence. She turned to the American. "But there must be some catch. A place like this, sitting vacant in the middle of one of the world's favorite vacation spots. Why?"

"Madam," the Greek interjected, "this is something of an embarrassment to the government. Originally, in the time of the Colonels, Greece was very friendly to the Shah. He was granted a ninety-nine-year lease of Practos and he built all this, a simple summer retreat for his court. But before he could ever occupy it, both he and the Colonels had been ousted. This creation has sat here ever since, a white elephant, a galling reminder of how undemocratic our nation had become under the military regime. No true Greek would live here, given who built the place. But it is too fine to just bulldoze back into the soil." He shrugged. "When it was suggested to us that a lady of your fine reputation might be interested in operating it as a resort, we were receptive."

It took an hour to survey the rest of the buildings. There were twenty cottages of varying sizes; a block of stables beside a polo field; broad steps cut in the rocks down to a white sand beach, an ocean pool, and a dock.

She completed her tour breathless and thrilled.

"Where do I sign?" she demanded. "I could fill this place a dozen times over. And it's ready now. All that's needed is a staff and furniture."

"I'm glad you approve." The Greek smiled. "The details can be attended to in Athens. But Mr. Judge still has many friends in the government and I think you will find that most problems have already been solved. The lease, I believe, can be purchased from the government for a reasonable figure. Staffing presents no problem: the people of the region have a long tradition of service in the great houses. You will find them diligent, honest, and anxious to please."

She bubbled with excitement all the way back to Athens. There was so much to be done if she was to have the resort open in time to catch some of the late-summer trade. Furnishing, the attaché promised her, would be no problem: there were many fine craftsmen in Athens who would build to specifications. But she had to find a manager and senior staff—Greek-speaking, ex-airline if possible.

"What's the procedure?" she asked Smith as they sped back to Athens in the embassy car. "Who do I see to get all the permits and permissions?"

"I'll put it all in motion tomorrow," he said. "There won't be any problems." He shook his head admiringly. "You have some very influential friends stateside." They dropped the Greek at his headquarters and she thanked him profusely. He bowed and wished her every success.

"I hope you're not tired," the attaché said as they reached her hotel. "There's a rather important event tonight, a dinner on Spiro Gravas's yacht. They called the embassy and especially asked if you would attend. I'm to be your escort. I should have mentioned it before but we seem to have been on the move all day."

She knew she had to accept. People were smoothing her way and she couldn't snub anyone.

She unpacked, rang for a maid to press her blue evening gown, and ordered a half bottle of champagne from room service. She reclined on the terrace of her suite and watched the crazy rush-hour traffic battling through the

ancient city. She finished her wine and ran a
hot bath, then luxuriated in the water, proud
of herself for coping with so much, so quickly.

She was waiting in the hotel lobby when
George Smith strode in. He looked her over
admiringly and escorted her to the car. They
retraced the route to Piraeus and rolled to a
halt at the dock. A platoon of white-and-blue-
uniformed sailors formed an honor guard
from the street down to the water where a procession of barges awaited the guests. Gravas's
yacht, *Sirena*, lay anchored in the bay. Almost
a thousand feet of gleaming white, its three
decks were lit from stem to stern. Another
rank of sailors was lined down the gangway of
the yacht.

Jill saw their host when they reached the
head of the gangway. Gravas was surrounded
by guests—there were already close to a hundred aboard. She recognized him from news
pictures. He was the last of the flamboyant
Greek shipping tycoons, a fat, florid man who
conveyed a sense of power and ruthlessness.
She stood beside Smith, waiting to take her
cue from him.

"George!" a Texan voice boomed beside
them. A big, silver-haired man had come out
of the crowd and was pumping Smith's hand.
"Glad you could come." He turned to Jill.
"And you, of course, are Jill Nagle. Delighted,
ma'am. I'm Dan Passage and I'm a friend of
Seb Judge and he said to be sure I took darn
good care of you." He gestured with his cigar

to their host. "Old Spiro is tied up for the moment. He's so seldom in Greece since . . . since the changeover . . . that when his boat does put into port, every wheeler and dealer in the place tries to get his attention." He led them aft, where there was less of a crowd. A steward poured champagne and left them.

"So what did you think of Practos?" Dan Passage asked her. "You going to take it over?"

"It's fabulous," she said. "If I can arrange the right kind of—"

"It's all arranged, honey," he said. "Seb has seen to that. I took the liberty of speaking to some people myself. Isn't it a great little island, though! Actually, I kept an eye on the construction work there for my friend, the Shah. Shame he never got to use the place. Still, you've got a nice, ready-made resort there. You'll get all the best people." He drained his glass and a steward appeared from out of the shadows. "You'll need some help staffing it. I understand this hasn't been your theater of operations until now. I'll be pleased to assist you. I might have just the guy to run the place for you. I'm staying on in Athens awhile, so you let me dig out a few people, right?"

He left them to greet someone he hadn't seen in a while, and George led her toward the main saloon.

"He's overwhelming," Jill told him. "I feel like he's taken charge of me."

"Dan Passage is quite a character," the attaché said. "Made his money out of oil, of course. A war hero, did a few jobs for LBJ's administration. These days he pretty much just gets around the world, knowing the right people, knowing how to get things done." He dropped his voice. "He's been very useful to us here. For a while after the change of power the Greeks were a little xenophobic. Some of them felt we'd been propping up the Colonels. Dan managed to keep some lines open. It helped. He does the same kind of thing for our host. A lot of the other tycoons didn't fare as well. Spiro, though he's not exactly hailed as a hero in Athens, hasn't had to resort to a foreign passport."

Spiro Gravas approached them not long afterward, nodded to the attaché, took Jill's hand, and pressed it to his lips. They were fleshy, moist lips, yet not repulsive.

"You're the young woman Mr. Passage was so insistent join our party," he said. "I can see why." His voice boomed. He didn't care who overheard. "My dear, you stand out as a beacon of youth and beauty among these pinched-faced, pursed-mouthed parvenus." He studied her for a moment. "Why don't you join my cruise?" he said. "Tomorrow we sail for Rhodes. I think you would enjoy it."

"I'm afraid I couldn't." Jill laughed. "I'm here on business."

"Business! A woman like you shouldn't be bothered with business. There are plenty of boring old men who have made all the billions they could ever use who would be happy to share their wealth with you."

"Jill may be taking over Practos, sir," George said.

Gravas frowned. "The Shah's folly? Yes, Dan mentioned it. My people—the Greeks, that is—would be very happy to see someone take it off their hands. It stands as an embarrassing monument to a former friend whom we rejected in his hour of need. A good man, the Shah—though a little too convinced of his omnipotence. He was my guest on this yacht often." He smiled at Jill. "Sit by me at dinner, and I'll tell you stories of what it was like before the world began to change." He looked around the throng. "In fact, we'll go in to dinner now. They've all had enough to drink."

She was swept along on his arm, the crowd parting, down to a huge dining room where twenty-four tables were set, all with gold and silver. Gravas led her to the head table and held out an ornate chair for her. He took no notice of the perplexed steward who whipped away the place card and scurried off to find another place for the Albanian duchess Jill had usurped. Gravas slumped into the chair beside Jill and glared at the other guests as they found their places.

"Such great times we used to have," he said. "*Real* kings and princes. Your John F. Kennedy and his lovely bride; Churchill, although he was in his dotage by then. The

Shah, the Aga Khan, Rubirosa—that scoundrel. And the girls! All so lovely, so young, so free. My last wife couldn't bear to come aboard *Sirena.* She called it my floating harem. And it was.'' He laughed, flashing his brown eyes at her. ''After dinner, I shall show you my stateroom. *That* will take your mind off business.''

She laughed. For all his conceits, his boorishness, Spiro Gravas was an endearing man. She caught George Smith's eye, down the table, and winked.

''I'd love to look around the yacht,'' she said. ''And perhaps, if and when I have Practos functioning, you will come visit me there.''

''I have my own island,'' he said, shrugging. ''Three times the size of yours. And if, as Mr. Passage tells me, you intend to operate some kind of tourist resort, your island will be packed with people like these.'' He dismissed his guests with a negligent wave. ''But I wish you well, and I shall direct a better class of clientele to you.''

The first course arrived, shrimp and baby octopus, and he set upon it with relish. There was no further conversation as dish followed dish: tiny quail bound in bacon, a salad of nasturtium leaves and mandarins, a pink rack of lamb with rosemary, a tangy sorbet, wild boar in black-currant sauce, a raspberry soufflé. He drank only Krug, but that copiously. At the finish of the meal he dabbed his lips with a damask napkin and burped loudly.

"Good, simple food," he told her. "That is the secret of my longevity. How old do you think I am?"

"I couldn't guess," Jill laughed. "But you appear to be in perfect health."

"I am eighty-nine years old," he told her proudly. "I have sired twenty-one children I admit to, and various grasping women have claimed twenty more were also mine." He stood up abruptly, catching the other guests in midcourse. Most of them began to struggle to their feet in deference. He paid no attention. "Come," he said to Jill, "and I shall show you around my yacht." She followed him from the saloon, accompanied by a rising buzz of whispers.

He was proud of the yacht. He led her through a procession of chambers, a fully equipped casino, a ballroom, dayrooms, evening rooms, bars, a gymnasium, the library. And finally to his own suite. It was, in comparison to the rest of the yacht, subdued. A big four-poster bed concealed by a gold-woven tapestry, crimson silk draperies, a thick burgundy carpet. An old, scarred oak desk, big comfortable leather chairs, a bank of telephones, and a video display unit. And on the walls, softly lit, five Renoirs.

"No individual has more of the master," he told her proudly. "He is my passion." She felt his hand on her bottom. "You like Renoir?" he asked softly. "I would give you one."

She concealed a smile and moved a single

step away from him. The pass, she thought, had been made only because it was expected of him.

"You're very lucky," she said, "to live in such splendor. You must be very happy. Are you?" He knew she really wanted to know.

"Actually, I'm lonely and quite bored," he said. "I wish you would stay aboard. But I can see you're a woman with a mind of her own. In time, perhaps, you will come to look on me as something other than a repulsive, fat old man." She saw the laughter in his eyes. "Until then, as your neighbor, I shall also be your protector." He held out his arm, she took it, and they proceeded to the ballroom. "Yes," he said as they passed down a broad companionway, "I shall keep a fatherly eye on you at Practos. Beginning with a warning: Dan Passage will be very helpful, but not everything is as it seems. For every favor given, one will be expected in return. Use Mr. Passage and his American friends, but be prepared to be used by them. Do not forget what I've said."

Later, when Passage sought her out for a dance, Gravas's warning came back to her. She wondered if she were not getting in over her head, but her heart was already set on taking over Practos, making it the ultimate Wings resort.

If Passage ever really did want his favors returned, she would owe him plenty, she soon realized. The next night he took her to dinner in Athens, accompanied by an American couple, Richard and Diana Moore. The Moores had lived in Athens for a decade. They were in their early forties, a handsome, self-assured couple.

"You probably have friends in common," Passage said when they were all seated. "Richard was Pan Am's manager here for many years. Then, when the airline wanted to send him back to a big job at Pan Am headquarters, he and Diana decided they loved Greece more than his career. They've stayed all this time."

"It wasn't a hard decision," Diana Moore said. "Richard didn't want to be a deskbound executive, and we'd come to think of Athens as home."

"I bet *you* don't miss working for an airline," her husband said.

"I miss the people I worked with," Jill told him. "Airline crews are like one big family. But the way things have worked out, almost all the Wings staff are out of the airlines, so I haven't lost my friends."

It was an easy, pleasant dinner. The Moores extended an invitation to their home whenever she was in Athens, and she knew she would accept. She already felt at ease with them.

When Passage dropped her back at her hotel, they stopped in the lobby bar for a midnight cognac.

"So what did you think of them?" he asked.

"A lovely couple," she said. "It will be nice to know someone in Athens."

"They can be a lot more than friends in Athens," he said. "Richard has done quite a few jobs for me here, but he really needs something challenging, something he can excel at. That's why I put you three together. I think Richard and Diana would be perfect as the managers of Practos."

"Would they want to do it?" Jill asked.

"They're wild for it," Passage assured her. "I sounded them out today. Diana's a cordon bleu cook; Richard knows everything there is to know about caring for tourists." He sipped his brandy. "I hope you don't think I've presumed on you, setting up tonight. But you've got so little time here and I thought you'd like to tie up as many loose ends as possible. The Moores, if you decide to take them on, could handle all your staffing, the refurbishing of the island—all the crap you won't have time for. As I said, Richard's done a few things for me and he's never let me down. I trust him completely."

"I can't thank you enough, Dan," Jill said. "If they want the job, it's theirs. If, of course, I get the island. That still has to be settled, you know."

"I've arranged a meeting with the government tomorrow for you," he said. "There'll be a lot of talk, a lot of bargaining, but I know the figure they'll settle for. At the meeting you'll sign a letter of intent, subject to finance, inspections, permits, et cetera, et cetera, et cetera. That'll give you time to arrange the money through Seb." He stood up and yawned. "The figure, the real bottom line, is half a million bucks for good will, half a million a year for the lease, and then whatever it's going to cost to furnish the place. I'd allow a half million for that, don't you think? So you get a great deal—one and a half million and you have one of the best islands in the world."

It was hard to sleep that night. Jill was scared by the figures Passage had tossed off so blithely. Sure, Seb had said the money would be there, but Wings was already heavily borrowed and this was a huge debt she was considering taking on. Still, Practos would make three or four times the money any of her other places were doing. And the business was already so big, it was impractical to keep it a one-person operation. Or two people, she thought guiltily, remembering that she hadn't even thought about Andy's reaction to all her grand plans. Doubts rose again: how happy they'd all been when it was just Wings, Hawaii. If only they could go back to that simplicity. But you never went back, did you?

The government negotiator did just as Dan had said he'd do: he wanted two million for good will. "What good will?" Dan snapped. "You should be paying Wings for taking it off your hands." And finally he came down to a half million. She signed a letter of intent, thanked Passage for all his help, and caught the afternoon flight to New York.

She was in Seb Judge's office at seven o'clock the next morning.

"That's good," he said, nodding, when she gave him her progress report. "I like to move fast on a deal like this. No need to sit around in endless meetings, running up bills. You see something you like, go for it."

He said he would put it to some of his investors. He would need the balance sheets of Wings, assets-and-liabilities statements, but it looked like he could raise a couple of million for around a 40 percent slice of the whole business. That would leave her with some working capital plus control of Wings.

She got into Honolulu at ten o'clock that night, desperately tired. Sam Chisolm was there to meet her and she gladly surrendered her bags. Sam, a bright, eager young man she'd recruited from United's booking staff, had quickly risen to assistant manager of Wings, Hawaii, but like everyone else on the island he was happy to do any task. He swung her bags into the cab trunk and held the door for her.

"I'm bushed," she said as she sank back in the seat. "The island is going to look real good to me. I could sleep for days."

"I don't think you'll get too much sleep." Sam grinned. "We've got a real lively crowd this week. If we were charging for drinks, we'd be making a fortune.''

''Who's there?'' she asked, almost too tired to care. ''Anyone important?''

''Just Ellen Brooks, her husband, and their entourage. She's supposed to be relaxing before her concert at the Bowl, but the way the whole crowd of them are carrying on, I wouldn't line up for tickets. Ellen's pretty nice, actually, but her husband, Doug Steed, is a real pain in the ass. He and the rest of her party are coking up and drinking all night. Ellen may be one of the most popular singers in the world, but her husband doesn't seem to be among her worshipers. They fight all the time.''

''Where's the coke coming from?'' she demanded sharply. ''If Sonny Ramos is dealing again . . .''

''No, Sonny's behaving himself. We keep an eye on him. They brought their own supplies, a kilo at least the way they're going. I hear Sonny did offer Steed a toot and the guy slapped his hand away and said he didn't do 'street shit.' Sonny was upset. But he's still playing his heart out every night, hoping they might need a backup musician for the concert.''

Jill pressed her hands to her temples. This was all she needed, a bunch of coked-out rock-and-rollers. The drug scene that accompanied some of their guests bothered her but there wasn't much she could do about it. Wings' ambience was built around its freewheeling style, and if some of the customers brought their own recreational drugs, what could she say?

She brightened when they were in the launch and out under the stars. The lights of Waikiki fell away behind them and she let the warm sea air flow over her. Going home, she thought. The island was home and she always wondered why she had left it, even for a few days.

Maggie Stewart met them on the dock. The manager was smiling but she looked almost as tired as Jill.

"Welcome back, honey," Maggie said. "I guess Sam's told you we're having a torrid old time right now. Show biz people! I wouldn't mind if we never booked them again. We don't need the publicity and they're always such a hassle."

"I didn't know Ellen Brooks was coming in," Jill said.

"They booked the party under her husband's name. And they said your pal Don Messner recommended the place."

"I'll have to ask Mr. Messner to stop doing us favors." Jill laughed in a singsong voice.

They reached Jill's bungalow and Sam placed her bags in the living room. The place was filled with flowers, and a bottle of champagne rested in a silver ice bucket. It was so good to be back.

She tiptoed into Jonathan's room. He was

sleeping easily, his nurse nodding in a chair beside the bed.

She bent and kissed her son. "How's he been? Did he miss me?"

"He's very good about it all," the woman said. "Yes, he misses you, but he seems to understand you have to go away a lot. And he knows you'll always come back." She stood up and yawned. "If you don't need me I'll go next door and get some sleep."

When Elsa had gone Jill stood by the boy's bed awhile. She reached down and gently brushed the blond hair from his forehead. He smiled in his sleep. She was so lucky, she thought, gazing down at him. Perfect health, a sweet disposition, a good-looking boy. She hated being parted from him. But at least he had the benefit of all the Wings staff doting on him like aunts and uncles. And Carl Cohen was grandfatherly and wise with him, a favorite companion. Her own parents' frequent visits Jonathan loved, too.

No, she didn't feel that she was leaving her son too often: it was she who was being deprived of love.

She walked into the bar half an hour later. Andy gave her a huge hug and Sonny waved across the room before playing his next song. She quickly spotted the show biz party, six of them around an outside table, noisy but no worse than the three inside tables occupied by other happy guests.

"How are you coping, Andy?" she asked. "I hear we've got some hell-raisers. Sorry to have left you at a time like this."

He shrugged. "Nothing we can't handle. The main thing's been to see they don't bother the other guests. But the stuff they're doing, they're not interested in anyone else, anyway." He looked up. "Ah . . . here comes the one who makes everything worth it." He smiled at the tall, dark woman walking toward them. "Hi, Ellen. I thought you'd turned in for the night."

"I couldn't sleep," Ellen Brooks said. "I was concerned about the boys. Are they causing any bother?"

"No." Andy smiled at her. "You needn't worry. This is Jill Nagle, Ellen Brooks."

The singer smiled at Jill. "I'm real pleased you're back. Don Messner said to be sure to say hey. I love this place—it's even more beautiful than Don described."

"Thanks," Jill said, finding herself drawn to the woman. "It's quiet and relaxed, which is the way most of our guests like it."

Ellen frowned. "Yes, it suits me, but I'm afraid the boys are getting a little stir crazy. I had intended visiting Wings on my own but my husband insisted on coming along. He'd be so much happier over on Waikiki."

"I'm sure they'll be okay," Jill said. "Anyway, you'll be heading back to the real world soon. You have a concert in a couple of days, right?"

"Yes. Will you come? I'd love you to be my guest."

"Sure," Jill said. "That sounds like fun."

The other guests drifted away soon enough, but the volume of noise from Doug Steed's table rose. Ellen had a soda with Jill and Andy and glanced nervously across at her husband and his friends, but she made no move to join them. Steed caught her eye and gestured for her to come over, and she moved hesitantly across the room. Jill and Andy watched her discreetly.

"Goddamn it!" Steed yelled at his wife, making no effort to keep his voice down. "What are you doing, lurking by the bar and spying on me? If you're going to hang around here, you better have a more pleasant attitude." They saw him forcing a dish of white powder on her. She tried to back away but he had a firm grip on her arm. "Get some of this into you," he demanded. Ellen's free hand swung loose and connected with the dish, spilling the powder all over the floor.

There was a stunned silence all around the table as Steed's friends gazed at the precious white powder spilled across the earthen floor.

"You stupid fucking bitch," Steed snapped. "You did that deliberately." He punched her in the side of the face. "Get down on your knees and pick it all up."

Ellen stood there, unable to move, and the next blow jerked her head back. Andy was moving by then, around the bar and across the floor. He pinioned Steed's arms before he could hit her again.

Steed was a big man, almost as big as Andy, and he managed to push Andy away. He grabbed a bottle from the table, smashed it, and turned on Andy.

"Keep out of this, Sambo," he said furiously. "I don't like the hired help interfering when I'm trying to teach my wife, the star, how to behave. Run along back to your bar before I carve you up."

Andy feinted to the left, slipped inside Steed's guard, and threw him to the floor. He slammed his foot down on the hand holding the bottle until Steed let it go.

"I don't want any trouble with you," Andy said. "But I won't stand for you hitting a lady. Now go on to bed quietly. Before I lose control."

Steed got to his feet and made a lunge at Andy. Again the bigger man feinted but this time Andy followed up with a solid rabbit punch to the back of Steed's neck. Steed staggered but came again and Andy hit him twice, roundhouse punches that caught him flush on the jaw and sent him down.

The others decided they should be doing something to protect their meal ticket. Three of them circled Andy, getting up the courage to rush him.

"Don't try it, punks," he snapped.

"No, don't," Sonny Ramos echoed. The guitar player had come out of the shadows to stand beside Andy. He had a two-foot-long iron bar in his hand and looked formidable indeed. Steed's people summed up the situation fast, picked up their boss, and carried him off to his bungalow.

"I'm sorry, Ellen," Andy said. She hadn't moved. She was just standing there, one hand exploring her bruised face. Suddenly she swayed forward and Andy caught her. He carried her over to the bar.

"I think a brandy might help," he said to Jill.

Ellen was crying softly.

"I'm sorry," Andy said to her. "I didn't hit him too hard. He'll be okay in the morning. But you're badly bruised."

"It's not the first time," Ellen said, taking the brandy and stifling her crying. "But it's going to be the last time. Please, there's nothing I can say to tell you how embarrassed I am. To bring an ugly scene like this to your beautiful resort—we'll all be off the island first thing in the morning."

"I don't think you're going anywhere for the next week," Jill said firmly. "You can't do a show with your face all banged up. I think you better stay here with us until the bruising's gone. The others can go back to Honolulu first thing in the morning. They're going to have to, anyway, to explain that your concert's been postponed for a few days."

Ellen started crying again; she looked so helpless with her battered face, her pride shattered, and the decision made that her marriage was beyond saving. Jill put her arms around her and held her for a minute.

"You can stay with me tonight," she said. "No one will bother you in my bungalow."

The brandy helped, and eventually Ellen slept. Jill, tired as she was, dozed only fitfully. She got up at dawn and walked out on the verandah to find Sonny curled up in a hammock, keeping guard on them. She woke Ellen only when Sonny reported the launch had gone to Honolulu taking Steed and his pals.

"Drink lots of coffee," Jill advised, "then I'll have breakfast sent over here for you. You might prefer to just hang around the bungalow for a few days. None of the other guests come up this way, so you'll be by yourself."

"I haven't been near a mirror yet," Ellen said. "How bad is it this time?"

Jill didn't want to know about the other times, so she said quickly, "It will fade soon. But there's no way you could have done the concert in the next couple of days."

"Thanks for being so kind, Jill, and so sensible. Most people would freak out over a scene like that. Trouble is, I'm almost used to it now. Poor Doug. We used to be so happy."

"Don't talk about it," Jill said hastily. She didn't want to know. She shuddered at the memory of the night before, the ugliness of it all. How could this woman, the idol of millions, allow herself to be abused like that?

"I do want to talk," Ellen said. "If you can stand it."

Jill nodded. She was involved already, she thought, so she might as well hear it.

"Doug and I have been together ten years," she said. "He found me when I was just a kid, waitressing in Oakland, trying for singing gigs. He was a hotshot talent agent, one of the best on the Coast, and he saw something in me. He quit the agency and devoted himself full time to making me a star. The early years were rough, but he had faith and I guess I had some talent. Things got better, slowly, but they did. Then I scored a hit single and an album that didn't do too badly. We were even confident enough to have a child, our little girl. She's all I have left of the marriage now." She kept talking, not watching Jill but gazing out at the ocean.

"Having Jessica and scoring a few successes should have made it all wonderful for us. But I got really big, superstar stuff, and Doug couldn't hack it. Funny, after trying so hard to set me up as a star, he couldn't stand my fame. People were insinuating he was just a hanger-on. Doug was never good with the media, anyway, and it got to be open warfare. It wasn't fair, the way they portrayed him, but it stuck and no one ever remembered he gave up his career for me. In the end, I don't think even Doug remembered. I'd dedicate songs to him, stuff like that, and he'd go into a rage.

"Drugs were his prop and at first I didn't

oppose them. Cocaine gave him some confidence and, God knows, he needed propping up. But then, like all real coke heads, his personality started changing. He became cruel, vicious, paranoid, always accusing me of sleeping with men—with women, too, for that matter—and claiming Jessica wasn't his child. The drugs have been getting worse and worse and so has he.''

She took a deep, shuddering breath, like someone who's been crying for a long time, though she hadn't cried at all. ''I'd quit performing if that would help, but it wouldn't. He's too far down the track now. The thing is . . .'' She began to cry. ''I love him.''

''No one will disturb you here,'' Jill said gently. ''Stay quiet and think everything through.''

But the first wave of paparazzi arrived in the afternoon. Three reporters and a brace of photographers landed on Wings' dock demanding an interview session with Ellen Brooks. They were representing mainland tabloids and insisted on checking out a story sweeping through show biz circles that Miss Brooks had been gravely burned in a drug-related accident. Something to do with cocaine and flames; freebasing.

Jill, backed up by Andy, refused to allow them ashore. There was nothing wrong with Miss Brooks, Jill said: she had a bad throat that had forced the cancellation of her Honolulu concert. Now she was resting for an additional week on Wings before resuming her concert schedule. The reporters were not happy but, confronted by Andy's bulk, there wasn't much they could do.

They came back the next day and there were more of them. Andy couldn't stop that many. Two parties landed and stalked Ellen Brooks for hours. They didn't get much: a few long-distance shots of Ellen hiding behind huge sunglasses and a floppy hat as she strolled on the beach with Jill, one fuzzy picture of the star apparently weeping in Jill's arms, and one shot of Andy bursting out of the bushes and chasing them all off. For the more sensational tabloids, it was enough.

The following weekend Seb Judge called her from New York.

"You should have let the dogs of the media get to Ellen Brooks," he said. "Denied access, they've made the most of it—made up a lot of stuff." He cleared his throat. "I have two papers in front of me. The uglier of the two features a sidebar all about the Wings resorts, happy havens for swinging jet-setters where 'anything goes.' The Wings resorts are run by, I quote, 'someone of their own kind, beautiful Jill Nagle, of the Boston Nagles, one of the oldest and most respected families in the nation.' "

"Oh, shit," Jill moaned.

"I suppose you could say any publicity is good publicity," Judge sighed, "but it's damned embarrassing to me, just when I'm raising the money for the Greek Wings." He laughed. "Don't worry. It'll all work out. It might just take a day or two longer."

When he hung up, Jill realized she still hadn't told her partner about their new Wings. She found him sitting on the beach with Ellen, who, since her bruises had faded, was no longer hiding.

"Hi, Jill," Ellen called as Jill approached. "I've got to go do something with my hair. Andy and I are going over to Honolulu for dinner tonight—my coming-out event. Will you come too?"

"No thanks." Jill sat down in the chair Ellen vacated. "I've got to talk business with Andy, then I've got to pack for tomorrow's flight."

Andy made a face.

"It's Saturday," he complained. "We should be taking it easy, not talking business." They watched Ellen walk up the beach to the bungalow. "She's a great lady," Andy said. "Too bad all her success hasn't brought her any joy."

Jill decided to come right to the point. "Andy," she said, "I haven't been holding out on you, but there hasn't been a chance for us to talk. While I was in New York a deal was offered for us to open a new Wings resort in the Greek Islands. I flew over and had a look. It's a great prospect. To finance it we'll have to sell off forty percent of existing Wings, but the increased take from the new place will cancel that out. I think we've got a manager already.

I can't see any problems. Will you go along with me?''

He shook his head slowly, sad but resigned.

"I'm sorry, Jill," he said. "I haven't been holding out on you either. But I need out of Wings. It's all gotten too organized for me. Having another place will make it even more complicated. I'm not pulling my weight around here as it is. You do all the traveling, you watch the books, hire the people. You don't need me and I feel like I'm not doing a full share anymore. I want to go back to what I was before you and David brought me aboard this venture.''

She was shocked cold.

"Forget about Greece," she said quickly. "It doesn't matter. We won't do it. I don't want to lose you, Andy. *Please.* Don't walk out on me.''

"I wouldn't leave if you needed me," he said gently. "But you don't. It's not walking out. This is your show and you don't need me." He put his head in his hands. "I've been thinking about this for a while, but something else has come up lately and confirmed it for me. Ellen. Ellen Brooks. We think we might be in love. She wants me to go with her when she flies back to the mainland next week, live together for a while, see how things work out.'' He tried to laugh and failed. "I always said I'd never marry again, but now I don't care what I said. Ellen seems to need me and I'm real happy with her." He stood up and brushed sand from his body. "I want to see if it'll work. Please cross your fingers for us, Jill." He bent and kissed her on the cheek. "We'll still be best friends, kid; you just won't have me around your neck all the time."

She stayed there long after he had gone, the sense of loss overwhelming. It was all her fault: She had been too busy to listen to Andy, to know what he was feeling. She had taken him for granted. Like a brother.

But she knew now she damn well didn't think of Andy as a brother. Somewhere deep inside her he had been her main hope of loving again. If she'd just had more time, hadn't been so preoccupied with business, she and Andy might have gotten together. Now it was too late. Now she was alone.

Chapter Nine _____

"ARE YOU LOOKING FOR ANOTHER partner?" Burt asked casually. They were sitting on the terrace looking across the lagoon toward the Penang beaches. Burt, who'd brought Jill in with a party that morning and was flying another party out that night, was drinking a Foster's in defiance of regulations.

"The airline's doing okay now," he added. "If you want someone to buy Andy's stake, I'd be interested."

She spread her hands in a helpless gesture.

"I don't know, Burt. Andy says he doesn't want any of his money out, at least for now. He's happy to take a dividend. My real decision is what to do about the Greek thing. Judge has the money ready; everything's set. But now, on my own . . . I don't know if I should plunge into anything so big."

"Bullshit! Go right ahead and grab it, Jill. I know you. You need to keep trying new things. If you don't grab every new opportunity, you'll never know what you might have made of the business. Hell, you're already the most talked-about woman in the travel business. A couple more resorts and you'll be on the cover of *Newsweek*. Instead of the sensational rags." He laughed. "Anyway, remember me if you need some new capital. Hell, I owe you. My airline grew on Wings. And I've got some big plans. You'll see."

"Thanks, Burt, I appreciate it. You've been a good friend to me."

"I'd be more than that, if you'd only let me," he said, reaching across to place his hand on hers. "I know you don't think of me that way, but I always hope someday you will. I'm there if you need me." He withdrew his hand. There was no point in trying to pressure Jill: his only hope was to play a waiting game. But for how long, for God's sake? He had loved her for years already, even before they both lost David, but he had hidden that love behind a facade of boisterous brotherliness. He studied her face, the strong bones framed by the beautiful hair. Maybe he'd hidden it too well.

After Burt left to fly the departing guests home, Jill felt fully the aloneness of her life, more so now with Andy leaving. She was glad when Jeff Thompson got free of his duties and joined her for dinner. They dined at a table set under the palm trees. Jeff was bright and attractive, ran the resort better than she could have, and was fun to be with. She studied his easy good looks, the bright green eyes and blond hair.

"The new crop of guests looks fine," he said, pouring wine for them. "The usual thing: They arrive off the plane all tense, looking for something to complain about. Then, gradually, they see that Wings delivers all it promises and more. By sundown on day one they're converts. It's a great formula, Jill. Kind of a tropical playpen. When I first joined I thought your staff-guest ratio was too high, but you were right. It makes all the difference, having all those people around who're happy to do anything for you."

"Your figures look good," she told him. "Ninety percent occupancy three months in a row."

He shook his head. "I just wish I had more bungalows. We could keep up ninety percent even if we were double this size. But I guess if we got too big it wouldn't be a Wings resort."

"That's the point. All of the resorts have to be small, select, and personal."

She glanced through the trees to the bar area; couples were dancing under the stars to the music of a Malay trio. The concept *did* work, the idea of a luxurious, sensuous, carefree vacation in the world's most beautiful locations. She still met some resistance to her no-children edict, but even the most doting parents soon realized they needed a break from domestic routines. She couldn't count the number of young mothers who had confided to her that, during their Wings vacations, their love lives had been rekindled. She sometimes broke her own rules by having Jonathan with her in the Hawaii Wings, but that would end when he started preschool.

"Don't look so glum," Jeff said. "Have some more wine and enjoy the music."

She let him fill her glass. She knew she was too serious, too intent. But it was the protective wall she had built for herself.

"Do you dance?" she suddenly asked Jeff. "I haven't danced in years."

"I'll try not to stomp on your feet," he laughed, standing.

They walked through the night-blooming bushes and stepped onto the outdoor dance floor. She moved into his arms and they mingled smoothly with the other couples. Jeff was almost a head taller than she, light on his feet, easy to follow. The gentle, familiar music relaxed her and she let her head rest on his shoulder as they moved around the floor in a soothing rhythm, around and around. She smiled to herself. She felt good.

They danced for an hour and in between drank wine. Why not? Why not enjoy herself for a change?

Later they strolled silently down the sandy path through the jungle. His hand was under her elbow and she could feel his strength. They stopped in the clearing outside her bungalow and stood a moment, bathed in moonlight.

"I don't want to do anything dumb," Jeff

whispered, ''but would you hate it if I kissed you?''

She smiled at him and he gathered her in his arms. His lips against hers felt good; all of him felt good. She returned his kiss passionately, pressing against him closely. He kept an arm around her as they started up the steps and into the darkened bungalow. They kissed again in the living room, and then he took her hand and led her to her bed.

Jeff undressed her slowly, almost reverently, and gently put her down on the bed. He knelt beside the bed and slowly, tantalizingly, began to stroke her, his hands smooth and warm. They roamed over her, exploring her toes, tracing patterns on her thighs, brushing her breasts slowly. She could just see him in the moonlight, his head moving forward until she felt his lips following the route of his hands. She almost cried out as he lightly kissed the inside of her thighs and she wanted him right then. His tongue traced circles on her nipples and the fire rose in her. She was so ready for him.

He lay down beside her, the cotton of his shirt and pants cool yet rough against her skin. She lay still as he continued to explore her, loving just lying there naked, vulnerable, listening to his breathing and feeling the beating of her own heart.

He broke away for an instant and she watched him stand up and flow out of his clothes. Then he returned to her, their bodies stretching away down the bed, skin to skin. She reached out and found him, hard and quivering to her touch, and guided him to her. He was light on her body, and she opened to him eagerly, taking him inside her. She began to move in rhythm and he matched it, stroking deeper and deeper, always letting her set the pace. His hands went under her buttocks and lifted her up, a rod of hot steel rising up in her, forcing a sudden crashing climax: it came in waves and lasted an eternity. Yet still he was there, bringing her on to new peaks, new joys of release. Her body seemed in command of his, taking all, not caring what it gave in return, exulting in the surges of passion. At last, exhausted, she felt herself sink back onto the bed. Only then did he let his own pleasure burst in her.

They lay in silence, listening to the night sounds of the jungle. She closed her eyes and felt him kiss her cheek. There was a gentle rustling of his dressing, and then she sensed he was gone. Sleep took her down into a deep, warm place.

The sunshine flooding in awoke her, warm on her nakedness, caressing her. She stretched and her body felt better than it had in a long time. A chattering mynah bird perched on the window ledge and fixed her with a bright yellow eye. She could hear the gentle surf and the morning breeze rattling the banana fronds. It was not a day for pressure and work, she told herself firmly.

She dressed and strolled down to the breakfast terrace for coffee and croissants. Then she went in search of the perfect beach. The island was a series of small white-sand beaches, each made private by jungle growth running down from the center of the island, which was densely wooded.

The largest beach, closest to the bar and restaurant, was the only one with any resort facilities. There were deck chairs and waiters, sailboats and windsurfers. But it was the smaller, private spots that appealed to most of the guests, and to Jill. She strolled around the island. An easy fifteen-minute walk took her to the farthest point. It was her favorite beach, a rock-enclosed cove hidden by thick lantana. She found the tunnel through the lantana and stepped onto the fine sand. There was nobody there.

Jill spread her towel on the sand, stripped out of her clothing, and flopped down. The sun was directly over her in a cloudless sky: she welcomed its heat on her naked body. She glanced down at her deeply tanned skin. She had been in the tropics so long now it seemed unnatural to be any other color.

At some point she dozed off, and when she awoke she felt her skin burning despite her tan. She got up and plunged into the warm sea, the salt stinging. She dried herself carefully, dressed, and set off to try Jeff's latest innovation at Wings—a massage.

''Hello,'' she called, stepping into the dark

little bungalow. From out of the back a tiny Thai girl, beautiful and smiling, emerged and greeted her warmly.

"Hello, missy," the girl beamed. "You come for massage, yes?"

"I got too much sun," Jill said. "I thought if you could put some oil on me. . . ."

"No trouble. I fix. You come through here, please."

She stepped into the massage room. Jeff had spent his budget well: a pair of massage tables were in the center of the room, on one wall was a shower stall, and against the other a plunge pool and whirlpool. She undressed in one of the changing cubicles, wrapped herself in a towel, and lay down on a massage table.

"My name is Kim," the girl said. "You like it here, at Wings? Is very good place." She undid the towel and Jill felt a pleasant chill as oil was gently poured on her burning back. "I been here only two months but I will stay long time," she said, her hands spreading the soothing liquid over Jill.

The girl continued to chatter as she worked, Jill mumbling an occasional reply.

"Mr. Jeff very good to me," said Kim. "Before I come here, life very hard." She was working the oil down the back of Jill's thighs, her hands quick and expert. "I come from Chiang Mai. Bad place in the north, many bad men there. Mr. Jeff find me there and bring me to Wings.'' She tapped Jill on her bottom. ''Turn over, please. Do other side.''

The girl poured more oil, making a little pool around Jill's navel, and began spreading it in widening circles. Chiang Mai? A long way to go to hire a masseuse. She hadn't known he'd been up that way. Still, the girl *was* good. She felt the small hands gently anoint her breasts and was embarrassed when her nipples became erect. Kim seemed not to notice. Then the girl was oiling Jill's legs, high up inside her thighs, and Jill felt a faint arousal. The supple fingers worked higher still, brushing her lightly.

''You like more?'' Kim whispered. ''Many ladies do.''

Jill shook her head. ''No,'' she said, ''I've had enough. Thank you. I feel much better.''

''Okay,'' Kim said. ''Better you don't shower now. Let oil get into your skin before you wash off.'' She watched Jill climb down from the table. ''You very beautiful,'' she said. ''Everyone come to Wings beautiful. Not like pigs in Chiang Mai. Here I happy to give men and ladies pleasure. Some, they try and give me tip, but that not allowed at Wings. Everything free. All are happy. You get burn again, or you get tired, come to Kim and I make you feel good.''

She dined with Jeff and two of his assistants that night, eating a magnificent coconut curry of coral fish and lobster. Appetizers had been local river oysters, fat and succulent. Dessert was a mango mousse followed by French cheeses and fine coffee.

"Of course we can always grill a steak, or anything the guests want," Jeff said. "But I find that after a couple of nights almost all the guests have become adventurous. They want to dine on the local produce."

They took their coffee on a terrace overlooking the beach.

"I had the treatment from your little Thai girl today, Jeff. She's very talented. Must be a big hit with the guests."

"She is," he nodded. "I was lucky to find her."

"I didn't know you'd been up to Thailand, not recently, anyway."

He toyed with his cup. "Just a quick weekend trip," he said. "I have a . . . commitment there." He passed her a brandy and she could see how nervous he was. "What happened was, I was flying for a charter airline some of the Vietnam vets set up toward the end of the war. I missed out on the war itself, so I thought that was the next best thing. Anyway, I was based in Chiang Mai for a few months and I had an affair with a local girl. She had a baby, and then she vanished into Cambodia. My son's being taken care of by her parents. I pay them. They won't let me take the boy away, so every now and then I go up there and see how he's doing."

She was stunned. She'd never have guessed. Jeff seemed so carefree, so *young*.

A bit later, she stood up and said she was going to bed. He didn't ask if he could escort her to her bungalow. He understood her message: there would be times when they would be lovers again, but she would set those times.

Next day she made the long trip to Garokan, six hours flying down Southeast Asia into Brisbane, Australia, then four hours out into the South Pacific. The Wings resort in Garokan was the most remote of all, hardest to get to, with fewer facilities than the other Wings. Still, it was the most popular of the three Wings because it was so beautiful.

Cindy was waiting for her on the white beach, waving happily. She had bloomed on Garokan, deep tan contrasting with sun-bleached blond hair. The pounds she had put on flattered her. She looked like a satisfied woman. When Jill stepped onto the beach, Cindy hugged her.

"It's so great to see you!" she cried. "You hardly ever come visit us these days. Even Burt doesn't make the run anymore."

"There's no need for me to come. You're doing such a good job, Cindy. The place seems to run like a dream."

"Thanks to Jean-Paul," Cindy bubbled. "He makes sure nothing goes wrong. His people do exactly as he tells them. It's great, having the chief on your side!"

Jill studied her secretly as they strolled up

the beach to Cindy's bungalow. Jean-Paul must be treating her well, Jill concluded. Cindy was blooming, prettier than ever.

"What about the Garokan government? The real government, over in Petit Bougainville?"

"Oh, they leave us alone," Cindy said airily. "Jean-Paul is the chief on Sabot and they don't mess with him. I think they're happy that he's happy, and not plotting an uprising or anything."

They waited until the tall young porter had deposited Jill's case in the second bedroom. A wooden ceiling fan moved the warm air around; brilliantly colored butterflies drifted in and out of the open shutters.

"I'd forgotten how quiet it is here," Jill said. "Where are all the guests?"

"Most of them have gone off on the wild-boar hunt with Jean-Paul's men. We do one every week—it's very popular. And tonight, after the hunt, we'll feast on the result." She laughed. "It's funny how quickly you go native here. My great joys are riding bareback on the sand, fishing, that kind of thing. Me! I used to think volleyball at the Outrigger Club was the height of athletics."

"You're happy, aren't you?"

"Oh, God, yes. I've never been so happy. I don't ever want to leave here."

They let the afternoon drift by, catching up with each other's news. Jill told her about Jonathan, and about Andy's departure. At sun-

216

down they walked down to the beach to watch the hunters return. There were thirty guests in the three canoes, proudly brandishing the bloody tusks of four boars.

"Look at 'em," Cindy said proudly. "That guy in the first canoe, he's a securities analyst on Wall Street. He arrived here all buttoned down, stitched up. Now he's naked to the waist, spattered in pig's blood, the great white hunter. No wonder they all love it here."

The feasting and drinking went on late into the night, everyone joining in with wild abandon. The handsome Sabots mingled with the guests, serving but not subservient. The chief was not there, but from the way Cindy kept anxiously glancing down to the beach, Jill figured he was expected. The dancing started late, lit by flares and moonlight. No one could escape the sensuousness of it. The native dancers were expressing primitive sex to an audience long weary of X-rated movies and explicit magazines. This was the real thing. The beat of the drums was like a racing pulse, summoning them to get up and join in the dance. Soon only Jill and Cindy were still seated.

"I'm going to bed," Jill said finally. "I feel like a voyeur. This is no place for a woman alone."

"I'll just wait awhile longer," Cindy said. She was still looking down the beach. "Make sure no one gets into any trouble. I'll see you in the morning."

Jill lay under her mosquito net, hearing the

drums and watching the flares reflected on the ceiling. She was glad for Cindy, being so happy in this faraway place. She slipped easily into sleep while the revels continued in the black silk night. She didn't hear the erotic whispers in the next bedroom, the frantic movement of the bed, or the slap of big, bare feet padding away at dawn. But the next morning she knew he must have been there: Cindy was radiant and exhausted.

The friends passed two pleasant days together on the island. Jean-Paul didn't appear until Jill was preparing to leave. He was polite but just a little ill at ease.

"I hope you are happy with the way things have worked out," he said. "Certainly, my people are. They have work that does not degrade them and they are mixing with Americans, which is good. Those peasants in Petit Bougainville are still trying to protect Garokan from the outside world. But we are more enlightened."

"You're not having any trouble with the central government then?" Jill said. "Because they could make it very difficult for all of us."

He dismissed the government with a contemptuous wave of his hand.

"Don't concern yourself. They are no-account people, people of lesser tribes. The Sabots are the only ones who matter in Garokan."

She had arranged for Biggles to fly her to Petit Bougainville to connect with a flight to Pago

Pago and on to Honolulu. He was waiting at the little Sabot airstrip.

"You won't be going to Pago Pago tonight," he said. "The plane hasn't left Sydney yet. Tomorrow sometime. I got you one of Woody's rooms for the night."

She was missing Jonathan, but otherwise she didn't mind being hung up for the night. "I'd like to talk to a few people in the capital, do a little public relations for Wings."

"Yes," Biggles said laconically. "That wouldn't be a bad idea. Go see our beloved president and tell him how much you appreciate being allowed to operate here. The old boy's nose is a little out of joint because Sabot is getting all the action."

It was easy to get to see President Tovare. He was available for public audience every afternoon in his small office in an old copra shed by the wharves. When Jill arrived there was no one else waiting for him.

Tovare was a small, worried-looking man. He was a Melanesian, very dark, thick lipped, hesitant, anxious not to upset anyone. Two centuries of his people's being exploited by blackbirders, traders, and missionaries had made him that way.

"An honor, Mrs. Nagle," he said. "Please sit down. I am so pleased you have found time to visit with me. Your island resort, it is all running satisfactorily? I hear so little about it, you see. The Sabot people are . . . difficult."

"Yes, Mr. President. Everything is satisfactory. My concern is that everything we do is acceptable to you. I don't want Wings to be seen as siding with any faction in your nation. We are simply here to operate a resort. I hope everyone in your country can benefit from it one way or another."

He shrugged. "There are benefits, of course. They spend in the duty-free store, they pay their departure taxes, a few of your guests add on tours to other parts of our beautiful country. That is as much as we can expect."

"I'm sorry it's not more. But Sabot is such a perfect place for our resort, and the chief is so helpful."

"Yes, Jean-Paul can be of great assistance to . . . those who can benefit him." He lit a cheroot and watched the smoke rise up to the corrugated iron roof. "I do not mind him getting so much out of your resort, but some people . . ." He coughed. ". . . some people fear he is using your presence to establish an American influence in the islands. You may know of the policy I have established in Garokan. The world laughs at us for this, but I am determined we will not become a pawn in the game between your country and the Russians. So neither of you are accorded diplomatic status here. It is sad, but the mistrust between the two great powers is so great that they will not accept our nonaligned stance. Because I accepted the credentials of the Cubans, America feels threatened. On the other hand, the Cuban ambassador complains that Wings is some kind of capitalistic hotbed.'' He laughed. ''Of course, you and I know that is not so. Don't we? Because if there were any kind of activity at your resort, anything at all political, I would have to ask you to leave our nation.''

''I promise you, Mr. President, we are not involved in politics. We're not interested. I am very much aware that we are guests in your country. We will do nothing to abuse your hospitality.''

He nodded. ''Thank you, madam. You reassure me. I shall tell the Cuban he is suffering from paranoia.'' He laughed. ''He won't believe me, but I will tell him.'' He came around from behind the old desk. ''If there is anything we can do to assist you, I am always here. Jean-Paul appears to be taking care of things, but, who knows, someday there may be something my modest government can do.'' He nodded politely in parting. ''Thank you for coming to see me.''

Clearly, nobody ever came to see him.

Clint Donnelly was in Woody's bar that night, and Jill remembered Woody's jibe about Clint being a CIA operative. She was curious about Clint's interest in her.

''It's all going well, then,'' he said after he'd bought her a drink. ''You're not unhappy you decided to set up a resort on Sabot?''

''No, it's even more successful than I thought it would be,'' she replied. ''The guests love the place. I could fill the rooms twice again.''

''It's rubbing off on me, too,'' Woody chimed in from over the bar. ''I get 'em coming and going from your place. Means I don't have to be so dependent on bums like Donnelly here.''

''And you're not getting hassled by the central government?'' he asked, ignoring Woody. ''I thought the president might be getting jealous, seeing all the trade flocking to his enemies on Sabot.''

''Actually, I dropped by the president today and he was courteous and helpful. He thinks any development is good for the whole nation—even if it's built on Sabot.''

''I wouldn't be too sanguine about that,'' Donnelly said gloomily. ''Tovare looks like your tractable coon but he's got a real bee in his bonnet about Americans. You know he's in the Cubans' pocket?''

''Hardly in their pocket, Mr. Donnelly,'' Jill said coolly. ''The way I understand it, the Cuban ambassador only turns up here twice a year.''

''There are others,'' he said. ''We hear reports of Cubans on the outer islands, posing as agricultural advisers, UNESCO people, teachers. You can be damn sure Castro's stirring things up here.''

''See!'' Woody crowed. ''Just as I told you! Donnelly's either nutty as a fruitcake or he's

one of your American spooks—both, more
likely."

Donnelly looked at her with real loathing.

"I wish there were somewhere else to drink
on this dreadful island," he said. "You have a
monopoly on liquor—and a monopoly on stupidity, too."

The big woman reached over the bar and
took Donnelly by the lapels of his grubby
white jacket. She dragged him halfway across
the bar and boxed his ears, not gently, before
letting him slide back onto his stool.

"Yank," she said calmly, "any more cheek
out of you and I'll bar you."

There was an uneasy silence after that, and
Jill finished her drink and went in to dinner;
she was beginning to feel some of the tensions
of these islands. Had it always been that way,
or was it something recent, this disturbing un-
dercurrent of electricity?

Chapter Ten _____

THE HEWITTS LOVED HER NEW JAPA-
nese-style house. They prowled around, playing with the gadgets in the super kitchen,
exclaiming over the sparkling bathrooms, rhap-
sodizing over the views from Diamond Head.
They had their own wing—Jill had persuaded
her parents to spend every winter in the islands
with her and Jonathan—and she hoped eventually to have them living in Hawaii permanently.
Watching them act like little old children in a
fantastic toy shop, she was reminded of how
hard life was in Chicago, especially in the
winter. They still could not encompass all the
things she had achieved; her life was beyond
their comprehension.

For a moment, standing on the terrace alone,
looking out to sea, she wondered if it wasn't beyond her grasp, too. It would be so much sim-
pler to be running a home, raising Jonathan,
caring for David. But that had all been decided
for her when David was taken.

She heard the doorbell and hurried to greet
her friend.

"Carl." She hugged him. "I'm so glad you were willing to make the trip down the mountain. I know how you hate to leave your place, but I did want you to see the new house. And Jonathan's so excited: he wants to take you on a guided tour, starting in his nursery." She laughed. "I've got to stop calling it a nursery. He's a big boy now. I know it's true because he told me."

Dr. Cohen shook hands with her parents and welcomed them back to Hawaii. They responded to his warmth with their own shy warmth. They were glad he was in Jill's life.

"Jill says you are going to make a nice long visit of it this time," he said. "That's terrific. At our age we don't want to be suffering the snows of winter, do we?" He shuddered.

And then Jonathan, trailed by Elsa, his nurse, came bursting into the living room. He flung himself on the new arrival.

"Uncle Carl! Uncle Carl!" he yelled. "Come look at our house. It's brand new! I don't think it's as good as your place, but it's next best." He grabbed the old man's hand. "Come on, I'll show you my room."

Jill watched them go. She worried about Jonathan. He had no friends his own age. He was deeply attached to Elsa and to the housekeeper, Mrs. Bunter. Dr. Cohen was, Jonathan had told her, "my special friend," and Burt Brydon made him laugh a lot. Now there would be time for the boy to get close to her parents.

"He's such a bright little boy and looks so much like his father," her mother said. "He must be a joy."

"He is. But it's such a wrench, having to leave him as often as I do. I wish I didn't have to travel all the time, but it's the price I pay for everything I have."

"Don't worry," her mother said. "As long as he knows you love him and will always come back, it's all right. People worry too much about children. When he was kissing me good night last night, he told me the new house was for you and him to live in together for the rest of your lives. He's a happy child, Jill."

"I hope you're right, Mom. His poor father had the strangest kind of childhood. They were rich and respected, but there was so little love in the house." She put her arm around her mother. "That's where you and Daddy made me richer than rich."

"Don't get misty-eyed, you two," her father said. "You know men can't stand tears."

The three of them and Carl had a relaxed meal under the stars, and by ten o'clock the three older people were yawning. Dr. Cohen had come by cab and Jill insisted on driving him home.

"A very nice house, Jill," he said when he was settled in her green Mercedes. "I'm glad you're starting to give yourself some of the finer things. You've worked hard for what you have, dear."

"Too hard? Do you think I've been too ambitious, or that it's costing Jon?"

"No," he said firmly. "The boy is fine. He misses you when you're away, but that's taught him independence. I think you need to be as involved as you are in your business. It's good for you."

"I guess I'm just nervous about the Greek Wings," she said, frowning, as she steered around a curve on the steep, narrow road. "The big opening is in two weeks, a cast of stars. I'm kind of scared it will all blow up in my face. The other resorts have always been low-key; this one's shaping up to be very jet-set. It seems to be getting out of hand. But dear old Spiro Gravas has appointed himself unofficial public relations man and he's pulling in all his famous friends for the opening. One doesn't say no to him."

"Gravas," Cohen said. "You didn't tell me you knew Spiro Gravas."

"I went to a dinner on his yacht when I was looking over the island. And then he was in New York the same time I signed the deal to finance it. He's a kind, funny man. I like him."

He chuckled. "I knew Spiro very well, a long time ago. Forty years ago. Since then, all I hear of him is what I read in the gossip columns. All those wives, all those women, all that money. I guess he's past it all now, though."

"He certainly is *not* past it all," Jill laughed. "He's still in there pitching. Although I suspect it's more for the sake of his reputation than his libido.''

''He's a good man, Gravas, playboy or not. I'll write a letter for you to give him.'' He chuckled again. ''It will be a real echo from his past.'' The car bumped up the rough drive to Carl's house, and he sprang out and bowed to her. ''Thank you for the ride. And I feel much happier about your new project, knowing Spiro is watching over you. I'll have the letter ready when you and your parents and Jonathan come over next week.''

The public relations woman was waiting for them in TWA's VIP suite at Kennedy Airport.

''I've only just gotten the final guest list,'' she told Jill. ''The duke and duchess of Cranbrook had to drop out, so there's going to be room for the Martecs. You'll like them—no money, but he *is* a real prince and they're both fun.'' She handed Jill several pages clipped together. ''They're all there, with bios. And I've got some early press clips for you. It's already being billed as party of the year. The media are livid, though. I decided the best kind of publicity for Wings would be the exclusive kind, so I only invited *Vogue*, which is your kind of market.'' She leaned forward, conspiratorial. ''But I happen to know young Tony Haden is taking his camera along 'cause he's got a deal with *People*, so we'll get that end of the market, too.''

Jill glanced through the lists. She recognized many of the names: the international set, English and European nobility, the latest generation of old American families. And some show biz people, including Don Messner and Ellen Brooks.

"It was a real coup getting those two," the PR woman said. "If Messner will take his shirt off, you might even get the *People* cover."

Jill smiled. It was good of Don and Ellen to make the trip, as busy as they were. And Andy would be along, too. He and Ellen were still happy together.

"My only worry," the woman said, "is about this outfit that's going to be flying them all in. No one knows anything about Royalty Airlines."

"There's nothing to worry about there," Jill smiled. "Come Tuesday they'll climb aboard their Royalty flights here and at Heathrow and they'll be in for the trip of their life. Royalty's going to be our exclusive carrier—an airline as luxurious as the resort it serves."

Diana Moore met her at the Athens airport.

"Richard said sorry he couldn't make it, but he's running around like crazy," she told Jill as they climbed into a cab. "It's a great country, Greece, but they don't have any sense of urgency. There's a hundred things still to be done before the mob arrives. But we'll get there. Thank God Gravas showed up in his yacht this morning. The refrigeration broke down for a few hours, so we put a hundred pounds of caviar in his freezer."

''His yacht's going to be handy. We pruned the list as far as we could, but there are still more people than there are cottages, so Spiro has offered to take the overflow. Thank heaven for him.''

''Wait till you *see* the cottages,'' Diana said. ''No one's going to want to stay on the yacht. The whole place is looking fabulous.''

It was. The transformation was incredible. The buildings shone white against the vivid grass; new plantings made a profusion of brilliant flowers everywhere. The island was groomed, immaculate, yet retained all its wild charm. The mansion house sparkled in the sun: rich Persian rugs covered gleaming floors, and solid teak furniture exuded the glow of antiquity. Fountains played, crystal sparkled, and the white-garbed staff scurried silently through the halls.

''We'll be ready in time,'' Richard Moore promised Jill when they'd found him in the kitchen. He was wearing jeans and T-shirt, in contrast to the team of uniformed chefs with whom he was arguing. He wiped his forehead. ''The air conditioning won't be working in here until tomorrow, but all the rest of the equipment is functioning. The chefs are hassling each other over who takes precedence. The Frenchman isn't talking to the Greek and neither of them can understand the Chinese. But they'll work it all out. Come on through to the garden and we'll toast Wings. At least the champagne is cold.''

They sat under an ancient olive tree while a Greek waiter served them. It was a divine spot, silent, as far removed from the twentieth century as any place could be.

"You've obviously both been working terribly hard," Jill said. "The effort shows, believe me. After the next few days, when the hoopla is over, we should be able to settle into a normal Wings routine." She lifted her glass to them. "In the meantime, here's to us—and getting through the grand opening."

Even the staff cottage set aside for Jill was lovely; the thick whitewashed stone walls kept it cool by day and warm by night. Brightly colored draperies and spreads, a polished wood floor, solid comfortable furniture, all gave the cottage a cheerful but definitely luxurious feeling.

The all-important power guests came ashore in two waves, Burt's party from out of New York first, then the London contingent. The cream of the international set, they were jaded, cynical, used to only the best. They had seen it all and they were not going to be easily impressed. But the combination of Burt's superluxury air service and the elegance of the new Wings pleased them and they were gracious enough to say so.

"Beautiful." "Different." "Romantic," they told one another.

Jill moved among them, listening to the plaudits and nodding when they complimented her. They would come again, as paying guests, some promised, and tell their friends about it. The opening was costing close to four hundred thousand dollars but it would pay for itself soon enough.

Seb Judge was everywhere, holding court or huddling with first this celebrity and then that one. It was as if the island were his creation. Still, he had put it together for her, so she couldn't let herself be too annoyed. He had already told her he would be reserving places for a dozen people every two weeks for the rest of the year.

"It's a long way from the other resorts," Burt said to her quietly as the two of them sat on a rocky outcrop high above the bay. It was midnight on the first day of festivities. Below them, Spiro's surprise for everyone—a superb fireworks display—was lighting up the black night. "It's going to be your biggest success," Burt added, "but I'm not sure either of us would be happy living here."

"I know," Jill said, glad he always understood her so well. It was lovely to have him there, comfy and constant, her refuge. "This place is just a business for us, Burt. Our home will always be Hawaii."

The elite guests were there for three days. They consumed copious amounts of champagne and cognac, cocaine and caviar, and seemed well pleased with the amenities. The Moores were in their element with this kind of guest, and Jill had little to do other than observe the proceedings. She was grateful to Dan Passage for finding her the Moores: they, as much as the superb location, would account for the success of this Wings.

On the last day, Andy came looking for her. They had not spoken alone during the long party because Jill was always busy and Ellen was always at Andy's side.

"I've been feeling lousy about leaving the business," Andy said. "I never meant to let you down. But you didn't need me, so I knew I didn't have to worry about you. You've done it all now, Jill. You should be very happy."

"I guess I am." She placed a hand on his arm. "Please, Andy, don't talk about feeling bad. I'm the one who owes you. You were there when I really needed you, you and Burt. I'll never be able to thank you for what you did for me through those awful times." They walked in silence, side by side, up through an olive grove to a place where they could see the neighboring islands. "How is it with you and Ellen?"

He shrugged and looked away, puzzling her. What was wrong?

"It's funny," he said slowly. "I was never going to marry again, never going to get involved, even. But Ellen . . . needs me. I don't think anyone needed me before. I'm just a bum, but I give her what she needs: a solid shoulder to cry on, no show biz bullshit, stability, I guess. We love each other in our funny ways."

"I'm so happy for you, Andy." But even so, there was that lingering sadness for what might have been for her and Andy. She grinned at him. "If you spend your honeymoon here, it'll be great publicity."

He scowled. "That's a big problem, coping with Ellen's fame. When we're alone she's just Ellen—a little scared of the world, a fragile, lovely creature. But when she's onstage, or anyplace public, she's a superstar. I feel way out of my depth and I hate it." He glanced around. "No, I don't think we'll honeymoon here. It's not my speed, thanks. But Garokan, now, that would be different. How's our Cindy doing?"

"Still enraptured with her chief. I don't know what's going to come of that, but in the meantime, she's looking wonderful."

"As far as I'm concerned, the jury's still out on Jean-Paul. Last time I was there it seemed he kind of had Cindy under his thumb. I guess he keeps out of the way when you're around, but with me—another Pacific native—he lets his guard down. I haven't figured his game out yet, but he's using Cindy somehow. You can bet on that."

The last night, Spiro Gravas gave a small dinner party on the yacht, just the pick of the guests. Jill was seated beside him again, and again she noted the impression this made on the others. He was signaling that she was under his patronage. It gave her confidence among all the princes and dukes and tycoons. He made a toast to her and spoke of how successful the new Wings was going to be, ''A place for people like us—I know you will all continue to patronize it.'' Later, he strolled on deck with Jill, their arms linked.

''I read the letter you brought me from Carl,'' he said. ''I did not know of your friendship with him. It makes me a little sad because it means I have to be your protector instead of a dirty old man offering you Renoirs for your favors.'' He chuckled, delighted with himself. ''But whatever Carl Cohen tells me to do, I do. I owe him my life. And my fortune.''

She must have registered surprise because he peered at her sharply through a cloud of cigar smoke, shaking his head slowly.

''Perhaps you don't know much about Carl's background,'' he said. ''He has always been a most self-effacing man. But there was a time when he strode the world stage, presidents and kings and generals seeking his advice.''

He was silent for a minute, considering how much he ought to say. ''At the worst time for the Allies in World War II your president called on Carl and he organized what has since been called the most successful espionage ring in history. I had a humble part in it. He had me snatched from Nazi captivity where I was under sentence of death. I had a tiny fleet of coastal freighters then, and he put me to work for the Allies. We had a long association, through the war and after, when he was the silent man behind your various intelligence agencies. He would accept no public honors. Everyone trusted and respected Carl Cohen. Grateful nations paid him in gold bullion. Even today, the remnants of the old guard in the Kremlin honor him and I hear he is still consulted by Washington and by leaders of other nations. The Entebbe raid, for example: those of us who like to think we're still in on international intrigues believe Carl was instrumental in that amazing episode." He flicked his cigar out over the rail and watched its trail of sparks until it hit the water. "So when Carl Cohen says I should take care of you, you can be sure I will take care of you."

He looked across the water to the lights of her new island.

"Wings will be a success here. But I would caution you to take nothing at face value. Mr. Judge, for example, is not in the business of doing favors, at least not for attractive young women. Young men, perhaps. And Dan Passage, I already sounded a faint alarm to you about him. These men have smoothed your path here and that is good for you. But be alert: they will at some time want something in return for their assistance. Don't forget."

There was nothing she could say.

"And I am very pleased for you," he went on. "If you have Carl in your corner, you'll be fine."

* * *

She stayed in New York awhile to huddle with Seb Judge, who had a new proposition for her, the result, he said, of investors who had been at the Greek opening and wanted to buy in with her.

"It's being handed to you on a silver platter," Judge said. "They'll finance, one hundred percent, Wings resorts in Jamaica and Haiti. They already own suitable operations there. I want you to do it. It won't dilute your holdings in Wings because they'll own the resorts and you'll operate them under a management contract."

"Slow down, Seb," she said. "I don't know whether I want any more resorts. I haven't got the time a new resort would—"

"Nonsense. You're a dedicated businesswoman. You've got to keep expanding or you'll stagnate. A couple more resorts and you'll be able to offer it all—the Mediterranean, the Pacific, *and* the Caribbean. You'll be grossing thirty million a year, minimum."

"But it's getting out of hand and it's happening too fast. Anyway, Jamaica and Haiti aren't good places for Wings. There's been so much trouble in both of them."

"Jamaica's settled down again," Judge assured her. "They need tourist money. And Haiti—Haiti's just had bad press, that's all. People in the know, wealthy travelers, love Haiti. Voodoo, exotic atmosphere . . . Haiti's a place you can sell to people who've been everywhere else."

"AIDS? How are you going to sell AIDS?"

"AIDS has nothing to do with Haiti," he snapped. "That was a bad rap and it's played hell with their tourism. It was all untrue. The scare is passing now, now that the god-damned media are getting bored with the story, but the damage has been done. That's one of the reasons it's such a great time to move in there. The government will make it real easy for us because they're desperate."

"I don't know, Seb, I—"

"Damn it, Jill, why do you think I'm spending so much time on your problems? I have faith in you. I want you to dare to be great. If you're content to run some little half-assed operation, then tell me now and we'll end our association right here. I want you to realize your full potential. Isn't that what life is about? You're on your own, responsible to no one but yourself. Go for it!"

She saw why Judge had such success with juries; he was making her do something she didn't want to do and implying she would be unhappy with herself if she didn't. But, in truth, he was right: she owed it to herself to be as successful as she could be.

"Okay, Seb," she laughed. "You're right. If you can put it together, I'll give it my best shot. Hell, I'm in way over my head as it is."

He smiled. "You won't be sorry." He glanced at some papers on his desk. "A limey is fronting for this new group. Name's Max Oram. He'll take care of all the details, new menus, staffing, whatever. In consultation with you, of course, but they'll want to move quickly, I warn you."

"I want to get home to Honolulu," she said. "I plan to spend one uninterrupted month with my son. If Max Oram wants to talk with me, can he come out there?"

"Sure. He'll want to visit the other resorts, anyway, to get an overview of Wings." Seb stood up and put out his hand. "You won't be sorry, Jill. I'm going to watch you become a very rich woman."

"At the moment I feel like a very tired woman. But it'll have to be this way for a while, I realize that."

She didn't get her restful month with Jonathan. Max Oram arrived in Honolulu four days after she did and she had to spend long days in the office with him. Oram was polite and charming, but he was also determined to know every facet of the Wings operation. It was only when they were going through the sketchy early records that Jill realized just what a seat-of-the-pants operation she'd been running.

"It's just grown kind of by itself over the years," she explained. "And we've always run Wings with people we know and trust, mostly former airline personnel. I'm sorry if it all looks messy, but this is the way I've done business."

"Our accountants can straighten it out," he said. "Don't you worry about it. The main thing is you've got a great little business which can clearly be made into a great big business."

Max had dinner with her and her parents, Jonathan, and Carl before he flew to Garokan and Malaysia. The Englishman was bright and funny, entertaining her parents with his army stories, playing with Jonathan, listening respectfully to Dr. Cohen's discourse on orchids. He was a charming guest and said flattering things about Jill's business successes and her brilliant future.

"I feel very confident about your joining forces with Mr. Oram and his associates," her father said when their guest had departed in a cab. "He understands numbers, that man. We had a talk about cost accounting and he was really interested in what I had to say. Even suggested he might have a job for me." Her father laughed. "I told him I was happy to be retired, but it sure was nice of him to offer. Made me feel damn good."

As usual, she drove Carl home. He was silent during the early part of the trip, but as they started up the mountain he asked abruptly, "Do you know who his investors are?"

"No. But from what Seb has told me, I assume they're wealthy Texans." She glanced across at him. "What's bothering you, Carl?"

"I remember seeing Oram's picture somewhere. It's probably nothing, but I'll make some inquiries." They drove up to his house and he asked, "Would you like to come in for a nightcap?"

"Sure." She was weary but she never missed an opportunity to be with Carl.

The Japanese houseboy brought them drinks on the terrace. The night was dark and it was so quiet, far from the traffic on Waikiki.

"Your business plans are interesting," he said to her, "and I'm sure you'll carry them out successfully. What interests me more, though, is your personal life." He looked into his glass. "I hope you won't hate me for meddling, but I worry about you. So do your parents. None of us is getting any younger, and the time will come when we won't be here."

"Don't say that, Carl."

"It must be said. I worry you will be left with nothing but your son and your business interests. I think you should be considering marriage."

She laughed ruefully. "Oh, Carl, I'm much too busy for that. And I'd make a dreadful wife. I'm always on the run, traveling, working. I've no time for a husband. And, anyway," she teased, "no one's asked."

He remained serious. "Your love for David, does it have anything to do with the shield you've put up around yourself?"

"No." But she knew that it did, a little. "What we had was perfect, and then it was gone. I guess I do steer away from men because I always compare them with David."

"David wouldn't want you to spend the rest of your life alone," he said firmly. "You need someone. And Jonathan needs a father."

She started crying, uncontrollably, as it turned out.

"I thought I was coping so well," she sobbed. "And now you tell me I'm a bad mother. What am I supposed to do?"

He put his hand on top of hers and let her cry until she was exhausted.

"You're a fine mother," he said at last, gently. "You know how much I love you, how proud I am of everything you've achieved. It's because you are so good and strong that I want to see you having a whole life again." He rang a silver bell and Obi padded out onto the terrace. "A brandy for Miss Jill, please."

When her drink arrived he went on, "I've been thinking about your situation for a long time and the thoughts become more urgent as my own time comes to an end. So I was most gratified when Burt Brydon came to me for advice. Advice about you. Burt says he loves you, and we all know he loves the boy. He wanted to know if there was hope for him, if there was any point in his—as he put it—continuing to 'moon around' after you. He's a fine man."

"Poor Burt," she said. "I *have* taken him for granted these past years. He's seemed like a brother. I haven't been able to think of him as . . . as a lover."

"Perhaps you should try to."

"Give me a little time, Carl." She was tired and confused. "But, about Jonathan, do you think it would help if I tried again with David's parents? Someday Jonathan is going to wonder why he has no contact with his father's family."

"No," Carl said sharply. "There's nothing to be gained from the Nagles. Leave them buried."

His reaction shocked her. Carl was always the most tolerant of men, the one who always counseled reconciliation. The bitterness in his voice was completely unlike Carl. It was advice she could not accept, not even from him. One day, she dreamed, she would bring Jonathan together with his other family and they would all be friendly. She owed it to Jonathan and she owed it to David.

"I'll think about all you've said." She stood up, yawning. "Thank you, Carl, for caring so much about us." She leaned down and kissed his cheek. "Please stop talking about time running out. You'll be here among your orchids forever. You have to."

He called her two days later, in her office.

"Still pressing Burt's suit?" she kidded him. "I never thought I'd see you playing matchmaker."

"No," Carl said, his tone serious. "It's not about that. It's Mr. Oram. I've been checking around and there are some things you ought to know. Can you come by my house this afternoon?"

"Sure," she said, "but—"

"Where is Oram?"

"He's on Garokan today; then he goes to Malaysia the day after tomorrow."

"I'll see you this afternoon." Carl hung up.

Chapter Eleven

SHE MADE SURE ORAM HAD MOVED ON before following him to Garokan. She told no one she was making the journey, taking the weekly scheduled flight via Samoa instead of using Burt's airline. She had Biggles fly her from Petit Bougainville to Sabot.

"Jill! You didn't say you were coming! It's so great to see you." Cindy was pleased, genuinely pleased, embracing Jill and leading her to the bungalow, chattering all the while. "Mr. Oram was just here and he didn't mention it. You've got to tell me all about the Greek opening. I wish I could have been there. I bet it was fabulous, huh?"

"We've got a lot to talk about, Cindy." Jill kept her voice friendly. She and Cindy had been together for so long; she still didn't believe Cindy could have betrayed her. "Where's Jean-Paul?"

"Oh, around the island somewhere. I don't know. He comes and goes. He's very busy, of course. His people look to him for everything."

"Did he have any dealings with Max Oram?" she asked.

"Yes, they got along real well together."

Jill was stripping out of her traveling clothes and putting on shirt and shorts.

"Let's go walk on the beach, Cindy. Something's come up."

They strolled down a long, deserted strand well away from the Wings buildings. Cindy was puzzled, but she waited for Jill to speak first.

"Something funny's going on, Cindy," Jill began when they were far from other people. "Jean-Paul is at the heart of it. I've good reason to believe he's planning an uprising against President Tovare."

Cindy shook her head. "That's just Jean-Paul mouthing off," Cindy said. "He's always saying how superior his people are. But there's nothing bad in Jean-Paul. The Sabots are gentle, nice people. They're not warriors."

"They would be if someone were stirring them up. The way I hear it, the island of Sabot—and Wings—is being used as a training ground for small groups of American mercenaries who are going to back the Sabots in a coup."

There was an uneasy silence.

"Why would anyone want to do that? There's no wealth here, no minerals, no trade." But even as she spoke, Cindy had guilty memories of the silent young men who came to stay and didn't behave at all like regular guests. The fitness sessions on the beach, the long treks off into the jungle with Jean-Paul's men.

"They don't need a particular resource," Jill said. "There are people around—fanatics, opportunists, whatever you want to call them—who dream of creating new, independent island nations. They set up tax havens, money-laundering operations, unregulated gambling, even gun running, or training camps to export revolutionaries. People can make millions and millions. A place like Garokan in the wrong hands—hell, they'd be financing international drug deals, giving refuge to every rich criminal in the world."

"Jean-Paul wouldn't let his island be used like that," Cindy protested firmly.

"He's just their dupe. They have to find some gullible local revolutionary to make the take-over look like political philosophy, a moral battle." She stopped walking and gripped Cindy's arm. "I know you're madly in love with him, but you owe me, Cindy. Tell me the truth. What is going *on?*"

"I don't believe I'm hearing all this," Cindy said. She felt the grip on her arm stiffen. "Please, Jill, please don't think I'd let something like that happen, something to hurt you and Wings." She stood with her head hung low. "Maybe there has been something going on," she muttered to herself. Then, all in a rush, she told Jill about the unusual visitors. "But they did no harm, they paid their bills. I never thought anything of it. It wasn't as if they were running around with guns."

"You wanted to believe the best about Jean-Paul." It was not a question.

Cindy nodded, miserable now. "If you're right . . . it means he's just using me." She shook Jill's arm away fiercely. "I don't think that's true. I know he loves me. And I love him. You're making all this up because you're jealous." She broke away from Jill and ran back up the beach to her bungalow.

Jill went to Jean-Paul's village in the early evening. She found the chief holding court in the dusty square outside his house. When he saw her he dismissed his tribesmen and motioned her to sit beside him.

"It is good to see you back on our beautiful island so soon," he said. "You enhance its beauty."

"I love Sabot and all of Garokan very much," she said evenly. "It's always a pleasure to be here." She nodded to his offer of a drink and waited while the lithe serving girl placed two gourds in front of them. "But this time I've come because I'm very concerned about something. I've been hearing things I don't like."

He smiled.

"My . . . friendship with Cindy?"

"In part, yes. Are you using Cindy in order to use Wings for an illegal purpose?"

"I don't understand you, dear Jill. Illegal purpose. What do you mean?"

"You've been bringing mercenaries in here to train your people and prepare for a coup against Tovare." She watched his eyes as she spoke. Something flickered there, contempt for her, or derision.

"You Americans! You see plotting where there is none, unrest where all is placid. There is no revolution being hatched here. Certainly my contempt for the puppet president Tovare is well known. But if I were to move against him, I would do it without the assistance of soldiers of fortune." He glared at her. "We Sabots don't need outside help. Oh, I have from time to time accommodated people at Wings. They were economic advisers, technicians, agriculturalists. I summoned them here to improve the lot of my people. We cannot forever live off the crumbs you throw us from Wings."

"Max Oram was a technician? Oram, the mercenary who crops up in Angola, Libya, Central America—anywhere there's revolution growing?" She stared at him. "If Oram has been here, your plot must be reaching a crucial stage."

He laughed.

"*You* sent Mr. Oram here, Jill. He was *your* emissary. He had a letter of introduction from you and I extended him hospitality. If anyone's planning a revolution, I guess it must be you. I think our president would be most interested to learn this: he is already paranoid about the Americans."

"I didn't know who Oram was until a few days ago," she said. "He was presented to me as someone else altogether. As soon as I did know—"

"Tovare is going to believe that? Even a man of Tovare's limited intelligence would not fall for that story. I think he would immediately close down your operation here and banish you from Garokan."

He was right, of course. If Wings had been used as a haven for mercenaries, if Oram was who Dr. Cohen said he was, she was deeply involved whether she'd been duped or not.

"I get your message, Jean-Paul. I have to shut up for my own good. But if there is trouble here, I'll know why, and I'll do something about it."

He remained seated while she stood up. He was indifferent to her. Poor Cindy, she thought. This man wasn't the least interested in Wings—or in Cindy.

"You're playing with very dangerous people, Jean-Paul," she told him. "If you go ahead with this insanity you might find yourself under a far harsher regime than Mr. Tovare's."

"Don't worry about me," he said coldly. "Mind your own business."

The sky was grumbling and gray when she flew out the next day. It suited her mood. She had gone there to take action, to stop the potential disaster Dr. Cohen had warned her about, but she had achieved nothing.

* * *

Dr. Cohen was not perturbed.

"Maybe he's changed more than just his name," he said when Jill finished talking. "Whatever, there doesn't seem to be anything you could have done at this stage, not without compromising Wings. I think you handled it just as you should have. What do you think, Burt?"

Burt shook his head.

"Those guys never change. Crazy bastards, running around the world looking for trouble. I've known a few of them. They settle into regular jobs but spend all their time reading those gun-for-hire magazines and dreaming about trouble spots." He took a swallow of beer. It was an unlikely place to be talking about insurrection, there in Dr. Cohen's tranquil garden. "He probably can't do much harm, though. And Jean-Paul is all talk anyway. I'd be more worried about the people on the next island, Latakia. Now, those guys could stage an uprising *any* old time. They're quite far around the bend—cargo cultists."

When Jill had no idea what he was talking about, Burt told her what he knew. "It all got started when the first white settlers came to the island and the Latakian chief got popular with his people by saying that all the white man's possessions—his cargo—had actually been meant for the Latakians and the whites had hijacked the goods on the way to the islands. He promised to retrieve it all for them someday. The cult grew out of that. They still build mock airstrips on the beaches and wait for the planes to arrive with their cargo. There are similar cults all over the Pacific, New Guinea particularly. The movement got its biggest boost in World War II, when the Yanks arrived with so much equipment. And they left so much behind when they departed, the cultists took it as a sign. Now the Latakians believe the central government has replaced the white man as the thief of their cargo.''

''What's President Tovare doing about it?'' Jill asked. ''He seems like a good man. I'm sorry he's got so many problems.''

''He is a good man,'' Burt said. ''I've spent a lot of time with him in the period I've been flying into Garokan. He didn't want to be president, but they convinced him he was the only person who could hold the islands together after independence. I would hate anything to happen to Tovare.''

''I certainly don't want Wings to be used by anyone making trouble,'' she said worriedly. ''Maybe I *should* have gone and talked to Tovare, after all. I'd have taken the risk that he would believe Wings isn't involved. I should have done it.''

''He'd have believed you,'' Burt said. ''But he wouldn't have done anything about it. He's a fatalist. If there's going to be an uprising, he'll face it when he has to. Meantime, he'll do nothing.''

Jill called Seb Judge that night and he told

her there was little to worry about. If Oram had been, in his past, some kind of soldier of fortune, so what? Seb's investors were well pleased with Oram. They didn't care about his past associations.

"If you start making noises over nothing, you'll frighten these people away," Judge said sternly. "If that's what you want, sure, I'll just call them up and say you object to their man. Then it's good-bye Haiti, good-bye Jamaica."

She listened to him, smooth, reasonable, reassuring. The awful thing was, once she had accepted the idea of Wings, Haiti, and Wings, Jamaica, she desperately wanted the new resorts.

When he and Jill were finished talking, Seb Judge left his office. The rolls of quarters ruined the hang of his beige suit but he would soon be rid of them. He fed coins into the phone at Grand Central and waited for the phone to be answered in Houston.

"Our girl isn't as naive as we thought," he said when his colleague answered. "She's tumbled to Oram. I've calmed her down but we're going to have to watch the situation."

He listened, then said, "Yes. She wants the new resorts, so she won't give us any trouble. But there's no time to waste. We have to have everything in place, and on schedule."

He hung up, used more coins, and dialed the Boston number. The voice that answered had that distinctive New England accent that

Seb disliked so intensely. It was the accent of old family, old money; it suggested that people who spoke the way Seb did were not to be tolerated.

"Just checking in to let you know it's all almost ready," Judge said. "A few more weeks and we'll all have what we want." He listened. "No," he said firmly. "You keep well away from them. We all have the same objective, but you and they have different reasons for wanting what we want. Trust me. I know what's best." He hung up as soon as he could.

Jeff Thompson drained his glass and rapped on the table for another. The sullen Malay waiter brought a third gin sling for him and more tea for Oram. The waiter left, and they were alone again in the old hotel on the George Town waterfront.

"I can't do it, Max," Jeff said quickly, getting the words out as fast as he could. He was rattled, and the drinks weren't helping the way they should have. "The risk is too great. It's an automatic death penalty. And I can't do it to her, either. Jill's given me a break. I can't help ruin her."

"You don't believe in our common goal anymore?" Oram said softly, gazing down at the table. "You disappoint me. I've always thought of you as one of our finest recruits. A young man like you can go far in our organization. So many of us are getting past our prime.'' He sighed, sounding deeply disappointed.

''I still support what you're trying to do,'' Jeff said miserably. ''But I'm leading a normal life now. I'm afraid—for myself and for other people.''

''Your little boy in Chiang Mai?''

Jeff nodded. ''What would happen to him if they caught me and executed me?''

''We would take care of him. But don't talk that way. You've done these runs before and you've never been in any danger. We need this shipment badly, Jeff. There are people to be paid off and they'll accept only those particular goods.''

''I'm sorry. I can't do it.''

Max Oram raised his eyes to meet Jeff's. ''You leave me no choice, then. If you don't carry out this mission, you'll never see the child again. He'll be sent into Kampuchea, like his mother was. She may have survived there. At least she was a beautiful young woman, so she had sex to trade for food. But a little boy—no, I don't think he'd last very long under the Vietnamese. Do you?''

Jeff's eyes blazed with anger. ''I've taken the most awful risks for the organization! I've been loyal. I've never refused an assignment before. Please, this time, leave me out of it.''

''No, Jeff. It's got to be you. You have a reason to visit Chiang Mai; you've made the trip several times before. You won't attract any attention.'' Max patted the younger man's arm.

"If it were up to me, well, I'd let you off the hook. But we're all just soldiers in this, obeying orders. And I have to tell you, if you don't do it, the child will be lost to you forever."

Jeff tasted the bitter dregs of his drink and wanted to vomit.

"One last run," he said. "When?"

"We'll be in touch. Just be ready."

Burt suggested he go along with Seb and Jill on their Caribbean inspection trip.

"After all, my airline will be flying your guests into the new Wings. I should check out the aircraft facilities. I just picked up a BAC-111 that would be ideal for the job. Why don't I fly you and Seb Judge around?" He desperately wanted her to accept; they were getting so little time together these days.

"That would be wonderful, Burt," she said, glad, as always, for his reassuring presence. She watched him now, playing on the lawn with Jonathan and the puppy he'd bought Jon for his birthday. Burt could make them a whole family, and she knew that was what he wanted. What she didn't know was whether she loved Burt.

Seb didn't approve of her obvious friendship with Burt, whom Seb treated as hired help. Burt didn't cotton to the attorney, either. Burt's big open face showed everything he felt, and he didn't approve of Judge's dress, mannerisms, or conduct. An hour out of New

York, Burt emerged from the cockpit and found Seb snorting coke.

"Mr. Judge," he said, his voice menacingly low, "I don't care what kind of shit you stuff yourself with, but if it's illegal, you don't do it on my airplane."

Seb carefully snorted another line, then placed the container back in his breast pocket. He looked at Burt with amusement.

"My, you antipodeans are really strung out about things, aren't you?" he said lightly. "Son, you just fly this airplane and let me worry about the law. Each to his own job, eh?"

Jill wondered if Seb realized how close he was coming to being thumped. But Burt restrained himself: he felt out of his depth with people like Judge, smart New Yorkers who knew all the answers. He glowered at him for a moment, then stomped back to the cockpit.

As the jet made a grand sweep over Port-au-Prince, Jill took it all in eagerly. She knew about the poverty in Haiti, but just then all she could see was the sheer exuberant beauty of the place: brilliant jungle climbing the sides of high peaks, mad Victorian gingerbread houses dotting the clearings, whitewashed buildings along the waterfront. And all around was the clear blue of the Caribbean.

Seb got a big welcome from the airport officials and they were whisked through customs without any questions.

"Poor bastards are desperate for new development,'' he explained when they were settled in a 1955 Cadillac taxi. ''The country was in enough trouble before, with all the bad press old Papa Doc and his Tontons Macoutes got. His boy, Jean-Claude, was just succeeding in cleaning up that image and bringing the tourists back when the AIDS scare started.''

They were driving down a narrow white road roofed with flowering trees; along its sides were bands of smiling Haitians. If they were the poorest people in the Caribbean, it didn't show. They looked happy and proud.

Judge had booked them into the Grand Oloffson, a huge wooden building madly embellished with turrets and cupolas. It sat on a rise above Port-au-Prince and, apart from the knot of drinkers in the bar, they were the only guests. Jill stood on the balcony of the tower suite and sipped a cool drink while he pointed out features of the town.

''The place you're going to be running is five miles down the coast road. It's a cottage complex started by a Frenchman five years ago. He went broke. The government's kept it empty but in good repair, praying another operator would come along. From what I've been told it could be started up within weeks. I'll take you over to see it in the morning.''

Jill's room was a crazy, eight-sided affair hidden under gables. There was a big four-poster in the center of the room with a canopy of brilliant paintings done by local artists. The furnishings were of rattan, sturdy and comfortable, and the room was sunny and cheerful.

There was a knock on the door and she opened it to find Burt towering there.

"I'm just down the hall," he said. "Isn't this a wild place? The builder must have been on LSD. Judge is right, though. Your kind of tourists will like this island."

A banquet had been arranged for the three of them that night, hosted by the minister of tourism. He was a small, bespectacled black man with a worried frown: it was, he confided to Jill, imperative she like Haiti. They knew of her successes on other islands and they would do anything to make it easy for her to operate on Haiti. Anything.

The banquet food was a marvelous blend of French and island flavors, much like Creole cooking. Giant shrimp, whole fish marinated in wine and ginger, tender chicken in tangy gravy, tiers of tropical fruit and French cheeses. The wines were French and the coffee was local—the most delicious coffee any of them had ever tasted.

At the end of the banquet the minister suggested a midnight tour of Haiti's attractions. An ancient limousine awaited them and they set out in the blackness. There was not a light showing anywhere, and no one was afoot: the people appeared to have a curfew. Their car turned down a dirt track that wound through dense jungle, and after a bumpy ride they stopped at a clearing in front of a long, low tin shed. As the engine died, they could hear, above the night sounds of the jungle, a low chanting coming from inside the shed. In the shadows were a knot of uniformed men, nervously cradling submachine guns.

"This way, this way," urged the minister. He pushed aside a burlap strip that served as the door to the shed, and they entered, blinking, into another world.

Inside, the shed was big and bare and lit with flares. A fine film of dust from the dirt floor danced in the flickering light. There were about fifty Haitians there. They paid no attention to the newcomers; their eyes were fixed, trancelike, on an altar in the center of the room. The chanting grew louder, a rhythmic sound pulsing from the throats of the Haitians.

An old woman, eyes glittering, hair awry, was standing on the altar, crooning to six white chickens. The chickens were mesmerized: only an occasional movement showed they were even alive.

The chant deepened and Jill felt Burt's hand grip her arm. From the dark recesses of the room emerged two men in crimson robes leading a tiny girl dressed all in white. As she came into the light, Jill saw that she was a teenager, but very small and fragile-looking.

"She is tiny because she's always been sick," the minister whispered to Jill. "The evil spirits are in her. They will be driven out now."

The girl's eyes were glazed and tremors shook her body as the men lifted her onto the altar. Then the chanting subsided and the room went silent. The men gently stripped away her white robe. She was naked. Her thin body had been anointed with oil and it shone even in the faint light. The old woman positioned the girl flat on her back. She led the participants in a new chant, a more savage sound that bounced off the tin walls. The tension in the room was electric; Jill shivered—and almost gagged, for the old voodoo priestess, in one swift motion, snatched up a chicken and bit off its head. As bright red blood spurted from the chicken's convulsing body, the woman moved the chicken's body so that blood flowed over the girl, across her small breasts, down her stomach, between her thighs. The audience moaned.

The rest of the chickens were dispatched in the same manner, and now the old woman whirled each decapitated chicken around her head, sending blood out in wider and wider circles, splattering the eager onlookers. The audience rose then and began a ritual dance, moving around the altar and the blood-soaked girl.

''We go now,'' the minister whispered, and Jill dashed out of the shed, shaken and upset by what she had seen. Deep down she knew she had been fascinated by the primitivism of it all.

''Your tourists would like that?'' the minis-

ter murmured when they were back in the car.
"It is most exotic, isn't it?"

She nodded dumbly. Her tourists, some of
them, *would* like that.

"Now would you like to see a cockfight?
And then we shall visit a gambling den, and
after that a special place with music and dancing."

"Not a cockfight, *please*, Minister," Jill said
quickly. "I think I would like to go back to the
hotel now."

"Me too," said Burt.

"Ah, the bourgeoisie," scoffed Judge.
"We'll drop them off, Minister, then you and I
will sample *all* Haiti has to offer the jaded tourist."

After they'd watched the limousine vanish
back down the drive, Burt held her arm and
guided her up the broad wooden steps of their
hotel.

"Judge is suited to this place," he said. "A
fine facade and evil just below the surface. I
know his type. They corrupt everything. He'll
score himself a native boy tonight and the
devil with AIDS."

"I guess there is something ugly about
Seb," Jill mused as they stood in the ornate
lobby. No one was stirring in the hotel; the
bell desk was unattended. "But look at all the
deals he's set up for me. He's a good business-
man."

"I wonder if we can get a drink," Burt said,
leading her to the lobby bar. It was dark and

deserted. "I've got a bottle of cognac in my luggage, if you'd like a nightcap," he said. "After tonight's exhibition, we need one."

"Sure. I'll see you in my room in a minute. You better grab a couple of glasses from behind the bar."

She waited nervously for Burt to appear at her door, knowing it was time to take the great step, to risk a wonderful friendship in hopes of a greater love. She looked in the mirror and saw the face she put on for the world: confident, resolute. She seemed the only one who detected the uncertainty deep in her eyes.

There was a soft knock on the door and then Burt stood there, moving uneasily from foot to foot, a bottle of cognac in one hand and two brandy balloons in the other.

"If you're tired . . . if you'd rather just go to sleep . . ." He was awfully nervous about stepping over her threshold. "It's been a long day, I know."

"No, Burt," she said. "Come on in." She glanced around the odd-shaped room. If she'd had a suite it might have been a little easier for them; this was so clearly just a bedroom; the bed itself loomed large in the center of the room, its covers turned back invitingly, chocolates placed carefully on the pillows.

As Burt poured their brandies a little of it slopped on the surface of the dresser. His hand was shaking. When he heard her muffled sound, he looked up and crossed to her, taking her hands in his.

"Jill, did I upset you? Please don't cry."

"Oh, Burt!" she gasped. "This is crazy!" And she let the laughter spill out of her. "Look at the two of us, nervous as a couple of kids on their first date. After all we've been through together." She squeezed his hands. "Don't just stand there, Burt. Do something."

He did. He put his huge arms around her and swept her against his chest. She was enveloped, and it felt safe and right. She lifted her face and felt his beard rough against her cheek. Their lips came together. The kiss, their first real kiss, was long and deep. His fingers fumbled with buttons and zippers and she had to help him undress her. When she was finally naked she led him to her bed and lay down.

He quickly shrugged out of his shirt and pants to reveal himself, all muscle and bone and tight-curled brown hair. Jill shivered as she ran her hands over him, so big and powerful, so different from David. She knew then it was time to put the physical memories of David behind her, to allow the flow of her life to begin again. And she surrendered herself to Burt.

For such a huge man he was a gentle, tender lover. Each explored the other, touching, stroking, kissing with a profound sense of wonderment. When he moved onto her body he kept his full weight from her. She was ready soon, and gave herself completely, feeling the bigness of him deep inside her, responding with wave after wave of passion, abandoning herself to the electric sensations pulsing between them. She felt him climax in a surging, plunging motion sending new shocks through her, and she came, again and again, small waves washing through her, not cresting until they reached her very core.

Their lovemaking went on a long time; they gave to each other and they took from each other, their bodies in harmony, the song as old as time itself. At last, replete, they drifted toward sleep, his arm around her, his lips by her ear.

"I love you," he said. "I've loved you for such a long time. I've dreamed about tonight, but I never really dared hope." After a moment, he whispered, "Jill, dear Jill, don't let us ever be apart again. I want to take care of you forever."

She kissed him. She had taken the chance and now she knew. She did love Burt. She kissed him again and sighed, a sigh of contentment—and a little relief.

"I love you, Burt. I think I have loved you for a long time, but I had to be sure. I had to wait. You understand, don't you?"

He nodded. "I would have waited for you forever."

Seb was late coming down for breakfast, and when he did appear he looked exhausted, certainly too tired to take notice of the new light shining in Jill's eyes. He grunted when she asked him if he had enjoyed his night on the town. He scowled when Burt suggested they all go swimming before driving out to inspect the resort.

"Why don't you two go down with the government man and look the place over?" Judge muttered. "I've seen it already, last time I was down here."

Their government escort was eager, desperately so, that they like the place. The villa complex, though unused for two years, had been kept in excellent condition. There were twenty-five bungalows, each with its own swimming pool. No expense had been spared to make Habitation Le Coq luxurious.

"The guests, in the great days, liked this arrangement very much," their guide confided. "They could swim naked in their pools, sun themselves on the decks, make love outdoors without interference. Mixed couples, gay couples—we have always been a most tolerant nation. The gays were very important to us until all the lies were invented about AIDS. Now we want the tourists to come back and enjoy our beautiful country."

At the heart of the resort was a handsome low white building that had served as restaurant, bar, and entertainment area. Oddly, it was almost a prototype for the Wings resorts Jill had already created.

"What do you think, Burt?" They were strolling through the fragrant grounds, their guide out of earshot. "It's certainly got the right appearance."

"Yeah. It's okay to look at. But this whole place kind of gives me the creeps. That stuff last night, and the kind of action I reckon old Judge was into—hell, I know Wings caters to a fast crowd, but do you think this place is the right image for you?"

"It *is* worrying me. That and the fact that it's still a dictatorship here. The Tontons Macoutes may have a new name, but you still get the feeling if you stepped out of line you might get a midnight visit. And besides all that, I'd still have to watch over things for a while. We're stretched too thin as it is." She took his hand, a little shyly. "I think I'll pass on it," she said finally.

"Good. I was hoping you'd decide against it. Maybe I'm just biased against Judge, or maybe I'm being selfish because I don't want you working so hard all the time. But this place just doesn't feel right to me. I don't like it."

Mr. Judge, they were told, had retired to his suite until flight time, so there was no chance to talk to him. She lay by the pool with Burt and let herself luxuriate in the joy of being in love. She watched him from behind her sunglasses, seeing him anew, liking very much what she saw. A big, gentle man, he was almost too rugged to be handsome but the more pleasing for his ruggedness. She watched his rippling muscles as he pulled himself, dripping, from the pool: it was difficult to believe what a gentle lover he was. She shivered at the memory and in anticipation.

"Are you cold?" he asked anxiously, putting a towel around her shoulders. "You've got to be careful you don't catch something in places like this. Once when I was in New Guinea—"

She put a finger to his lips.

"Stop babying me, Burt. I can take care of myself." She saw the flash of hurt in his eyes. "If you must know, I was thinking about us last night and I got goosebumps." He blushed. She smiled to herself. Burt, for all his size and experience, would have to be handled with the utmost tact: she would need to suppress her take-charge attitude a little. She smiled. That was a tiny sacrifice to make for receiving so much.

Seb was back to normal by the time Burt had them in his plane and on their way to Jamaica. He waxed expansive about the beauties of Haiti, the magnificent deal he had swung for Wings. She let him go on until he declared, "We'll get the whole thing rolling inside of three months. No point in waiting. We'll get the new tourism in Haiti off to a bang with Wings."

"No, Seb," she said. "I appreciate all your efforts, really I do, but I'm not going to do it, for all kinds of reasons. I don't get the right vibes from Haiti. Also, I haven't got the staff to guarantee it'll be up to the Wings standard.

And to top it off, I'm not going to have the time to cope with all the problems it'll present.''

Very slowly, Seb turned in his seat and looked at her. For a moment the hoods lifted from over his eyes and she felt the full force of the ice-cold blue gaze.

''I never figured you for a stupid woman, Jill. I wouldn't have wasted all this time with you otherwise. You're obviously not thinking straight today. I know what you and the fly-boy got up to last night. I got chapter and verse from my people in the hotel. It's your business if you want to sleep with a jerk, but it becomes my business when it affects my interests. Before you got involved with him you were all for this project. Therefore, I suggest your judgment is clouded because of this affair.'' He waved a dismissive hand toward the flight deck. ''Use him in bed if you want, but listen to me when there's business at hand. I'm telling you, Haiti is going to be damn good business for all of us.''

She kept her anger under control. She did owe him a great deal, after all. She spoke carefully. ''Seb, I've thought this through for myself and I'm not going to do it. You've helped me enormously, but there comes a time when I have to ask myself how much further I want to go. I've reached that point. I don't want to do this. Thank you for your help, but no.''

He watched her, reading her as he was used to doing with juries. He saw a determined woman who would not be swayed, a woman made even stronger by an inner glow he hadn't seen before.

He shrugged, telling himself he shouldn't be surprised. After all, she was just a little stewardess who'd gotten lucky for a while. Now she was about to get very unlucky.

"Tell your boyfriend to change course," he said. "If you won't take Haiti, you don't get Jamaica. We may as well head straight for New York. I've wasted too much time on you as it is."

She wondered if he was bluffing and decided she didn't care. She returned his gaze and watched as the hoods came down over the eyes again. Seb Judge cut her out of his sphere of interest in three seconds.

He paid no attention to her for the rest of the flight to New York. At Kennedy, after they had passed through customs, he left her without a backward glance.

Judge stopped at Grand Central before going to his town house. He found a vacant phone booth and lined up his quarters. It was lunchtime in Houston and the number answered immediately.

"The cunt's stopped playing ball," Judge said. "She won't buy Haiti." He listened. "Yes, it's a nuisance. But we can always find some other way to use it and use Jamaica. They weren't vital, anyway. So, as far as I'm concerned, you people can move whenever you want to. She's of no further use to us."

The Boston number rang a half dozen times and he was about to hang up when the voice finally answered. You prick, Judge thought as he heard the lofty drawl, I hate bringing you good news.

"It's all fixed," he said. "It'll all start happening now and you will get what you want." He listened. "Yes, you've been patient, I know that, but a thing like this couldn't be hurried. The timetable can begin now. No, nothing can go wrong. You're going to be very happy."

Chapter Twelve _____

JEFF THOMPSON LAY ON THE STAINED mattress under the yellowed mosquito net. The air in the tiny room was fetid; when any breeze did stir it, the stench of the polluted *klong* flowing beside the small hotel was wafted into the room. He reached down for the bottle of bourbon on the floor and took a hefty swig. In the two days he had been waiting in the room, he had consumed four bottles. But the liquor had had no effect; he remained tense, fearful—waiting, as instructed. He had not yet tried to see his son—they had been precise about that. The heroin had to be collected first. Only then would he be allowed to see the child.

Later that day, he heard footsteps coming up the outside stairs and then two figures moved along the verandah outside his window. He struggled off the bed just as there was a knock on his door.

They were Vietnamese, short, solidly built men, both faces blank.

"Mr. Thompson," the younger of the pair

spoke. "We have the packages for you." He nodded to his companion, who was carrying an airline bag. "You will check the contents please."

The bag was placed on the dusty dressing table and the Vietnamese stepped back from it, waiting. At first Jeff could not move; he felt a loathing for his visitors, for the goods they had brought, and for himself.

"Hurry," the one who did the talking hissed suddenly. The silent man let his cotton jacket fall open and placed his hand on the butt of the pistol stuck in his belt.

Jeff unzipped the bag. The heroin was in four packages, each embossed with a thick red seal, a crudely drawn elephant. It was, he knew from past courier operations, the stamp that declared the product was the highest-grade, purest heroin. The contents of the bag—when cut by all the dealers who would handle it from the heart of the Golden Triangle to the streets of New York—would be worth about ten million dollars.

"It is right," the spokesman said. It was not a question.

"Yes," Jeff said, physically ill after touching the evil cargo.

"Sign," the Vietnamese ordered, slapping a handwritten form on the dressing table. It was in Thai and Jeff couldn't read a word of it, but he scrawled his name at the bottom. The Vietnamese folded the form and placed it in his wallet. They both scrutinized Jeff carefully for a few moments, as if committing his features to memory. Then they turned and left the room.

Jeff's hand was shaking as he picked up the bourbon bottle and took a big slug. Nothing, he thought, was worth this much terror. It had been different when the heroin he'd couriered was for the Agency; all of them knew there was no risk of getting caught. And if some customs man wasn't in on the arrangement and happened to do a search, the Agency fixed it.

But he wasn't working for the Agency anymore, just for a bunch of crazies who wouldn't admit the war was over, who refused to go home and live like normal people. There was no more protection for Jeff: he was on his own and looking at a mandatory death sentence if he got caught.

He reached into his wallet and took out the photograph of his son, a shy, solemn little boy gazing into the camera. He would make this last run for the child's sake and then he would return and take the child from his grandparents and bring him home. It was worth all the risks if he could achieve that.

The visit later that day was awkward: little Peter's grandfather would not leave them alone together. Jeff guessed he had been ordered not to let the boy out of his sight. His masters knew if Jeff could somehow snatch the child and escape with him, they would have no hold over him, and their heroin would not be moved.

Jeff was nearly in tears when he finally kissed Peter good-bye. It was early evening and time for his flight. In the cab, clutching the flight bag to his chest, his worst fears took over. It was dank and humid but a cold sweat soaked him. He knew he had to get himself under control or else the first official who looked at him would know he was smuggling.

With the help of more bourbon he got through the airport formalities and settled in a window seat in the rear of the plane. The rest of the passengers were tourists, tan, brightly dressed, laughing. What he would give to be so carefree again, he thought. They were bound for the beaches of Penang; maybe some of them were going to his own resort. He thought about Wings and the happiness he had found there. And about Jill, the woman who had given him his chance at success and who had, for one ecstatic night, even given herself to him. Maybe, when this terrible journey was done, when the horror was forgotten, there would be a future for him with his son and Jill. He tried to recall what her son, Jonathan, looked like, to imagine the two little boys together, with him and Jill. But all he could think of was the airline bag.

He'd been through customs at George Town many times; he knew most of the officers and tonight he was relieved to see the head man was one he'd entertained at Wings.

"Hi, Tan." Jeff smiled as he stepped over to the officer's counter. "It's good to be back.

Thailand isn't my idea of fun. Too many people, too many hassles. I wouldn't go at all if it wasn't for my child being there.'' He knew he was talking too much, prattling on nervously. They'd taught him, in the old days, the right way to act when making a run: be cool, haughty, arrogant. But the training had fled; this was real.

''Hello, Mr. Thompson,'' Tan said. He smiled, a sad smile, Jeff thought. ''Would you come straight through, please? There are some people who wish to speak with you.''

Thompson looked past the customs officer and saw three khaki-uniformed men at the back of the hall. His stomach lurched and he had to swallow hard to stop himself from throwing up. The customs man beside him, he walked across the hall to the waiting military.

It only took a couple of minutes. They hustled him into a small office, opened the airline bag, ran a basic test on the contents of one of the packets, and administered a swift, savage beating. He was only barely conscious when they carried him to a jeep and drove to George Town's jail.

Burt insisted on flying Jill out to Malaysia; he was guilt-ridden over Jeff Thompson's arrest because he had introduced Jeff to Wings, and the whole Wings organization was in jeopardy because of this. Jill herself was angry but bewildered. She thought she had known Jeff so well, a good man, an excellent administrator, loyal. And a fine lover, a memory she now blocked out in deference to her newfound love for Burt.

"Don't be so angry with Jeff," she pleaded with Burt as they waited in the public prosecutor's office in George Town. The prosecutor said nothing after the introductions were made, sitting silently at his desk, watching.

"I'll break his neck if they'll let me close enough to him," Burt swore. He was rigid with the fury that had been coursing through him from the moment they received the news in New York. "The bastard has imperiled everything you've achieved here. He's let us all down."

Jill went cold when they brought Jeff into the room. He was supported by two guards; his feet dragged behind him and his arms hung limp at his sides. There were no marks on him but it was obvious he'd been hurt severely; his eyes were dead, his body defeated. He looked at them with recognition but without hope.

"You shit!" Burt said, starting toward him. "I told you what I'd do if you fucked me over again." He raised his fist. The guards made no move to stop him. But Burt looked into the dull eyes and saw there was nothing there. He dropped his hand. "You've really done it this time. No one's going to get you out of this." Jeff nodded agreement.

"I'm sorry," he said, looking at Jill. "I didn't do it for me. You *must* believe what I tell you. They had my son and I would never have seen him again. I never wanted to bring any trouble on you. You gave me the best chance of my life." He moved his head painfully so he could look at Burt. "You won't believe me, Burt, and I don't blame you. But they forced me into doing a run for them." He glanced at the guards, who seemed not to be listening. "It's too late for me, Jill," he said. "But you be careful. There's something funny about all this; somehow, I think it was you they were trying to implicate. Something's not right about this."

"Bullshit!" Burt snapped. "You made this run for the bucks. It had nothing to do with a kid, or Jill. Why don't you try and be a man for once?"

"I don't care what you think." Jeff shrugged. "They're going to hang me anyway. The only thing I care about now is my boy. If I could have gotten him out of Thailand . . ." He slumped forward. The guards grabbed him roughly by the arms and legs and frog-marched him out of the room.

The public prosecutor rose from behind his desk. He spoke with grave politeness, addressing Jill and Burt as one.

"There is, of course, nothing that can be done for Mr. Thompson," he said. "Our laws are inflexible, for we are determined to stamp out the drug trade. The danger for you, madam, is that there will be pressure to close your resort. He was your manager, your official representative. Already I hear some people have approached my government, suggesting your license to operate here be revoked." He lowered his voice. "Large sums of money have been offered for you to be banned and the resort simply given to new owners."

"They can't do that," Jill said sharply. "I've sunk a fortune into Wings. I'd be bankrupt if I lost it. Hell, I can't be blamed for my manager's actions. It's not as though Wings were being used as a drug-trading base. Jeff acted alone."

"I understand," the prosecutor nodded. "But I am warning you there are those who would like to take over your resort."

The next weeks were hectic. Jill kept the resort going and groomed Jeff's assistant, Jenny Ferguson, to take over its management. At the same time she was diligently lobbying government officials to save her license, and she learned that the prosecutor's warning was well based. Someone was mounting an intensive campaign to have her declared persona non grata in Malaysia.

"I think you will survive all this," the prosecutor told her as she sat in his office late one afternoon. He had become her ally, guiding her through the maze of officialdom. "Mr. Thompson will pay the ultimate price for his crime and then things will settle down."

"There's no hope, no appeal?" she asked for the umpteenth time. "I mean, if I just gave up everything, gave Wings to your government or whoever seems to want it so much, could I save Jeff?''

He shook his head. They had covered the same ground over and over.

''Our laws are inflexible when it comes to serious drug offenses. I am sorry to see a young man die, but there is nothing to be done.''

She visited Jeff once more before she left Malaysia. He seemed in better shape physically than in the days right after his arrest. He was pale and thin, but there were no more beatings.

''They want a whole body for the trial,'' he said. ''No point in stringing up a body that's half-dead already.'' He tried to smile but it was a twisted grimace. ''I'm resigned now. Except for my son. I have nightmares every night where I see Peter in exactly the same situation I'm in now: sitting in a prison cell waiting to be executed. It's not just a dream, either. It could be his fate. His grandfather is the conduit for a hell of a lot of the heroin passing through Chiang Mai.''

Jill was shocked: was there no end to the things she hadn't known about Jeff?

Back in Honolulu, reunited with Jonathan, Jeff's anguish was intensified for her. She had long since forgiven him for the heroin run. She knew, when she looked at Jonathan, that she'd have done the same thing to save her son.

Her friend the prosecutor called from George Town. The connection was bad but his message was clear.

"Mr. Thompson has escaped," he said. "Someone outside engineered it. The seaplane you kept at Wings? It is gone, too. There is no trace of Mr. Thompson. For your sake, he must be found soon. The government has shut down your resort, seizing it as a bond against Mr. Thompson's return to stand trial."

She consulted lawyers in Hawaii; Jenny Ferguson camped on the doorstep of the American consul in George Town; Burt told all his old flying cronies in the Far East he wanted Thompson found. But nothing happened.

Wings stayed shut and her whole empire was in jeopardy. The banks, recently so eager to lend her money to expand, began demanding fresh collateral because, without Wings in Penang, the whole Wings structure was coming apart.

She even tried calling Seb Judge. On the fourth attempt he agreed to speak with her. He was cold, distant.

"You're out of your depth, Jill," he said. "The banks don't like being involved in a scandal like this, and your cash flow is going to be so diminished with the Malaysia resort shut down that they'll have grounds to foreclose on you." He sighed. "I gave you your chance but you wouldn't take it. Now I must look after my own clients, the people I got to invest in Wings. We'll try a scheme, put in some more capital, get the whole Wings on a sound footing.''

''Where would that leave me, Seb?'' she asked, barely succeeding in keeping her voice flat.

''Nowhere,'' he said. ''You'll come out with a little money when everything's cleaned up, but I don't believe it's desirable for you to be involved in the management any longer. Wings will be turned over to professionals.''

''I'll see you in hell first,'' she said quietly and hung up.

Burt took charge. For all her defiance of Seb, Jill felt beaten. She knew her balance sheets well enough—God knew, she had worried over them for years. She knew she couldn't operate with one quarter of her empire shut down. The borrowing to establish the Greek resort was a burden she could bear only if every part of the Wings chain was functioning. Two good years were all she'd have needed, but now she was sunk.

''Don't give up,'' Burt ordered. ''We've still got a few weeks to get everything straightened out. I've arranged to pay this quarter's interest charges, so that gives you some time. Keep the other Wings going until we see what happens.''

''I can't take money from you, Burt,'' she protested, close to crying. ''I'm not going to drag you down with me.''

''I'm going in the morning,'' he said. ''If

you need any help, Carl Cohen is standing by.
He'll know where to find me if anything urgent comes up.''

Burt hated being a passenger but it was the
most unobtrusive way he could arrive in Hong
Kong; he gazed down mournfully at the
dense-packed city as the jet did a hard turn to
starboard and dropped down on to Kai Tak.
He didn't relax until they were alongside the
terminal.

The message he'd received in Honolulu
from the stewardess had been like something
out of a movie. The piece of white stationery
had written on it: ''Your old copilot needs to
see you in the Kimberly.''

''Where did you get this, Gloria?'' he'd
asked her.

''The letter was in my box when I went to
get my key at the Sheraton,'' she'd said. ''Addressed to me. Inside the envelope was the
message for you. I figure it's from someone
who knew I'd be flying to Honolulu. But
that's *all I want to know* about it, Burt.''

He sat in the taxi and sweated as they
inched through the Nathan Road traffic and
turned into Kimberly Road. He paid the taxi
driver a block before the faded white building.
It looked as decrepit as ever, laundry hanging
from the tiny balconies. He remembered it all,
the smell and clutter of the place, the way the
other residents walked softly with downcast
eyes. The Kimberly Hilton, he and Jeff had

christened it ironically, back in the days when they were both always broke and it offered a room for six dollars a night. The rest of the tenants were prostitutes and small-time hustlers, and a few old men for whom the Chinese family system had failed. It was seedy, sad, suitable for a fugitive.

Burt prodded the ancient *amah* dozing in a chair by the front door. She could have been the same woman from all those years ago when he and Jeff had stayed in the flophouse: the same toothless smile when he extended a handful of Hong Kong dollars, the shrill Cantonese when he asked where the American was.

He trudged up six flights of concrete stairs. The top-floor door was closed. He banged on it loudly and heard rustling inside.

"It's me. Burt."

The door opened slowly. He walked in only far enough to stand in the doorway. Jeff was on the far side of the room, holding a pistol pointed at Burt's chest.

"Come in quickly and shut the door," Jeff said. "Sit there on the bed and don't move. I've got to tell you some things. I'm sorry about this," he added, glancing down at his gun, "but I figured you'd just beat the shit out of me if I didn't get time to talk to you."

Burt nodded. "You're thinking right," he said. "But you look like hell. I almost didn't recognize you."

"Yeah, and living in this flop doesn't help.

But as for my new yellow coloring—I got hepatitis in the George Town jail.'' He shrugged. ''It doesn't matter. I'm dead, whatever happens. But I owe you and I owe Jill.'' With the gun still pointed at Burt's chest, he reached inside his grubby shirt and drew out a thick envelope.

''It's all written here,'' he said. ''That guy Jill sent out to inspect the operation? Oram? He's someone I used to know when I . . . worked for the Agency. He forced me to do the run, threatened to take my boy if I didn't. I had to go along. But the funny thing was, as soon as I hit customs I knew I'd been set up. Oram and his people *wanted* me caught. He sent someone to see me in prison. The guy said his group wanted to take over the Wings operation, and they thought getting me busted would help.''

''We've heard the same thing,'' Burt said.

''Well, apparently the scheme didn't work. Jill wasn't implicated. She has friends in high places and the resort has an unblemished reputation. The authorities in George Town were content just to have my carcass. So Oram and his crowd had to do something else.'' Jeff rubbed a hand across his eyes. ''Oram's man said I had to make a statement implicating Jill and Wings in the heroin deal, saying the drugs were for our customers, a service we'd provided for some time.''

''And if you didn't make the statement?''

''They'd kill my son.'' He glanced down at

the pistol, now shaking in his hand. "Burt, for Christ's sake, let me put this thing away. You'll hear me out now, won't you?"

Burt nodded and Jeff sank into a chair, dropping the pistol on the bed.

"I knew it wasn't an idle threat. These people are tough. So I busted out of jail. You've seen the George Town prison. It was easy to get out of. I got to Wings, took the seaplane, and flew down to Sarawak where I knew there was a guy who'd help me. He fixed me up with a false passport and enough money to get here."

"You know I'm going to have to take you back with me," Burt said slowly. "Because Oram, or whoever's behind all this, has gotten what he wanted because of your escape. Wings has been closed."

Then Jeff surprised him.

"I'm going back with you. That's why I sent for you." He shuddered and gulped from a bottle of whiskey. "My diseased liver can't take this stuff anymore, but what the hell. Burt, I need one last favor. I've got no right to ask, but I'm going to. Will you come with me to Thailand and help snatch my kid? If we do that, Oram's got no hold over me. We could use one of your planes for the run, be in and out of there in one day. Then I'll come back with you and give myself up. I've got a few grand stashed away for the boy's keep. Maybe he could stay at Wings? I'll give you power of attorney over the money. I'll also give you a sworn statement of what Oram's man asked me to do to damage Jill. It's all here, in the envelope.''

He tossed the bulky package to Burt, who caught it.

''Actually,'' Jeff continued, ''she shouldn't need the statement, not when you deliver me back to them.''

''I shouldn't do this for you,'' Burt said wearily. ''You've let me down twice now. Worse, you've hurt Jill. But I guess I believe you about the child.'' He stood up. He wanted out of that awful little room, away from the sadness and desperation. ''I'll be in touch. It'll take me a day or two to round up the right plane.''

It was, in the end, easy. Burt found that his company had a chartered jet arriving in Hong Kong the next night. He flew it to Chiang Mai with Jeff as copilot. Brydon Airlines was well known throughout the East and no one hassled them about their flight plans or anything.

Peter and his grandparents were living in a squalid apartment block near the town center; Burt and Jeff parked their rented car in the narrow street and walked up the four floors to the grandparents' flat. It was a grim slum, the end of the line. The grandparents, it was obvious, were not getting much out of their work in the drug trade. They were trapped in the system and would stay there, just as the smiling little boy would stay there, trapped. He ran to hug Jeff's legs when Jeff and Burt walked into the apartment.

They talked in Thai, Burt knowing enough of the language to be able to help Jeff's scheme along with a word or two. Burt, Jeff told the old man, was here to make a major buy. He would be sampling the product in the evening. In the meantime Jeff was going to show the newcomer around and he intended taking the little boy along for the outing. The old man didn't like letting the child out of his custody, but there was little he could do about it: his visitors were big, muscular, and determined. And if the bearded one was going to make a major buy, perhaps he would be able to wangle himself a commission somehow. So he shrugged and stood aside, letting them take the boy.

They drove straight to the airport, through the airport perimeter, and strolled through the aircrew gate out to the tarmac where the 727 sat waiting; Burt had ordered it refueled and they would make the flight to George Town in one leg.

Jeff had been shaking from the time they entered the old man's apartment, a mixture of fear and jaundice. Once they were safely in the plane and cleared for takeoff, he settled down. They completed their climb to cruising altitude and he held his son in his lap, watching with delight as the child stared at the instrument panel, fascinated.

Apart from the usual pre-takeoff checks,

Burt hadn't said a word since they'd left the apartment. He knew how precious was every moment Jeff had with the boy. A few minutes after takeoff, he stole a glance at his copilot and saw tears in his eyes.

"Oh, shit," Burt said roughly, blinking back his own tears. "I'll take care of the boy. Don't worry about his future. I'll raise him to be a pilot, like his old man, who, apart from being a fuckup, was always a damn good flyer. By the time they free you—"

"They're not going to free me, Burt. You know that. There was too much of the stuff, and the government's having a crackdown on foreign smugglers. No, it's all over for me."

"Maybe you can throw yourself on the mercy of the court? Plead duress or something?"

"Burt, I know what's waiting for me back there. All I want is for the boy to be looked after and no retribution to be taken against Jill and Wings. The documents I gave you should insure that." He smiled shyly and looked Burt full in the eyes. "I figured you'd come to my rescue yet again: one of the papers I've given you makes you his guardian. Thanks, Burt. I couldn't have turned to anybody else."

They circled a couple of times over George Town and made one sweep past Wings, gleaming white in the sun, a jewel in the blue sea. Burt took the jet down and taxied up to the terminal.

"How do you want to do this?" he asked

gently. ''You don't want the boy to see you . . .''

''Being arrested, handcuffed, beaten . . . ? No. What I'd like you to do, Burt, the one last favor, is take the boy through first. Tell them you've brought me back and I'm waiting for them out on the tarmac.''

Later Burt would wonder if he'd sensed Jeff's intent all along. He climbed down the steps of the plane, briefcase of documents in one hand and the tiny fingers of the child clinging to the other. He marched straight across the tarmac and into the customs hall. Sammy Lum, an officer he knew well, was the only person on duty.

''Hi, Sammy,'' he said. ''You better get some police over here. I've brought back Jeff Thompson. He's waiting out there for you. This is his boy,'' he said, patting Peter's head. ''I'd like to take him away before the trouble starts.''

Lum waved them through. He was already shouting for the police when they heard the single shot. Burt kept moving, almost too fast for the child to keep up, striding out of the airport and into a cab. It was two days before he could steel himself to look at the newspaper closeups of the body of Jeff Thompson sprawled on the tarmac, the little automatic clutched in his lifeless hand. He had, the papers said, saved the nation the trouble of a trial that would surely have ended with the death penalty. The prosecutor said that although

Thompson had been manager of the Wings resort, he accepted that the owners and staff of the resort had not been involved in Thompson's drug running.

Back in Honolulu Jill cried, off and on, for two days. She took Peter to her bosom and clutched him protectively. She would always see to his welfare, she swore.

"Burt," she sobbed, "what a waste of a young man's life. I'm responsible for his death. If they hadn't wanted to get at Wings, this wouldn't have happened."

He tried to console her; he loved her, and one of the things he loved most was her capacity to care for others.

"Marry me now," he whispered as they lay in bed in her bungalow, the tropic moon pouring in the window as if none of the tragedy had happened.

"Soon," she said. "Soon. Give me time to get over all this," she begged. And then she spelled out the thing that had also been troubling Burt for a long time: "I've got to discover who's trying to destroy me, and why."

Chapter Thirteen _____

SEB JUDGE TRIED NOT TO BREATHE IN the phone booth: it smelled as if a family of six had been living there for months. He waited impatiently for his ring to be answered.

"It doesn't matter, the Malaysian thing," Judge said. "So Thompson let us down, with his stupid sense of loyalty. It still shut Wings down for a while, and she's on her knees now. We can complete the take-over after the big event."

He listened, nodding.

"Yes, it's time to unleash the dogs. Washington won't give us any trouble, I've been assured of that. No one will even know, officially, that we're behind it. Let the coon take all the glory. Then we'll all have what we want." He listened, nodded again, and hung up.

Carl Cohen was on the phone, too, but he didn't have to use phone booths. Technicians from Langley, Virginia, had years before installed a sophisticated scrambler telephone in his quiet house among the orchids. They still serviced it regularly and Cohen knew it was safe to talk to any of his old contacts on that phone. He made four calls that morning before he was satisfied he had the whole picture. Only then did he stroll out into the garden where Jill nervously awaited him. He took his time, ordering fresh green tea for them, showing Jill a prize new bloom he'd imported, admiring the fine day. Then he settled down, sighed, and told her.

''David's father is the prime mover against you. He got himself involved with Sebastian Judge and a group of extreme right-wing Texans who all had a single purpose for varying reasons: the taking over of Wings. Most of them are ex-Agency people, emptied out of Langley in President Carter's purge. They want Wings because they see it as the ideal cover to get them back in the intelligence business. The Malay resort, the Greek Islands, Haiti and Jamaica if you'd gone along there . . . all are close to places of great interest even to the current CIA masters. They thought they could get back in favor by providing safe houses via your various Wings resorts. They also genuinely admire your little business and wouldn't mind making quite a lot of money out of it while playing superpatriots at the same time. Finally, there's the real clincher—Garokan. Stir up a revolution, install their own man, create a new nation with no rules.'' He sipped his tea. ''The only thing I don't understand is why old Nagle has been so particularly venomous about you. The others in the scheme have been patient, letting things roll along, but he's been screaming for action for months now. He wants you destroyed, quickly, and his motives don't seem to be solely right-wing or solely mercenary.''

''Why?'' She was at sea.

''My dear Jill,'' he said patiently, ''that I don't know. I think only you could find that out. In the meantime, it's essential you keep Wings afloat. The Thompson affair hurt you badly, and when the trouble comes on Garokan . . .''

''But surely,'' she protested, ''now that you know about this crazy scheme to start a war, they'll be stopped.''

He shook his head. ''I know of the scheme, as do a few people in Washington. But no one will act until they actually start their revolution. And then, if they have swift success, it may be too late to do anything. You must realize, Garokan's brave attempt to remain neutral does not endear it to either of the great powers. There are people in Washington who wouldn't completely disapprove of these people taking over.''

''But if there's a war on Garokan . . .'' She stopped, thinking of all the implications. ''My business will be shot to pieces. I'm only getting by now on Burt's charity. Any more setbacks and I'm through.''

''I've been thinking about your problems

and I've come up with a solution,'' he said. ''You have many friends. As for the war, perhaps when it starts I'll be able to exert some pressure in the right places. Meanwhile, there remains the mystery of Mr. Nagle and his campaign against you. It seems much more spirited, more spiteful, than merely a desire not to have his proud name involved in the resorts business. What's behind it?''

She kissed him.

''You say I've got friends, Carl. I need only one friend when I've got you. It's time the Nagles and I sorted this whole thing out. I'll fly to Boston tomorrow.''

He wouldn't take her call. His secretary was firm, almost rude. Yes, Mr. Nagle knew who was trying to reach him. Yes, he was in his office. No, he would not speak to her.

Jill took a cab to the Nagle mansion, marched determinedly up the wide gravel drive. It was eerie, approaching her late husband's boyhood home like that, the twilight making the house loom large before her. She looked at the broad lawns and thought of the young David playing there. David had been sad amid all this grandeur; she had had a secure childhood in the little walk-up apartment in Chicago.

She climbed the steps to the imposing main doors and found the bellpull. She could hear the bell tingle somewhere in back of the house, then slow footsteps until the door opened.

"Good afternoon, madam." The stiff butler made it more of a question than a greeting.

"I've come to see Mrs. Nagle. Would you tell her Jill Nagle is here?"

"I shall see if the mistress is receiving," he said. "Perhaps you would care to wait in the hall." He bowed her into a large reception area and silently vanished into the depths of the house. Jill waited a few moments, and then the butler was back.

"I'm sorry, Mrs. Nagle," he said. "Madam is not receiving today."

Jill gave him her sweetest smile.

"She probably didn't catch my name. I'll just go speak to her myself." She stepped around him, brushing off the hand reaching out to stop her, and started off down the hall, heading where the butler had gone. She found Celia Nagle easily, sitting stiff and alone before a roaring fire in a small sitting room off the main hall. Jill stood in the doorway unobserved for a moment and looked at her mother-in-law. The woman was quite old now but more than age had withered her. She appeared to be willing herself to sit upright; she had an unhealthy pallor and there were two red blotches on her cheeks. Jill took in the large, half-empty glass on the table by the woman's elbow. She coughed, but Mrs. Nagle continued to stare into the fire. Finally she went into the room.

"Don't blame the butler," Jill said. "But I insisted on seeing you. Your husband refused to take my call, so I decided to come here and meet with you. I've come a long way—"

"It's no use. You must leave at once. I have nothing to say to you." The voice meant to exercise command, but it was slurred and cracked. Jill's suspicion was confirmed: Celia Nagle was a lush.

"You could at least offer me a drink," Jill said. "I've brought some photos of Jonathan. I'm sure there must be some neutral ground between us."

The mention of her grandson stirred something in Mrs. Nagle. She raised a limp hand to the butler hovering nervously by the door.

"Get . . . get the young woman what she would like, Masters."

"A martini, please," Jill said brightly. "Straight up, very dry, an olive."

"You can't come bursting in here black-mailing us with photographs of David's child," the woman said crossly. She had some difficulty focusing on Jill. "All that is in the past. We have put it out of our minds. David made his choice and had to live with it."

Jill waited until the drink was at her elbow and the butler had withdrawn and closed the door behind him. She watched the firelight reflect in the beads of condensation on the glass and sipped gratefully at the strong cocktail.

"I'm not here to blackmail you," she said quietly to Celia Nagle. "I am here to discover why you and your husband are hell-bent on destroying me. In the past few days I've learned precisely what's been done to me and what's planned. Now I want to know *why*. I never did a thing to you. I tried and tried to re-unite you with your son. I loved him so much, I couldn't understand why you didn't feel the same way."

"Get me another drink, please, from the de-canter," the old woman said. She watched Jill cross the room and return with a crystal con-tainer of brandy. She nodded when her glass was filled again, and reached out a hand to touch Jill's. "We have been terrible to you," she said. "I'm sorry." She gulped her drink. "Could I . . . could I see the pictures? Please?"

Jill took the pictures from her bag and passed them over silently. She was surprised at the flat admission. Why had Mrs. Nagle said that? Did she believe it?

She watched her mother-in-law blinking over the pictures, trying to hold back the tears.

"A beautiful little boy," the woman said. "So like his father. Thank you for showing them to me." She hesitated, suddenly shy. "Do you think I could keep one?"

"Of course." She rushed ahead. "If the pair of you would stop this insane feud against me, you wouldn't need a picture of Jonathan. You could see him whenever you like. I want him to know his grandparents, to try and know his father through you. I don't understand you and I never have. What's wrong with you?''

The brandy was drained and Jill moved for the decanter without being asked. The old woman nodded as her glass was filled again. She began to talk then, her words badly slurred. ''No one can possibly understand what it's been like, being forced to cut yourself off from your son for so many years, and then from your grandson.''

''Nobody forced you to—''

''It *was* forced on me!'' she said fiercely. She paled, the alcohol blossoms on her cheeks even brighter. ''It was. There was never anything I could do about it.'' She shivered and a little brandy spilled from the glass onto the shawl covering her knees.

''Well, you're going to have to do something about it. I have enough evidence to take your husband and Seb Judge to court for conspiracy, not just against me but against the interests of the nation. All I want to know, before I act, is *why*. Why did you do all this to me?''

''You're very strong, aren't you?'' the old woman muttered. ''Perhaps if I'd been strong . . .'' She put her head in her hands and began to sob. Jill waited. ''I think I am going to tell you what happened,'' Mrs. Nagle finally said. ''It would be a relief to tell someone, and you, of all people, deserve to know.''

There was no farewell party when David

Nagle shipped out for Vietnam, Celia Nagle told Jill. She, with memories of young men being farewelled at dances in the Ritz-Carlton before heading out to World War II, had wanted to organize something for her son. But her husband was bitterly opposed to the boy's going to Vietnam. And he had the support of Marion, David's wife of two months. Father and Marion were united in contempt: if David insisted on climbing into uniform, there could be a comfortable Pentagon job for him until he came to his senses and joined the Nagle firm. But he was going off to be cannon fodder. Celia was bewildered by their hatred but powerless before it. John had always dominated her, and now, in Marion, John had a new ally, as tough and unrelenting as he was.

So Celia went alone to see him fly away to the war, dashing in his crisp officer's uniform, pain in his clear blue eyes. She tried to patch things up. It was natural, she told her son, that Marion would be bitter over losing his company so soon after their marriage. And his father entertained such high hopes for him in the Nagle business. Just give them time to get used to it all, Celia told David. They would all be one loving family again soon, she knew.

''Poor Mother,'' he said, bending to kiss her cheek. ''Such an optimist after all these years. We've never been 'one loving family' and we never will be. We're Nagles! That's just one of the reasons I'm going. I have to break out of the pattern. I thought Marion understood, even if I never expected Father would. But it seems she was marrying a name, not a person." His mother winced. Poor Mother, he thought, all those years of putting up with the old man's philandering, pretending it wasn't happening. And the pompousness of it all, as if the Nagles were some kind of royalty. He would be damn glad to be away from them. If Marion came to her senses, well and good. She was beautiful and dangerous and he had been attracted to her from the moment they met at the Yale game the previous fall. He knew they shouldn't have rushed into marriage, but events had gotten out of hand: she had so many suitors; his own father for once totally approved of one of his girls; the war was getting worse. So he had plunged into marriage with a girl he scarcely knew, and now, it seemed, the marriage was already over. Her bitter words of the night before had told him that.

"Don't think I'm going to sit around being a Boston matron while you play hero. You bastard, David! You immature bastard."

He wanted to make love to her—their passion was the only thing that overcame the terrible rifts between them—but she shoved him away.

"I guess things will all work out, Mother," he lied. "And I promise I won't take any risks over there."

Celia cried all the way back home, not caring that the chauffeur kept glancing at her in his mirror. As she watched her son's tall, proud figure striding across the tarmac, she'd felt all the good things coming to an end.

Even the glorious summer on Cape Cod could not lift Celia's spirits. While the round of parties went on, she stayed inside the huge, rambling old summer house reading and listening to the news from Vietnam, imagining her boy flying over those foreign jungles. She began to hate her husband and daughter-in-law: they carried on as if it were just another summer. They went to the parties together, played games, entertained others. All Celia had were the nightmares: within a week of David's embarkation she was taking pills to help her sleep and John had moved to another bedroom so she wouldn't be disturbed.

The night a bad summer storm hit the Cape was a particularly bad one for Celia. Even the pills would not stop her dreams, dreams of fiery crashes, of helicopters falling from the sky like wounded geese, of David broken and maimed, dying in a rice paddy.

The thunder and lightning pulled her into full wakefulness. The shutters were trying to tear themselves from their frames and water was seeping in her windows, forced in by the driving gale. Celia felt real terror then and she stumbled from her bed to find help. She blundered down the corridor to the room John had taken and felt through the dark room to his bed. It was empty. She became even more panic-stricken. What if he were out in the storm? Along the corridor was Marion's room and Celia headed for it. She had to speak to another human being. She tapped on Marion's door but realized no one could hear her above the thunder, so she opened the door and stepped inside.

A sudden series of lightning bolts illuminated the room and she saw clearly the tall, gaunt figure of her husband naked on top of Marion, writhing and jerking in passion as if propelled by the storm. Celia shoved her hands against her mouth but nothing could muffle the scream that burst from her; it was so piercing, so heartrending, it rose above the noise of the storm and the passion on the bed.

John Nagle turned to the doorway and saw his wife standing there. She could see mad lust in his eyes—and anger, anger at her! In shock, Celia wondered what she had done to make him angry. She feared his rages. She'd always tried to please him. Now he was shouting at her, ''Get out! Get out!'' And he climbed out of bed and advanced on her, his fists clenched, his huge erection threatening.

She slammed the door and ran back down the corridor to her room, flung herself on her bed, and began to cry bitter, hopeless tears. That he could betray her was one thing; that he could do it with his son's new bride was something far more evil. She would leave in the morning, leave the shelter of the massive Nagle summer mansion.

At breakfast, the storm over, the events of

the night before an ugly dream, Celia was less sure about leaving. She was, she knew, essentially a weak woman. How would she cope on her own? Whom would her departure help? Not her son. There was no rage in her by then, just a numb, sick bewilderment. John came down to breakfast and gruffly ignored her, taking scrambled eggs, bacon and sausage, juice and coffee from the maid. She watched him eating at the other end of the long table in the bright breakfast room. She became physically ill and would have run from the table, but Marion entered, beautiful, tough Marion. Her eyes were puffy from sleep and sex. Her hands on her hips, eyes flashing, she spoke.

"Last night, Celia," Marion said, "what you saw. What are you planning to do about it?" It was a challenge, tough and direct.

Celia couldn't speak. She fumbled with her napkin, staring down into her lap to conceal her tears. She stole a glance at John but there was no help there: he was gazing into his coffee cup, not remorseful, content to let Marion take over.

"If I were you, Celia, I wouldn't do anything," Marion snapped. "Because I'm pregnant, and it can't be by David. You make any trouble and I'll tell him who the father of my child is. What will that do to your family? If you just keep quiet and accept the situation between John and me, no one needs to be hurt. I'll write David today and tell him the happy news that he's going to be a father."

303

"John?" Celia managed at last. "This can't be—"

"It is," he snapped, "and you'd better listen to Marion. We want this child. The Nagle family needs a new heir. David's proved himself unfit."

"But . . ." She was foundering badly. "But David will *know* the child's not his when he sees him growing up. A father can always tell, can't he?"

"I'll have divorced him before the child's a year old," Marion said. "I would have, anyway. Our marriage was a stupid mistake. I thought David had some sense, for God's sake."

"Don't speak of him like that!" Celia shouted. "Don't you dare speak of my son that way after what you've done to him!"

"Not just me," Marion said smoothly. "His father, too." She sat down and poured herself coffee. "You'll get used to the arrangement, Celia. We'll be one happy family. Although, after the child is born, I intend spending most of my time in New York. You'll have the baby to raise, if you want to."

In a strange, hopeless way, Celia Nagle got used to the arrangement. Her heart ached for David but there was nothing to be gained by revealing the hideous truth. Celia allowed herself to retreat into a dreamworld, drifting through life as a proper Boston matron, shut off from the rest of the world by wealth, privilege, and heavy secret drinking.

John's incestuous love affair with Marion went on, but at least not under her own roof anymore. The boy, young David, was fit and healthy and Celia's one joy. Alcohol was always there. The only thing threatening her was Marion's increasing demands. As the years passed, Marion wanted more money from them, more freedom, more authority. She got everything she wanted because she held over them the ultimate threat: she would tell both her ex-husband and, as he grew older, her son who his father really was. Even John Nagle, so arrogant at the beginning of things, gradually bowed under the weight of Marion's threats. He became bitter and resentful but he was trapped, just as Celia was trapped. It wasn't just fear of exposure, of being a pariah in the world he was used to ruling. It was the certainty that, if the truth came out, he would lose the love and respect of the only person he loved, the boy who thought he was John's grandson.

"So you see, Jill," Celia Nagle said, staring red-eyed into the fire, "there was nothing we could do but live this lie for all these years. I was not allowed to make overtures to David while he was alive. Marion wouldn't hear of it. John didn't care much, anyway. He was terrified that if we got close again, David would discover the truth. He was relieved to have David away from David Junior. We lived for years in some kind of truce and then David married you. It enraged Marion. She didn't want my son for herself, but she sure didn't want him to have anyone else. As you two got more successful and happier and happier, her spite turned into rage. She ordered John to run you out of business. Even after David died she was still full of hate. She said the boy was showing interest in who you were, what his father had been like. You had to be gotten off the public stage, she said.''

After more brandy, Celia continued.

''She put on even more pressure after you and young David met, saying you were dangerous, you had to be stopped. And that,'' she sighed, ''is all I have to tell you.''

There was a great wound in Jill, and rage over what these people had done to the man she loved, to the young man they had so cruelly deceived. She thought about David Junior, their evenings together, how much like her husband he seemed.

''Thank you for telling me all this, Mrs. Nagle,'' she said softly.

''I had to tell you. I've lived with it too long. And you deserve to know. Because he *is* going to ruin you, you know. He has no choice. John has to do as he's told.'' She shuddered. ''I don't know where all this will end. I'm so afraid. He and his partners are going to take over an island where you operate.''

She looked at Jill one last time. ''Remember, he has no choice where Marion is concerned.''

Chapter Fourteen _____

"THIS IS ABOUT AS BAD AS IT GETS," Woody told her apologetically. "The only good thing about our wet season is, it's only for two months. But for those two months, there's an average of five inches a day, *every day.*"

She and Jill stared glumly out of the bar into the noon dark of the rain-lashed road. Nothing stirred; even the scrawny chickens had taken refuge under the pub's verandah. Jill was waiting for Biggles to arrive and tell her when he was willing to attempt the flight to Sabot.

"People go crazy in the wet," Woody continued, pouring them both a drink. "Someone who has, say, two gins regularly before lunch turns into an alcoholic in the rainy season. A couple who've lived happily together for ten months are suddenly at each other's throats. Mothers discover they hate their children. Everybody gets cranky. Even me."

Jill grinned wryly.

"Yes," she said, "I'm on a pretty short fuse myself."

She had flown in the day before and gone straight to see President Tovare. He was as imperturbable as ever when she told him about the plot being hatched on Sabot.

"Our defense force is tiny," he said. "Just the police, the military band, and one platoon of regulars. There is nothing we could do to stop a determined attack. We must just pray it doesn't happen." He smiled sadly. "At least, if there is trouble, it will not affect you at Wings. No guests in the wet, eh?"

"Uh . . . no, just a skeleton staff." She couldn't understand the man's attitude, more concerned for her operation than for his own government. "Look," she said desperately, "couldn't you ask for outside help? Some troops to fight on your side?"

He shook his head.

"No. Our policy of nonalignment means that no one will come to our aid." They sat a moment and listened to the rain thundering on the corrugated-iron roof of his office. "Thank you for your concern, and I appreciate that this—if it happens—is none of your doing. You're not to blame. All we can do is wait and see what happens."

Woody was watching her across the bar.

"You're a worried girl," the old woman said. "Is it the funny business going on on Sabot?"

Jill nodded. "What have you heard?"

The usual crazy talk you hear in the wet. The Sabots are gearing up to take over Garo-

kan, aided by those cargo cultists from Latakia. *And* fifty or so tough-looking guys who
definitely aren't natives.''

''It's not just crazy talk, Woody. They mean
business.''

''Hell, it won't alter anything here. What's
to take? This place is worthless. Wings is the
only thing to happen here since Independence
and it won't make any difference to you who's
in power. Or to me.''

''Yes it will,'' Jill said fiercely. ''This isn't
just tribal rivalries we're talking about. There
are some very ruthless people stirring this pot.
If they get their way, Garokan will never be
the same.''

''Amen to that,'' Biggles said, splashing
into the bar. The pilot was drenched, despite
the oversized multicolored golf umbrella he was
using for shelter. ''Any changes in Garokan
could only be for the better.''

''You people! You're both as bad as your
president,'' Jill said, exasperated. ''You don't
give a damn what happens to your country.
You'd let a bunch of pirates take over without
lifting a finger.''

''We do care, but there's not much we can
do about it, honey,'' Woody said soothingly.
''Old Tovare's right. We're in no shape to resist anyone.''

''Well, *I'm* going to do something about it,''
Jill said. ''Biggles, when do you think you can
get me over there?''

''This afternoon, I guess. There's been an

hour's break in the rain around four P.M. every day for the past week. We could get in and out in that time.''

Jill went into Woody's office to use the radiotelephone.

''Cindy?'' she shouted. The connection was bad. ''It's Jill. I'm at Woody's. I'm coming over this afternoon. Will you get one of the boys to wait for me at the airstrip? What do you mean, I *can't* come? I'm damn well on my way.''

She was angrier than ever. Even through the bad connection there'd been no mistaking Cindy's tone. She'd been shocked at the idea of Jill's arrival. Well, revolution or no revolution, she was still the owner of Wings and she would drop in whenever she damn well pleased. The idea!

Even with all Biggles's flying skills, it was a hairy landing at Sabot. The strip, not in the best shape anyway, was under a couple of inches of water and the little plane bucked and skidded when Biggles put it down.

''I can't wait around, love,'' he said to Jill. ''Got to get back before the rain starts again. I see your jeep's waiting for you, so I guess you'll be okay.'' He looked at her with that endearing crooked smile. ''You take it easy, hear? If any trouble breaks out, keep your head down.''

She scrambled out of the plane and picked her way across the strip. The driver in the waiting jeep did not get out to greet her. It was Oram.

"I've been wondering if you'd show up," he growled when she climbed into the front seat. "Judge figured you would." He threw the jeep savagely into gear. "You shouldn't have come. Nothing you can do will stop what's going to happen."

"You seem to forget, Mr. Oram, this is *my* resort. If you think I'd let a bunch of lunatics like you and your employers go ahead and ruin everything I've done, you don't know me at all."

"We'll see about you." He shrugged. "Who knows, maybe you can be useful to us. As useful as little Cindy has been."

There was nothing more to say; they bumped down the track, past the village, and out on the coral road to the edge of the lagoon. The skies opened again as the jeep stopped, and they were thoroughly drenched before they had settled in the dugout canoe. It was the heaviest rain she had ever seen, sheeting down as if they were actually underwater.

Cindy came running down the beach to meet them, her clothes plastered to her. She held out her hands to Jill; the look in her eye was pleading. She got a cold stare in return.

"Cindy," Oram ordered, "take Jill up to your bungalow. Both of you stay there—out of harm's way. We're going into Phase Red now. If I have to, I'll put armed guards on you. Just see that Jill cooperates, and there won't be any need for that."

When they were inside the bungalow, water streaming from them, Jill turned on her old friend.

"You didn't listen to me!" she cried. "Look what you've gotten us into. Those lunatics are about to start a *war*. We're smack in the middle of a war! People are going to get killed because you wouldn't see the truth about Jean-Paul."

Cindy wanted to defy her but the whole situation was out of control. She sank down in a chair, her head in her hands, and began to cry.

"I'm sorry, Jill," she sobbed. "You were right. All along, Jean-Paul was only using me. But I was so in love with him." She sobbed harder. "Now I don't know what's going to happen."

Jill let her cry. She was so angry with Cindy, but the girl had been cruelly betrayed by a man who had never loved her at all.

"What's the situation?" she asked. "What are they going to do? Do you know?"

Cindy nodded. "They'll start the revolution in the next couple of days." She stopped crying. "First they take over the government post on Sabot. There are only ten policemen there, so there'll be little resistance. Then they've got this powerful radio transmitter which can ride over Radio Garokan. They're going to proclaim a new republic and order everyone in Petit Bougainville to lay down their arms. If they don't, they'll send a force across and attack them. Jill," Cindy said desperately, "there are at least fifty foreigners here, real professional soldiers, *plus* the Sabots *and* a bunch of crazies from Latakia. They're going to succeed, I think."

"And Jean-Paul? He's going to be the new president?"

"They'll let him call himself that, but it won't mean a thing," Cindy said scornfully. "He's just their dupe. They're using him but he can't see it. Oram is running this show and, believe me, the first sign of trouble from Jean-Paul, they'll get rid of him. But for now, Jean-Paul is living out his dream of conquering Garokan."

"How do they treat you?"

"I'm kind of under house arrest," she said. "I'm supposed to keep out of the way. But I know their plans because . . ." She blushed and looked out the window. "Because Jean-Paul still visits me most nights. The poor bastard really believes he's in control of this army—just the way I believed he loved me." She stood up. "I'm very sorry I got you into this, Jill. Now you're a prisoner too. There's not a thing we can do to stop this from happening."

They were clustered around the old radio in Woody's bar, straining to hear the announcement above the constant drumming of rain on the roof. All day Radio Garokan had been jammed; periodically a strange voice advised all to stay tuned for an important announcement. Now, above the static and the rain, came the excited, self-important voice of Jean-Paul.

"Fellow citizens!" He sounded exultant. "Today we have a new nation. The rule of Tovare and his lackeys is over. Today we overran the government post on Sabot. They fought bravely but were easily overcome by our superior force. I am sorry to have to tell you that there was some loss of life. I speak to you now in order to stop further bloodshed. Unless Tovare and his inept government step down immediately, we will move on the capital. Then there will be a great loss of life. I urge you to renounce Tovare now and accept with open arms the new order.

"To ex-President Tovare I say this: you are beaten, old man. Stand aside or I will crush you." The radio went dead.

"I suppose this is your doing, you slimy little spook," Woody shouted into the silence at Clint Donnelly. "You bloody Americans! Always meddling, killing! Why the hell couldn't you just have left us alone?" Now that the revolution was a reality, Woody found she did care. The old woman was in tears for the first time in years. "Garokan might not have been much of a place but, hell, these people were trying to run their own show. Now it's all going to be ruined."

Donnelly said nothing. In truth, he was as

much in the dark as the rest of them. He had reported all the rumors, all the preparations, all the tension to his superiors in Langley, but he had gotten no feedback and no orders. He still didn't know whether this was a sanctioned operation. There were Americans on Sabot, but no one had told him how many or whom they were working for.

The rest of them were speculating on what Tovare would do. They agreed he had pitiful defense forces to call on. On the other hand, Jean-Paul would have his hands full mounting an invasion at the height of the rainy season. It looked like a standoff until the rains ended.

The AP stringer was excited: In the year he had represented the news agency in Garokan, he had sent only two pieces, and both had ended up on the weekend feature wire. There was enough in the revolution story—foreign mercenaries, a tropical paradise—to guarantee a good play around the world.

In the White House there was a great deal of confusion. Garokan was a new name to most of the officials and they didn't know what to do. There was no man on the spot, no ambassador to talk to.

"I don't even know where in hell Garokan *is!*" the president shouted, thumping his desk in the Oval Office. "And those bastards in the United Nations are already accusing us of doing another Grenada! I'm not taking a black eye over some godforsaken place I never heard of.'' He wheeled on his security adviser. ''I thought we had a tighter rein on the CIA. If they've done this without consulting us . . .''

''It wasn't them, Mr. President,'' the security adviser said carefully. ''We've been checking for days. No serving member of the Agency is involved, I guarantee it.''

''Well, then we're in the clear,'' the president said, relieved. He had more important things to worry about than a revolution on some tin-pot island nobody cared about.

''Not exactly, sir. We do have something of a problem. The mercenaries seem to be all Americans, many of them ex-Agency. And the men behind it are also Americans, some of them rather prominent. Including a member of your Texas committee.''

''What are we going to do, then?''

''We could do nothing. Garokan has always refused to give us diplomatic representation, so there's no lobby here for the Garokans. We could just let the revolution run its course and declare it has nothing to do with us.''

''We can't! We got away with Grenada, but a repeat would be disastrous public relations. If there are Americans involved, no one will believe we didn't send 'em.''

He paced the office, brooding. Did he have to do *everything* around there? All he really wanted to do was settle back and watch the Super Bowl.

''Okay, here's what we do,'' he said. ''Order the Agency to round up a force, however many they think it will take to stop this. Have 'em flown in by commercial airlines, induct them into the Garokan Army, and put this revolution down as fast as humanly possible. He raised a hand to stop the protest. "I don't care who's backing who over there. All that matters is, it makes us look bad if we seem to be interfering in the affairs of an independent state." He grinned. "When it's all wrapped up, we'll leak it that we unofficially came to the defense of a tiny, struggling nation. That'll give those bastards at the UN something to wonder about."

Clint Donnelly called on President Tovare late in the evening. Donnelly was, he explained delicately, representing the U.S. government and help was on the way.

"We do not want your help, Mr. Donnelly," the man said. "I would be willing to turn over power to the Sabots. Nothing is worth the loss of life. But my cabinet insists we must fight, so fight we will. Outnumbered, outgunned, we will fight."

"Then, please, let us contribute, sir. The men who will come here will be made members of your forces, under your command. We are embarrassed because Americans are involved with the other side. We feel we must redress the balance."

Tovare thought awhile. He was sickened to see his vision of an independent nation vanishing. If he accepted the American offer, Garokan would become just another client state, an American protectorate. But the Young Turks in his cabinet insisted they must fight the revolutionaries, no matter how bad the odds against them. He sighed. Better alive and aligned than dead.

"All right, Mr. Donnelly. Send your men to help us." He studied the man standing before him. "And as soon as this is over, if it goes our way, you will be expelled from our nation. You have been operating here under false credentials."

"I understand, sir," Donnelly said, and slipped out of the office, back onto the soaking main street of Petit Bougainville.

The media loved it. They flocked to Garokan to cover the "Mango War" and they filled most of the beds in Woody's longhouse. They couldn't move much because of all the rain, so they had to invent most of the color and drama. The arrival of the Cuban ambassador gave them a whole new angle; were the Cubans going to turn this into another Angola, this time supporting an established government?

It was a Washington newspaperman who got the first real scoop. He received a tip about late-night activity at the airport, took a cab out there, and arrived in time to see one of Burt Brydon's planes disgorge 150 tough, lean men, all dressed in look-alike civilian suits and

carrying odd-shaped bags. The reporter figured they were not a symphony orchestra. He
watched them hurry through the little terminal and into waiting trucks. Hard, tough
men; identifiably American.

So Tovare wasn't going to lie down and let
the revolution roll over him, the reporter
mused. Tovare wasn't so dumb after all. Imagine him going out and hiring his own guns—
American guns at that. Suddenly the Mango
War wasn't looking like such a joke.

The new arrivals, carrying unflagged combat uniforms along with their weapons, were
inducted into the Garokan defense force
shortly after midnight. They were briefed by
the tiny nation's defense minister, and then
they bedded down in a wharf shed to wait for
dawn. The first Oram's spies in Petit Bougainville knew of their presence was when they
filed aboard an old copra trader comman-
deered for the occasion, and set course for Sabot.

The lookouts on Sabot saw them coming
ashore before Oram was told about the new
arrivals; runners took the news back to him at
the command post he had set up in Wings'
main building. For once, he was shaken.

"Where in hell could Tovare get that many
men?" he fumed. "I don't believe it." He
turned to Jean-Paul. "Your boys are seeing
shadows. Or maybe it's the police band Tovare's sent to flush us out."

319

But as he finished speaking they heard the angry chatter of small-arms fire at the far end of Sabot; it went on for a quarter hour, then stopped. One of Oram's mercenaries arrived then with his report.

"A big force, sir," the man said. "Many more than a hundred. We took heavy casualties and we've withdrawn into the jungle. Thank God for the rain! They're having trouble following us. But we're way outnumbered and these guys are as good as we are." He looked bitter. "Hell, I think I even recognized some of 'em. I think they *are* us! We've been double-crossed."

"Shut up, Simpson," Oram snapped. "We've still got the Sabots and the Latakians to throw at them. You get back to your men and hold these fellows off as long as you can." The man left. Oram, ignoring Jill and Cindy, who had listened, horrified, turned to Jean-Paul.

"Okay, Chief, it's time for your people to show how much they care about their independence. We're going to mount one mighty ambush."

Jean-Paul's nervousness showed. He had been assured there'd be no real fighting. Tovare was supposed to just fold in the face of their vastly superior forces. Jill watched him and decided to make a move.

"Give up, Oram," she said. "You've caused enough tragedy. How many more people are going to have to die before you admit you're beaten?" She faced Jean-Paul. "And you, the people's beloved chief, are you willing to take the lives of people who trust you? Your own people?"

He could not meet her eyes. Cindy crossed the room and hugged him. He made as if to shove her away. Then Oram spoke again.

"Keep out of this, Mrs. Nagle." His voice was menacing. "And you," he snapped at Cindy, "get away from him. We've got work to do."

Cindy stepped away from Jean-Paul, but as she did so she pulled the .38 from the band of his sarong. She stood in the center of the room and aimed the gun carefully at Oram's chest.

"Tell your men to lay down their arms, Mr. Oram," Cindy said calmly. "It's all over, this whole crazy thing. Poor Jean-Paul—you conned him into this. Well, now I'm stopping it."

Oram snarled and took a step toward Cindy, then another. And then the room was filled with noise, a great boom more powerful than thunder, and Oram sank forward on his knees, both hands clutching the hole in his chest. Cindy watched him die, then turned and faced Jean-Paul. Only a slight waver in the gun barrel showed the strain that gripped her.

"Okay, Jean-Paul," she said. "You're *really* in command now. What's it going to be? Will you tell your people to lay down their arms, or do I have to kill you, too?" There were tears in her eyes. "Because I will kill you, Jean-Paul." They knew she meant it.

Jean-Paul's broken dreams showed in his

eyes. He nodded speechlessly to Cindy and started for the door.

"Yes, you're right," he said before he stepped out into the rain. "I thought I was doing the right thing, restoring my people to their place at the top, where we belong. But we were used. Now it is time for the killing to stop."

Jill and Cindy watched his departing figure. The rain continued to pour down and, for another hour, there was sporadic gunfire. Then Sabot was silent.

The Cuban ambassador did not know what to put in his report. He could not fathom what had happened on Sabot and there was no one who could tell him. Americans had been fighting Americans; that he knew but could not understand. Clint Donnelly was equally confused but did not ask questions. He simply packed his bags and prepared to leave Garokan.

The media never really got to the guts of the story; they were denied access to Sabot and they caught only glimpses of the captured mercenaries being herded aboard a Brydon Airlines charter.

Tovare did, finally, agree to a press conference. It had all, he explained, been just a little tribal fighting. The leader of the dissidents had been placed in prison for a while, but all other participants had been pardoned. Now Garokan could return to normal.

But what about all the foreign troops? the press demanded.

"Just soldiers of fortune," Tovare shrugged it off. "They have been expelled."

And the foreigners fighting on his side?

"Volunteers who heard of our plight and wished to help." He stood up. "I'm sorry. I am very tired and these events have distressed me. I hope you will return to Garokan in quieter times, and after the rain has stopped."

After all, it was Cindy who bolstered Jill's spirits. It helped ease the estrangement between the two old friends.

They were sipping hot tea to ward off the rain and the shock, when Jill said, "What a price we've all paid for Wings." Her voice was bitter. "Jeff Thompson dead, blood spilled all over these beautiful islands, you heartbroken . . . it wasn't worth it."

"Don't talk like that! I won't hear it!" Cindy was suddenly the strong one. "You've still got a fight on your hands." She touched Jill's cheek. "Fight for all of us. Because, if you'll still have me, I want to stay here and repair what we had. I thought I was in love with Jean-Paul. In fact, it's this place I love. I know it will take a long time to build a reputation for this particular Wings, but, if you'll let me, I want to dedicate myself to doing just that. I'm determined to get the place going again."

"If you're willing to try, I suppose I should be willing, too." Jill began to sound more like herself. "I've fought bastards so long now, another round or two shouldn't matter."

Chapter Fifteen _____

SHE STOOD ON THE SIDEWALK OUTSIDE John Nagle's office building, shivering in the cold. His limousine was waiting at the curb, so she knew she hadn't missed him. It got colder and darker there on the street; the atmosphere exactly matched her mood. She glared at his chauffeur, sitting snug and warm with the heater going in the long, black car. When she saw the chauffeur open his door and look toward the building entrance, she caught sight of Nagle, dapper in a dark cashmere topcoat, emerging from the revolving doors. His mind was far away and she had to step right in front of him before he saw her. Then he recognized her and tried to push her out of his way.

"Mr. Nagle," she said, her voice level and determined. "This time you're going to talk to me. Because I know who fathered Marion's child."

It stopped him like a blow. He stood frozen, his hand still reaching out for the open limousine door. His face crumpled. The hand fell back to his side and he turned toward her.

"What . . . do you want?" he mumbled. "I'll give you anything."

"I think we better find a place to talk," she said. "There's a little bar just down the block. Tell your driver to wait. We'll walk there."

They made the journey in silence, Jill steeling herself with reminders of what this man had done to her. Worse, all of what he had done to David. She glanced across at him in the dim light; he no longer seemed much of an adversary. He had shrunk in every way. She had to open the door of the bar and guide him in, a hand on his elbow. The bar was quiet, almost empty, and she steered them to a booth in the rear.

"Two brandies," she ordered when the waiter approached. She took off her scarf and gloves and waited for the drinks to arrive. Nagle sat hunched forward, staring at his hands, silent. When she finally began to speak, his hands shook.

"I always knew there had to be something very wrong," she said. "David, *my* David, was such a wonderful man and you shunned him. Why all the bluster about letting down the family? Even a family like yours couldn't have been so unforgiving. And the vendetta against me made no sense. If you'd only left me alone, I'd have done what David told me to do years ago: forget you. But you wouldn't leave me alone, Mr. Nagle, and you came close to ruining my business. As it is, the damage you've done . . ." She sipped her drink and paused for emphasis.. "Well, I am going to fight back, Mr. Nagle, fight dirty."

He raised his hands from the table in a gesture of surrender. But she was not going to let him just cave in; she wanted to hurt him first.

"If you don't do exactly as I say, I am going to tell young David—the light of your life—just what happened. How you and his mother betrayed your *other* son. Incest. Maybe not technically. But biblically . . . Mr. Nagle . . ." She couldn't stop the tears. "Oh my God, how could you do that to your own son? To your wife?" She gulped back the tears. "The only thing I can stand is that David never knew the truth. And even that I can't be sure of. He was a very savvy man. Maybe he did know, or suspect, at least. You are a terrible human being, Mr. Nagle."

His hands were old, manicured and smooth and white, but old. They fluttered in front of her, trying to rise from the table, a plea.

"I . . . accept everything you say. I know what I did. I've lived with it forever, it seems. It cost me one son and it destroyed my wife. As it has virtually destroyed me. But can't you understand, from all this damage, one thing emerged, one good thing? The boy. I swore he would be protected, assume his proper place in the family, make up for all the evil I had done—including the evil of fathering him. But Marion, Marion was so vicious about it all, so demanding. I gave her anything she desired but there were some things no one could give.

She wanted David obliterated from all our memories, and for a while it was that way. Then he married you and suddenly he had a life again.

"After the tragedy, Marion was still blind with rage and jealousy. It was not enough that David was dead; you had to be humiliated as well. There was nothing I could do but go along with it. And no matter what I do now, she will always have this weapon, this threat, this hold over me." He made a choking sound and cut it off with a swallow of brandy. He looked around vaguely, caught the waiter's eye, and signaled for two more.

"Just tell me what you want me to do," he finished wearily.

"All I want is for this business to cease. You'll have to buy Marion's silence any way you can. And I want sole ownership of Wings returned to me. You and your cronies just cut your losses, tear up the notes you're holding, and we'll all forget we ever knew each other." She smiled grimly. "The loss of four million dollars won't hurt you people, and I figure you've cost Wings at least as much with all the damage you've done to its reputation. You'll have to come with me to see Judge in New York tomorrow, tell him to call off his dogs. Make him stop."

He nodded.

"There's only one thing, though. The others involved in the project to take over Wings, their motives were quite different from mine. They are all members of a very wealthy foundation dedicated to conservative causes. I don't know if they'll go along with what you want. They are very angry about the way things turned out, and they're not what you'd call reasonable men. I will do my best to persuade Judge to persuade them, but . . .''

"I think I can handle Judge and his Texas reactionaries," Jill said. She stood up. "I'll see you on the nine A.M. shuttle to New York." She began wrapping herself against the cold waiting outside. He stood and put out a hand to touch her arm.

"One thing, please." It was not easy for John Nagle to plead. "Just tell me one thing. What was David like in the years you knew him? Was he happy with himself? I need to know. You see, despite what . . . I loved him. I always did. I thought about him all the time, but I never told anyone."

His voice cracked. Jill decided not to make it easier on him, so she said nothing until he asked again.

"What was he like? Please tell me something, anything."

She pulled on her gloves and then looked at him and started toward the door, speaking as she moved away.

"He was the most wonderful man I ever knew. Kind. Happy, most of the time. A proud man—and brave, David was always a brave man."

She hoisted her bag more securely over her

shoulder and finished. "You missed a lot, not knowing your son."

She turned away and left him.

Sebastian Judge was annoyed when his secretary told him John Nagle was in the outer office. Seb had a full schedule. But Nagle had been burned badly in the Wings affair; he figured he'd better humor the old man.

"Send him in, Janice, and bring some fresh coffee."

If he was annoyed at Nagle's intrusion, he was furious when he saw Jill accompanying him.

"I've washed my hands of her, John," he snarled. "We've nothing to talk about in front of her."

Jill smiled. She could afford to.

"Seb," Nagle said, "hear me out. Things have . . . changed. I've decided I should never have done the things I did to my daughter-in-law."

Judge gazed at Nagle with mounting wrath.

"We've got to tear up the paper we hold over Wings," Nagle continued. "I'll take the whole loss personally, just me. The Texans needn't lose a dollar. But Jill must walk out of this with no liens against her. She's entitled to make a fresh start."

"I don't give a fuck what you want, Nagle," Judge snapped. He finally deigned to look at Jill. "You ruined our plans," he said. "My friends and I aren't used to being obstructed, particularly not by a nobody like you. We're going to make you pay for causing trouble. What's left of your resort chain is the payment price.''

''Oh, no, Mr. Judge,'' she said. She was quite enjoying Seb's fury. ''I paid the price. Now it's your turn. You will back off, as Mr. Nagle wants, or you and those crazies will all go to prison for conspiring to overthrow the legitimate government of another nation. You'll also be exposed for trying to set up spy bases in countries we're supposed to be friendly with. That won't endear you to our government, as you must know. And, finally, the papers will be given the story of how the mighty Seb Judge and some Texas crackpots conspired to cheat a poor widow out of the business she and her brave husband built.''

''You can't prove anything against me,'' he snarled. ''And the government wouldn't listen to you. You're nobody and nothing.''

''You're quite right, Seb. For that reason, I've brought along someone who *will* get a hearing, someone who just has to pick up a phone to have the ear of the president or anyone else.''

She strode to the office door.

''Carl, would you come in, please?''

She enjoyed watching Seb Judge's expression as the bent old figure entered the office. Carl Cohen looked out of place, somehow, away from his beloved orchids and his private paradise. But his smile was hypnotic and the strength about him caused Seb to deflate completely. There was more authority to Carl Cohen than Sebastian Judge had ever dreamed of having.

"Hello, Seb," Carl said casually. "It's been a long, long time." He eased himself into a chair. "This city is too much for me, Jill. I don't know how people can stand to spend their lives in places like this." She moved to Carl's side. "Anyway, I guess we shouldn't waste more of Seb's time than we have to," he said. She could feel the energy running through him and she was awfully glad he was on her side. "Seb," he continued, "I'm looking after Jill's affairs in this matter. If you don't do as you're told, I'll be releasing a public statement detailing everything that's happened, everything you've done. You'll remember the last time we crossed swords in public and you'll remember who won. It took you two decades to get back in favor with the powerful people you like to ride with. You'd never recover from this disgraceful episode, never. You know that."

There was a long silence in the office while they all watched Seb, whose eyes never left Carl's face. The two men stared silently at each other, neither moving, the old man quietly gathering strength while the middle-aged one lost even the bravado that was all he had left to fight with.

John Nagle stood at Seb's side; Jill was beside Carl; the three waited for Seb to cave in. After a long silence, he did.

"Okay, Carl. We'll tear up the papers and forget there was ever any connection between my associates and Wings."

He bared his teeth, a mockery of a smile, as he glowered at Jill. "There's nothing left of Wings now, anyhow. It's ruined. No cash flow, a lot of bad publicity—"

"Oh, but Seb," she said quietly, "I have a new investor now. Spiro Gravas. He's promised to keep the wolf from the door until we regain all you cost me. So Wings is fine. And" —she put her arm around Carl's shoulders— "I'm merging. With a very successful airline, as a matter of fact."

She started for the door and Carl rose and followed her. Then she turned and looked at the man who had been her father-in-law.

"You don't have to worry anymore about the holy Nagle name being used in trade, Mr. Nagle. I'm flying home to Hawaii tonight and, in three days, my name will be Jill Brydon."

She and Carl left the office without a backward glance. In an hour they would be airborne, headed for their beloved islands in the gentle blue Pacific.